Abigail's Song

Hearts and Harmony Book 1

Alina Rubin

Publisher: Alina Rubin

ISBN: Paperback 979-8-9855378-6-4

Cover Design: GetCovers

Editor: Kirsten Rees| Book Editor and Author Coach

Dedication

To the family I've lost and the family I found.

To Vitaly with all my love.

And to Elanna, who inspires me to write without fear and to love without limits.

Leave a Review!

I would love to know what you thought of Abigail's Song! You can write a review at:

Amazon

Goodreads

BookBub

Be the first to know of new releases by subscribing to the newsletter at alinarubinauthor.com

I love hearing from my readers! Please connect with me!
Instagram: Alina.Rubin.Author
Facebook: Alina Rubin Author
Email: alina@alinarubinauthor.com

Contents

Part 1

Chapter 1

*D*eath is scarier and more agonizing than I imagined. The oblivion won't come. My nose and ears fill with water. My limbs no longer move. Only my mind refuses to stop telling me to save myself.

Death, take me already. I want this pain to be over.

From the darkness, a figure of light appears, advancing on me. With trepidation, I recognize my mother. As my eyes no longer impede me, I can make out every detail of her white clothes, even the necklace of pearls I lost as a child.

"Abigail, come to me. We'll be together at last."

Another figure blocks my mother's way and faces me. She is young and has a heart-shaped face, a classical beauty. When she purses her mouth as if she tastes something sour, I recognize Amelia.

She shakes her head at me. "You need more time, Abigail. Rise! Live!"

Time for what?

Memories tumble into my fading mind. The strongest one immerses me. It's the day my mother died, and the night I met Amelia.

Seven Years Earlier

Crouched in the corner, I hummed a gentle song over the cradle as my brother and sister slept. The women in the room, my ma's friends, called my name several times... *Abigail, Abigail*... I didn't look up.

Tending to Julian and Josie was my job. Since their birth, I'd stayed home, watching them while our ma worked at the mill. Whenever I itched to run off and play with other children, the babies' cries pulled me back to their soiled clothes or empty bellies. Ma would get home late, and just before going to sleep, she'd sing to them. I wanted them to hear Ma's lullaby before leaving this home.

"You're all still here?" The shrill voice of the landlady, Mrs. Levy, rang from the door.

Continuing the song, I hoped the dreaded woman wouldn't notice me and remark on my dirty clothes or tangled hair.

"I told you to take her belongings and go. I need to clean this room for a new tenant. And I must strip the bed." She slammed the door on her way out.

My eyes shifted to the bed where Ma and I slept, huddled to each other for warmth. My brother and sister were born on that bed. And early this morning, on December 24th, 1809, my ma took her last breath on it.

Ma's three dresses, a coat, and a shawl lay on the table where we normally ate our meals. Verna, Lulu, and Mabel stood over them. That table, two chairs and the bed were the only furniture in our room where Ma, the babies, and I lived. The three women avoided the bed, even though Ma was no longer there. She now slept deep in the frozen earth of the cemetery, in a grave marked with a little wooden cross I made myself.

We long ran out of wood, and our room was unheated. My fingers grew stiff from the cold. A cough seized my chest, and I spit thick saliva on the floor. The women stared at me with alarm.

"Is she sick with whatever killed Nellie?" Verna's mouth twisted. "Abigail, don't hover over the babies. They'll catch your illness."

I wiped my mouth and came to the table. The women were bending over Ma's clothes, checking them for holes and rips.

"This blue dress would look good on me," Mabel declared. "Nellie wore it to the church picnic with her pearls."

"Where are the pearls now?" Verna's eyes narrowed.

The women gazed at me. I lowered my head. "I've lost them."

Verna grabbed my arm and shook it. "Where? Tell me."

The guilt stiffened my breathing. My body trembled from crying.

"Abigail Jones," Verna hissed. "I need all I can get to raise Julian and Josie. I made a promise to your mother and to God when I agreed to be their godmother. If you don't want them and my son to starve, you'll tell me where those pearls are."

Because of my foolishness, my poor brother and sister might starve. Wails closed my throat, and I doubled-over, coughing.

"Leave her be," Mabel said. "Abigail lost those pearls a while ago. Nellie was so distraught that day."

"She should've sold them when she could," Lulu added with a dreamy expression. "They looked like real jewels."

They were real jewels. Ma said so. Even when we went hungry, she couldn't let go of something so beautiful.

Verna stared at me like I was a revolting worm. "Nellie also wore earrings and a bracelet. Did you lose those too?"

My voice quivered. "Mrs. Levy took those, Ma's good shoes too. And all the money she found in Ma's pockets. We owe two months' rent."

"But what if those jewels are worth more than the rent? That Jewess has no right." Verna's face reddened. Her fists balled as she stepped towards the door.

"Nellie made her bracelet and earrings from beads she cut off from an old skirt. Those were worth nothing," Lulu said as she ran her fingers over the blue dress.

"Ha! The joke's on the greedy landlady then." Verna nodded in satisfaction.

The door flung open. Mrs. Levy's face was a mask of fury. "If you're not out in five minutes, I will bring a constable."

Verna laughed. "That's an empty threat. A British constable won't help a Russian Jewess."

Despite Verna's words, my body trembled. Ma was afraid of constables, and her fear echoed in me. Another coughing fit forced me to crouch.

The women gazed at the landlady with crossness.

"Can't Abigail spend the night here? She's sick." Mabel looked at me sadly.

"Where's your heart? The children's mother died. And it's Christmas Eve," Lulu added.

Verna scoffed. "Jews know nothing of Christian compassion. All they care about is money."

The landlady's face remained blank. I believed that her heart was a stone. She was always cross with Ma about late rent and the crying babies. I never saw her smile.

With swift movements, Verna threw on the coat and draped the dresses over her arm. "Well, since I'm the one to raise the babies, I should take all this. What I can't wear, I'll sell to feed them."

The women nodded and donned their coats. I gaped at them in confusion.

"But... where am I going?"

"With Verna." Mabel gave me a smile. "She's your godmother."

"Am not." Verna's lips tightened. "The babies are my godchildren, not Abigail."

My mouth gaped. "Who's my godmother?"

Verna shrugged. "Who knows."

"Take her to help you with the babies. Or you can bring her to work with us," Lulu offered.

Mabel studied my bony figure. "She just turned ten but looks much smaller. She'll exhaust herself to death in a week. Or lose an arm, like Jenny's daughter."

Bile burned my throat. Ma often said that watching over babies might be hard, but it was better than breaking my back at the mill.

Little Josie fussed. At six months, she was a poor sleeper. If not comforted, she'd waken Julian. My brother, almost two, had a mighty scream. I stooped to rock their cradle and whisper to them.

A hand touched my shoulder. I looked up at Verna. Her gray eyes had a sparkle and her thin lips smiled. "Abigail, dear. If you listen to me, you could save yourself and your brother and sister. You could come live with me, and we all go hungry. Or you do as I tell you. You, Josie, Julian, as well as my husband, my baby son, and I, will no longer worry about the cold or hunger. What do you choose?"

Ma wouldn't have let me outside after dark, but Verna said I would be fine. I trudged through my small town, Churcham, in South Yorkshire, to the address she gave me. I passed the textile mill where my ma and her friends worked. The university our town was famous for loomed in the distance. Pinnacles of churches reached for the black sky with no moon or stars on such a cold night. Only the dim light of oil lamps showed me the way on the icy cobbled road. Wind went right through my thin coat. The warmest item of clothes I had on was my mother's shawl that Verna had allowed me to keep. My ungloved fingers froze.

When I found the one-story house, my heart leaped. Candles lit the windows, and the smoke rose from the chimney. The aroma of meat broth wafted in the cool air, making my mouth drool. Eager to warm myself and fill my belly, I knocked on the door.

No one answered, so I knocked louder, pounding it with my fists. The beats of my heart as loud as my knocks.

A well-dressed woman, fair-haired and round, answered the door. Two small girls clung to her skirts. I ogled their clean faces, their hair woven into pretty braids. Warmth escaped from within and caressed my cheeks, while the crackling of the fire taunted my ears. A whiff of roasting meat made my belly rumble. A man's voice came from within, demanding to know who was at the door.

"Another beggar," the woman said through her teeth and scowled. "I gave enough to that sick girl by the church. Go somewhere else." She closed the door before I opened my mouth to speak.

Verna told me to be persistent. I spurred myself to knock again.

This time, Mr. Howard answered the door. His broad shoulders filled the entire space of the doorframe. I couldn't believe a man this large was my father and the father of Julian and Josie. But Verna assured me it was him.

He crossed his arms and frowned. "My wife told you to leave, little girl."

No recognition in his eyes, even though he visited Ma many times. But then he hardly looked at me. He'd throw me a coin and tell me to go somewhere. I didn't mind. After his visits, Ma paid back Mrs. Levy for the rent or rushed to buy us food. Except later, when her belly swelled, she cursed Mr. Howard.

I filled my lungs with frigid air, stifling a cough. Verna instructed me to hold my coughs or sniffles as if my life depended on it. No one would bring in a sick child and risk their family catching the illness.

"Merry Christmas, Dada." I smiled at him. My lips were so chapped that it hurt to grin. "My Ma... gone to Heaven this morning. Please let me live with you. I'll be a good daughter."

The woman behind him shrieked. "What? What is that little wretch saying? She's your daughter, Jim?"

He hit me. Hard. My teeth rattled. Tears welling in my eyes.

"Shut up, girl," Mr. Howard said through his teeth and swiveled his head to his wife. "She's lying, Sally."

The woman stepped around him and grabbed my shoulders, breathing into my face.

"Who's your mother?"

Tears ran down my cheeks. In my head, I prayed to Our Lady to save me from the coughing fit that was squeezing my chest. "Nellie Jones," I rasped. "I'm Abigail. If you let me live with you, I will do any chores and care for your children." I was sure it would be my duty to wipe the children's bottoms and wash their soiled clothing.

She pushed me hard, and I fell backward, landing in the snow. My vision blurred. I struggled to sit up. My clothes became icy and wet. Mr. Howard's giant figure, and the smaller one of his wife, loomed over me.

Sally's chin trembled as she spoke to her husband. "I knew you were not working all those late nights. But a bastard daughter? Any other bastard children I don't know about?"

"My brother Julian and my sister Josie," I hurried to report. "They are only babies and would live with their godmother. She'll need money to feed and clothe them."

A boot hit my ribs, making my insides shoot with pain. "I told you to stay quiet," Mr. Howard clipped. He grabbed his wife's hands and kissed them. "Sally, I may not be perfect, but I've provided for you and our children. Didn't the pastor say that people should forgive each other on Christmas Eve? Go open your presents. They should make up for my... mistakes."

Sally chewed her lip. "They better be very fine. And I never want to see this girl again."

"You won't. I promise." After she disappeared inside, Mr. Howard gripped my arm and yanked me to my feet. "Who told you to come here and call me Dada? Tell me."

I shook my head. Mr. Howard was the overseer of the mill. He could sack Verna.

"You said the babies are with their godmother. Who's she? I bet she came up with this scheme."

I could no longer hold my coughs. A fit rattled my chest, and I spit into the snow.

He gasped and bolted from me. "Go away and never come back. Or I swear I will find out who sent you."

The door slammed shut. I stood for ten more heartbeats, unable to move my feet. Eventually, I began walking on my unsteady legs, trembling from the wind, and pulling my wet coat around my shoulders.

I did not know where I was walking or for how long. I only craved dry clothes and a warm bed. God, in his mercy, watches over lost children. When a church tower emerged in the distance, I took it as a sign of Heaven's mercy and urged my exhausted legs to keep walking.

A cheerful song sounded from the church, and my heart lifted. This was not the church I attended with Ma, but surely there would be kind people here who would help me.

As I approached the steps leading to the doors, my shoulders tensed. The church appeared somber in the soft glow of oil lamps. Tears flooded my face again. I wanted Ma to hold my hand. But the singing coming from inside charmed me. After a few breaths, I climbed the first step.

The tall doors flew open before I made it to the second. In that instant, I thought they opened to welcome me. But then a large man and a haggard woman appeared on the threshold. To my shock, the man shoved the woman and kicked her in the back.

"Get out of here! Go to a poor house," he yelled as the woman slid down the steps.

She turned to him. "The church is supposed to care for the deprived."

"I saw how you stole the lady's handkerchief and coughed into it. Don't come here again." He closed the doors.

"Bloody bastard!" She yelled after him with a rasp and spit red into the snow.

A moan came up my throat. If I were to cough, that man would throw me out, like he did with that woman. I hid my face in my freezing hands. My weeping prompted another coughing fit, worse than the ones before it.

A hand touched my shoulder. It was the woman who'd been thrown out. "Did you want to warm yourself in the church? Don't bother. These people talk about charity all day and then throw the poor people out into the cold," the woman said. Her face was heart-shaped, and her eyes were large with long eyelashes. She was young and a very slender lady. Beautiful, if not for her fallen-in cheeks.

I kept on shedding tears and sobbing, while she patted my hair. A carriage stopped by the steps and a well-dressed man got out.

"Please, sir, spare some change," the woman begged while rubbing my shoulders.

The man sighed and removed a coin purse from his pocket. "Buy your daughter some new clothes. Merry Christmas." He sped inside the church.

The woman jiggled the purse. Coins inside clicked and chimed.

"They never gave me this much before." A wide smile spread on her lips. "Little girl, I'm Amelia. What's your name?"

Chapter 2

Amelia and I huddled as close to each other as possible to keep ourselves from freezing on the icy steps. While I told her about my ma, Verna, and Mr. Howard, the musician inside the church played a vigorous melody. I envied the worshippers who sat at the pews, sated and comfortable. My teeth chattered, and I whimpered, exhausted from sitting on the frigid steps, from hunger, and from the despair that gnawed in my chest.

A couple came out, passing near us. Amelia nudged me. "Your turn."

I cried the words she just taught me. "Kind sir and lady, please spare us a few coins."

The lady kept walking, but the man checked his pockets and spilled his change into my cupped hands.

"God bless you," I said, encouraged by my success. Amelia kept quiet and turned her face away.

The man caught up to the woman and offered his arm. "You have such a kind heart, my darling," she said as they walked to their waiting carriage.

Amelia grimaced. "You have such a kind heart, my darling," she mimicked the woman's voice, distorting it. "Damn you, Katherine. I should be the one sitting in the carriage next to the baron."

"You, in the carriage?" My eyes rounded.

"You don't believe me?" Amelia's lips pursed. "I've rode in that carriage many times."

Before I could ask her why, a cough squeezed my chest. My eyes watered as I hacked. Amelia cocked her head, staring at me.

"You said your mother died from a cough? Did she spit out blood?"

"No. No blood. She started coughing and shivering from a fever a week ago. Grew weaker each day, until she didn't leave her bed, and then she ..." My lips trembled, unable to say the chilling word.

"Only a week? I wish I could die that quickly. Consumption is a slow torture. The doctor at the charity hospital said I could live another six months."

"You're dying?" I gasped. "Are you afraid?"

She shook her head. "Last February, I wanted my parents to buy me a new horse and take me on a holiday. When they refused, I swallowed a handful of sleeping pills. I should've died then. It would've been so easy and painless."

Righteous anger filled me with a spark of energy. My fists balled. "You wanted to kill yourself over a horse? If you died, your soul would suffer in hell for all eternity. You should say a prayer of thanks." Weekly services were not wasted on me. When other children fidgeted or snoozed, I took to heart every word of the pastor's sermons.

"Well, the caretaker is not keen on letting me in to pray," she said, glancing back at the closed doors of the church. "And I believe it was the doctors at the hospital who saved me that day. This handsome medical student, his name was Alan Parker, tended to me. He was the first to suggest that I should become an actress." She ran her fingers through her hair. Then another coughing fit made her spit a mouthful of blood. With a sob, she dropped her head. "Now dying will be painful and lonely."

"You need to pray for Our Lady to guide you to Heaven." I put my hand on her arm. "Ma was afraid to die, to leave me and the babies. She also fretted about her sins. But last night, I heard her pray to Mary, Our Lady. In the morning, I found her smiling. She wouldn't wake, but she was at peace."

"Fortunate woman," Amelia whispered.

"Our pastor says that all true Christians will go to Heaven," I encouraged. "Are you a true Christian?"

She narrowed her eyes. "What's a true Christian?"

"That's easy." I stood to stretch my stiff legs. "True Christians go to church. Toss a coin into the basket. Celebrate Christmas and Easter. My ma was like that. And her friend Verna, who's taking care of Julian and Josie, my brother and sister. When Verna dies, she'll go to Heaven, just like Ma." My eyes glanced up at the stars that lit the way into Paradise where her soul now rested.

"And who won't get into Heaven, according to your pastor?" Amelia tilted her head.

I cringed and stomped my foot. "Our landlady, Mrs. Levy. She's a Jew. Always cross with my ma, she yelled at me when the babies cried. Today, after we buried Ma, she threw me out. A wicked woman like that won't be permitted into Heaven."

"She sounds like a terrible person." Amelia stood and wrapped her arm around my shoulder. "But that's not because she's a Jew. Some people choose to be kind, and some choose not to be."

Unsettled by Amelia's statement, I shook my head. "She's a bad person because she's not a Christian. She never learned kindness."

The church doors burst open, and a group of worshippers ambled out.

A smile curved Amelia's lip. "According to you, all those churchgoers are kind and decent. Let's see how generous they'll be to the poor." She spread her hands and cried, "Please spare some change. We're hungry."

Tired and chilled, I drew breath into my aching chest and thought about Julian and Josie. Since Mr. Howard won't provide for them, I needed to get money another way.

"Good sir, good madam, please help us." I addressed a young couple, and the man took out his money purse and gave me a handful of coins. "God bless you both."

Next, came a bearded man, but he shrugged and rushed past us. A pretty girl asked her mother for some coins to give us. The woman winced at Amelia's cough and pulled her daughter away. A few more good people stopped to give us a coin or two, but most sped by us to their waiting carriages.

"The big finale, Abigail," Amelia said into my ear. "Make them weep."

I had no idea what she meant but pleaded as loud as my parched throat allowed to the dwindling crowd of worshippers. A young man in a warm coat approached us.

"Please, kind sir, would you spare any change?" I rasped.

Amelia echoed. "Help the poor and hungry."

The young man, dark-haired and handsome, gave me some silver coins. I thanked him profusely, but he wasn't looking at me. His eyes were on my new friend.

"Amelia Hearts?" he squealed in a high-pitched voice that didn't match him, as if it belonged to a younger boy or a woman.

She raised her chin and pursed her lips. Then her head dropped. "Mr. Parker, what a meeting."

From their conversation, I understood he was the medical student Amelia mentioned before. He was about Amelia's age, or even younger. When he asked who I was, I tried to tell him. Coughing so much, I could barely speak.

"You will both come with me to the hospital," Mr. Parker said. His voice no longer sounded womanly, but of someone who wouldn't take no for an answer.

Ma used to say that in the hospitals people catch more illnesses and often die. I was so cold and tired, I didn't care. Besides, if I died, Our Lady would guide me to Heaven where Ma waited for me.

Eventually, when I became too tired to walk, Alan Parker wrapped me in his coat and carried me. Amelia shuffled next to us, coughing up blood as she walked. I must have fallen asleep in his arms.

When I opened my eyes, I found myself in a large chair next to a wood stove. Heat spread from it, reviving my frozen limbs and fingers. An unfamiliar night dress covered me, soft and dry. I started, unsure where I was. My head hurt, my mouth dry.

"Are you awake, little one?" a man asked, and I turned to him. He was shorter than most men I knew and had hazel eyes. He grinned at me, but those eyes remained concerned and fatigued.

"I've asked for some hot bottles to warm the bed for you," he said. "Meanwhile, you can sit by the stove."

As the fire breathed life into my chilled body, I gazed around, taking in my surroundings. The stove was in the center of a large room with many cots, a few hidden behind curtains. All the beds I saw had a child in them. Whimpers, sneezes, and coughs sounded from every corner. The stench of piss and vomit made my nose wrinkle. It reminded me of the nights when the babies were ill.

"Are you a doctor?" I thought a healer would be older. This man appeared not even twenty. But then, Mr. Parker looked and sounded even younger.

"I'm a medical student. My name is Mr. Higgins, or you can call me Oli if you prefer." He retrieved a journal. "Your name is Abigail Jones, right?"

I nodded.

"And you are... about six?"

"Ten." People often thought I was younger.

He leaned in to see me better. "Malnourished," he muttered and jotted some notes. "Now, please open your mouth wide."

He peered down my throat and clicked his tongue. "All red and swollen. Have you been coughing?"

I nodded. As he put his ear to my chest, his thick curls tickled me. I inhaled his smell that reminded me of honey cake.

His long fingers felt my neck and forehead. Then he examined my fingers and toes. "Healthy pink. Although very cold." He rubbed my palms, warming them. "Alan said he found you begging on the church steps. How long did you sit there in the cold?"

My tongue was too sluggish to form words, and my eyelids grew heavy.

He nudged me. "Before you sleep you need to drink medicine for your cough. It won't taste good, but I'll give you raisins after."

Oli left for a minute and returned with a bottle and a spoon. I winced at the bitterness of the medicine and wanted to spit it out, but he rubbed my back. After I swallowed, he plopped raisins into my mouth. I chewed them, delighted by their sweetness. Warm, dry, and cared for, I no longer felt death breathing down my neck.

"The bed is ready, Mr. Higgins," a woman's voice sounded.

"Thank you, Mrs. Grace," Oli replied. He took my hand and led me to a bed. I spied Amelia lying on the cot in the corner. Mr. Parker hovered over her. She was the only adult patient that I could see.

"Should Amelia be here?"

Oli sighed. "No. But we have nowhere else to place her." He covered me with a blanket. The sheets were warm from the heated bottles. My body grew heavy.

I rested my head on a pillow. "Amelia said she's dying."

"She's very sick." His shoulder hunched as he glanced towards her cot.

"And me?"

He gave me a smile full of warmth and patted my head. "You are going to get better. We'll take good care of you. I'll check on you soon."

His words comforted me. I thanked Our Lady for bringing me into this hospital where I would be cured and fed. My eyes closed.

When I woke up, the room was bathed in sunshine. Amelia stood over me, dressed in her ripped coat. Her cheeks regained a bit of color. She would be pretty, if not for her haggardness.

Confused where I was, I blinked and gazed around. Instead of Oli and Mr. Parker, an older man walked around the ward. The children in beds to my left and right were finishing their porridge.

I bolted upright. "Did I miss breakfast?"

"Don't fret, you'll get your breakfast, little one." Amelia smiled, becoming even prettier. "I wanted to wish you a speedy recovery and Merry Christmas. I'm leaving now."

My scratchy throat ached dully. Last Christmas Day, Ma gave me a new comb and told me stories on our way to church. *I'll never have Christmas with Ma again.*

"Merry Christmas, Amelia." My voice lacked holiday joy. "Why are you leaving? You are sick."

I'd only known her for one night and barely understood who she was, a beggar or a rich man's daughter, but I wanted her near me.

She bit her lip. "There's no cure for consumption. They need the bed for a sick child. At least I got one night of proper sleep and a couple of hot meals."

"Where are you going?"

"I don't know." Her shoulders slumped. "I asked Mr. Parker to talk to my mother. She and my father didn't believe me when I told them I'm dying. Maybe if she hears it from him, she will let me come home."

"Why won't they believe you?"

"Because I became an actress." She raised her arm in an elegant manner. Then she dropped it and sighed.

"When I was recovering in this hospital from taking sleeping pills, Mr. Parker told me that I should try acting and stage a play with my friends. I loved it so much that I ran away from home and joined a theater troupe. A girl from high society can't do such a thing. My parents renounced me. They think whatever I say or do is only an act. I told them how I was robbed, how I became ill. They didn't believe me. Or didn't care."

My chest churned for Amelia. Not only did she lose her nice life, but she also lost her parents' love. My ma had so little, but she always said she'd love me no matter what. Even when I lost her necklace.

Amelia blinked away tears. "I am scared, Abigail. Last time I saw them, my father yelled they have no daughter anymore. My mother had this look of revulsion, like I'm the lowest thing on this earth. I don't even know what to say if I see her."

My brow furrowed in thought. Amelia sighed and walked away with her head down.

Church bells chimed in the distance. I straightened because I knew what Amelia was supposed to do. "Wait!" I yelled. Raising my voice made me cough.

Amelia returned. "Are you alright?"

I gulped air to stop my coughing fit. "You should pray to Our Lady for help. She'll guide your mother to you. Tell your mother you are sorry."

Her face squeezed like she bit into something sour. "You don't know my mother. All she cares about is what her friends will say. She won't forgive."

"She will. She's your ma." I clenched her hand. "My ma had this pearl necklace, the most precious thing we owned. One day, when she went to work, I donned the necklace and snuck out to the street. I wanted to show it to these girls who mocked me for my patched clothes."

I broke into a cough, and Amelia poured me a cup of water from a pitcher that stood by my bed. After I swallowed, she nodded for me to go on.

"Those girls ... snatched the necklace right off my neck. It was too long for me, and my head fit through. The strands of my hair were caught in the clasp, but they yanked hard and ran away with it. All day I was shaking and crying, thinking what I'd say to Ma. I started praying every prayer I knew and then I added a few I made up. When Ma came home, I told her 'I'm sorry'. She didn't even understand what for, but I repeated and repeated how sorry I was. When she understood what happened, she ran out to look for those girls. I didn't know their names or where they lived. No one owned up to stealing the necklace and we never got it back. Ma didn't punish but instead forgave me."

Amelia covered her face with her hands. When she withdrew them, tears ran down her cheeks. "Oh, Abigail. You are special. I'd hug you, but I fear giving you my sickness." She squeezed my hand instead. "I will go to the church and pray for my mother to forgive me. If the caretaker won't let me inside, I'll pray on the steps."

Before leaving, Amelia gave me all the coins we received from begging, and I hid them under my mattress. I made a plan to take the coins to Verna for my siblings' care as soon as I got out of the hospital.

I had my breakfast of porridge with honey, and then the doctor checked on me and gave me the same bitter medicine I had yesterday, but this time without raisins. With my belly full, I dozed off.

Loud steps and a woman's trembling voice woke me up. A lady with curly silver hair, wearing a beautiful coat, hurried through the ward.

"Where... where is she?" she implored, glancing from the beds to Mr. Parker, who sped behind her. "Where is Amelia?"

A gray-haired doctor approached, telling them that he discharged Amelia, and she left. The woman, who I guessed to be Amelia's mother, put her hand on her heart. Her expression was crestfallen and lost.

I sat up. "She said she will go to the church and pray that her mother will forgive her and take her home."

"I forgive her a million times!" The lady exclaimed and ran out of the ward.

There was only one explanation in my mind. Our Lady had heard Amelia's prayer and made a Christmas miracle.

In the evening, Oli examined me again. He beamed at me when I opened my mouth and stuck out my tongue.

"Better," he said after he finished prodding me. "I see from the notes that you ate your breakfast and dinner and slept during the day. That's exactly what you need to be doing to get over your illness."

I grinned back at him, happy for once.

After giving me the bitter medicine and raisins, he gave me a serious look. "Abigail, I heard you lost your mother. I'm so sorry. Are there any relatives to take you in when you are better?"

There was Mr. Howard, but he had already told me not to bother him. And Verna would struggle to feed me, my brother and sister, and her own family. I didn't answer.

"It's very important that you think of someone you could live with," Oli prompted with a concerned look. "If there's no one, you would go to the orphanage."

"All right. I have nowhere else to go."

Oli bit his lip. "Yes, it may be all right. In the orphanage they would feed you and hopefully school you, but I think it would be better if you had a family."

I released a heavy sigh. *Didn't I just admit I had no family?* There was no use wishing for one.

"Mr. Higgins, please see to ... what's his name? Second bed on the right," the gray-haired doctor ordered.

Oli raised his head. "Do you mean Ezra?"

"Yes. What kind of name is that for a boy? Anyway, he needs bloodletting."

Oli squeezed my hand and left to care for the patient. The child cried, and he spoke with a gentle voice to comfort him. The ward grew darker as evening changed to night. Cries of pain and fear changed to a quiet whimper, and I closed my eyes, listening to Oli whispering to the boy. When most of the children grew quiet, the doctor left some instructions and stepped out. The boy sobbed again, and then a mesmerizing, heartbreakingly beautiful tune pierced the silence. It took me a second to understand where it came from. Oli was singing a lullaby.

The song stole my breath away with its serenity and sadness.

Mrs. Grace shuffled in, and Oli stopped the song abruptly. "How is Ezra?" she asked in a soft voice.

Oli didn't reply, and she tiptoed closer.

"Oh," she paused, "poor child. I'll sew the bag. Maybe more than one, seeing how many patients we have with pneumonia."

"I hate to agree with you, Mrs. Grace, but yes. When you have time, please prepare several bags."

There was a moment of silence, then Mrs. Grace spoke again. "Mr. Higgins, would it be appropriate if I say my usual prayers for Ezra?"

"Yes, I don't see... Why are you asking me?"

"I thought you would know about... their customs."

"No, I don't." There was an edge to his voice. "I believe, however, the Lord welcomes all prayers."

She sighed. "The Lord does, but the people are less accepting. Well, if it's not forbidden, I will pray for the departed soul as usual."

My ma prayed to Our Lady more often than to the Lord. When I asked why, she said, "Because Mary was a woman and a mother. She understands why I sin sometimes. And she'll watch over you if something were to happen to me."

While Mrs. Grace uttered her prayers, I climbed out of bed and kneeled. "Holy Mary, mother of God, please take the little boy Ezra into Heaven. Amen." My head bowed as I remembered saying such prayer only a few days ago over Ma's grave.

Oli pivoted and gave me a long look.

Chapter 3

A silver-haired doctor with a pointed beard and a deep voice ambled through the ward. A flock of his students and assistants hurried after him. His name was Dr. Miller, and I knew he must be the most important doctor here.

While they examined patients, I was playing with rag dolls Mr. Parker gave me. He told me to call him Alan. A couple of days ago, he'd decorated the ward with yew branches bringing a smell of fresh pine. I asked what he was doing, and he said he couldn't stand such a miserable Christmas season for all the sick children. And then, he gave a present to each child. I was too big to play with dolls, but I needed something to pass the time. They reminded me of Julian and Josie, but unlike them, dolls never cried or soiled themselves.

With a frown, Dr. Miller approached my bed and lifted my wrist. His squeeze on it was tight, but I didn't squirm, knowing that he would leave me alone in a minute. It was Oli who took his time, sometimes making me stick out my tongue more than once or take deep breaths till I was dizzy. He would apologize, saying that he was still learning, but I liked that he gave me that much attention.

Finished with the exam, the doctor asked his assistant to give him the notes on me. After a glance, he asked Alan a question about pneumonia treatments. The student rolled his shoulders back as he gave a detailed answer. When he stopped, Dr. Miller clapped.

"Excellent answer again!" He shifted his gaze to Oli who stood by Alan. In their group of doctors and medical students, they were the two shortest people.

"Mr. Higgins, since you've been answering poorly all morning, I'll spare you from a medical question, but answer this. I asked you a couple of days ago to discharge this child home. Why is she still here?"

It had occurred to me that I was the only patient still here since Christmas Eve. All other children either left with their parents or were carried somewhere inside the bags Mrs. Grace sewed.

Oli stepped forward with his face flushed. "I'm sorry, Professor, but she needs to finish her course of medication. And..." his voice quieted, "she has no home."

The doctor shrugged. "Since when is that a reason to keep a patient here? As usual, you didn't follow a simple instruction." He turned to a black-haired, twenty-something man who supervised the ward most nights. "Dr. Shaw, arrange for the constable to escort the girl to the orphanage tomorrow morning."

Without another glance at me, the important doctor moved on to the next patient. My throat became so constricted I could hardly breathe. Oli rocked in place and regarded me with worry in his eyes.

"You've done all you could to find her family. Even let your studies suffer." Alan put his arm on Oli's shoulder. "I have an idea. Let's make a donation on her behalf so she's treated well."

"That's a good thought. I'll take tonight's shift and find out where she'll be going." Oli rubbed his chin.

His friend nodded and hurried after the professor, while he remained in his spot as if lost in thought.

A cough churned in my chest. Oli hurried over and brought water to my lips. "You need to finish your medicine, or you'll get sick all over again," he muttered.

"Mr. Higgins, how long do we need to wait for you?" Dr. Miller called. "Present the next case."

"Sorry, Professor." Oli winked at me and hurried to rejoin the group.

I could hear my heartbeat in my ears. A constable would come for me tomorrow, like the landlady threatened. If he learned of my ma's debt to Mrs. Levy, he could throw me into the debtor's prison. Ma said this happened to one woman who was sacked from the mill.

After Dr. Miller and his students left, Mrs. Grace brought dinner, but I could not eat it.

Her head, streaked with silver hair, shook. "No, Abigail, that won't do. You must eat." She sat down, and spoon-fed pea soup to me. My uneasy stomach refused it. She grabbed a bowl just in time to catch my vomit.

"That bad, huh." She chewed her lip. "Why don't you say your prayers, dear? That should make you feel better. I need to feed the other children."

I prayed to Our Lady, but the prayer did little to comfort me. In my mind, a constable with a club was coming to take me to a cold cell. The spasm in my belly made me twist and hug my knees. When Oli arrived for his evening shift, he glanced at me and rushed to my side.

"Are you alright, Abigail? Did your cough grow worse?"

I wanted to answer, but my mouth went dry. He listened to my lungs and checked my forehead.

"Your lungs sound almost normal, and you have no fever. Is something else ailing you?"

"My belly hurts," I whispered. "I think I need to stay in the hospital longer."

Oli's lips tightened into a line, an expression I saw on him often during the night shifts. He pressed his fingers on my belly over my nightdress, prodding me in various places. At least twice, he pressed in the lower right and asked if it hurt there. I shook my head. He then took out a silver pocket watch and squeezed my wrist, his eyes focused.

"So fast," he muttered. "All you need is a stomach illness on top of your other problems right now."

Frowning, he checked the journal. Then he called Mrs. Grace, who was feeding another patient.

"Mrs. Grace, you added a note that Abigail vomited her dinner. How many times did she retch today?"

The woman approached. "That was the only time, Mr. Higgins."

"Has she eaten anything since?"

She cocked her head. "Mr. Higgins, I'm not a doctor, but I believe the child has a case of nerves. When my parents decided to send me to a boarding school, I couldn't keep food down for days."

His cheeks reddened, but the tension on his face ebbed. "Of course. Thank you, Mrs. Grace."

"I'm glad my limited experience helped." Her hands smoothed her apron.

"Your help has been invaluable for the children." He bowed his head. "And students as well."

The woman's eyes gleamed, and she walked away with her back straighter.

With a sympathetic smile, he rubbed my belly. His touch, warm and gentle, eased the pain a bit.

"Sorry if I frightened you. When you are around terribly ill patients, it's easy to forget that most bellyaches are not dire. I'll order you some chamomile tea." He rose and stepped toward the next bed.

I didn't want him to leave me. "Would you sing me a lullaby? Like you sang to that boy?"

He glanced around. "If you wish. But I have a few things to do first."

Mrs. Grace served me the bittersweet tea and then eased my stomach with a warm compress.

"There, child. It will be alright," she spoke in a soothing voice. "I was like you when I arrived at the Reading Abbey Girls' School, ill with anxiety and homesickness. But it was all over nothing! Soon I found friends, joined the choir, and found the library where I read every book twice. Those were wonderful years."

"Did you study medicine?"

She shook her head. "Medicine is a male pursuit. I don't officially work in this hospital."

"But you are here almost every night."

Her eyes blinked rapidly. "The only thing that keeps me going is helping other little ones. After my children died from smallpox, I despaired. So here I must be." She petted my head and bid me good night.

My mind kept showing me a cruel constable and a jail cell. I couldn't sleep and sobbed quietly into my pillow. When snores and labored breaths of other children sounded through the ward, Oli returned to check on me again.

"Looks like it was only nerves after all, thank goodness. Is your bellyache better?"

Instead of an answer, I burst into tears and sobbed.

"Shh, you'll wake up the others," he said, sitting down beside me. "Talk to me. Your belly hurts that badly?"

"It's better, and that means ..." I wept, unable to finish my sentence.

"Is it the orphanage? You are scared to go?"

"The constable," I sobbed.

"The constable who would take you there?"

"Yes."

"Oh that. Would you feel better if I took you instead?"

I bobbed my head.

He tucked my blanket under my chin. "Well, that's what I will do then." When he was about to walk away, I grabbed his sleeve. "The lullaby."

He smiled. "A bit later." Oli turned to address the doctor who entered the ward. "Dr. Shaw, did you make arrangements for Abigail?"

They moved away, speaking among themselves. I tried to listen.

"I will explain the instructions for her medications," Oli said.

The older doctor covered a yawn with his hand. "You can take her, but I don't see why you need to bother."

A girl on the bed next to me began thrashing and moaning, like my ma did when her fever rose. Oli and the doctor broke their conversation and hurried over. I turned to my side to avoid seeing them bleed her.

When all was still and quiet again, and Dr. Shaw stepped out of the ward, Oli sat next to my bed.

"I won't sing the same lullaby I sang to Ezra. I knew he didn't have long, but I didn't expect him to die as I sang to him." His breath caught. "There's another nice one I know.

He cleared his throat and sang into my ear.

I did not know the language, but I understood in my own way. The song was telling me, 'Sleep now because you don't know what the next day will bring'. My chest squeezed.

"Why are your lullabies so sad? And why are they not in English?" I asked when he finished.

He shrugged. "Because there's a lot of sadness in the world. And people sing to their babies in all languages."

"But what language is it? Where did you learn these songs?"

"From my Mama and Papa. They sang to me and my brother and sisters when we were little." He touched his face and glanced down. "I'm sorry. Inconsiderate of me to bring up my family."

"No, that's all right. My Ma sang too." Trying not to wake the other children, I sang her lullaby in a soft voice.

When I finished, he beamed at me. "That was beautiful. You have an ear for music."

"Singing is easy." I shrugged. "I know all the songs from church."

"It's not easy for everyone. Musical ability is a gift. Perhaps the orphanage would have a choir." He inclined his head and smoothed my blanket. "Please try to get some sleep. I've settled everything for tomorrow."

"No constable?"

"No constable. I'll accompany you and make sure it's a good place."

I turned my head to go to sleep. Then a thought made me bolt upright.

Oli's eyes widened. "What's wrong, Abigail?"

My ma wouldn't approve of me trusting Oli or anyone else with the money, but I saw no other choice. After scanning the room to ensure that everyone around us slept, I reached under the mattress and retrieved the small sack with coins.

"Please give this to Verna Bax." I whispered and gave him the sack. "And please tell her that Mr. Howard won't help her. When I'm big enough to start working, I'll share my wages with her. Until then, I'll pray that her family and my brother and sister, Julian and Josie, don't starve."

He stared at me with his mouth open. After a minute of silence he stammered, "Why didn't you tell me?"

Chapter 4

After Mrs. Grace coaxed me into swallowing a few spoonfuls of porridge, she brought my dress, stockings, and shawl, all clean and newly patched. I held the shawl to my nose, hoping to catch the scent of Ma on it, but it now smelled of laundry soap. Mrs. Grace helped me to pull my dress over my head.

"It's too small for you," she said, clicking her tongue. "They should give you a new one at the orphanage. I also found you a pair of boots and a coat. The shoes you had are no good."

Studying my face, Mrs. Grace made the sign of the cross over me. "Go with God, Abigail. All will be well."

"Amen," I whispered, and she embraced me.

Oli walked in, wearing a long coat and mittens. "The coach is waiting outside. Are you ready?"

My heart jumped into my throat. I was going to a new place that I knew almost nothing about. It took all my willpower not to break into tears. I stole a moment to look around for any familiar faces to say goodbye, but so many children came and left since I arrived, I didn't recognize anyone.

We climbed inside the coach. As the horses trotted on the cobbled road, the seat shook violently.

"It's not far, just on the outskirts of the city," Oli said. "Are you alright?"

I nodded. The lump in my throat made it hard to talk.

"I saw your brother and sister last night. They are doing well."

I gaped at him.

He gave me a sheepish smile. "Verna and her husband were not too pleased that I knocked in the middle of the night. The babies woke up and bellowed. I don't blame Verna for being angry with me. But the babies are healthy. And you don't need to worry about them not having enough to eat. It's taken care of."

"Mr. Howard will pay?" I gasped.

"No." Oli shook his head. "That visit went even more poorly. Is he really your father?"

"That's what Verna said."

"Strange, but he didn't deny that your brother and sister are his children. He wanted nothing to do with them but didn't refute that he fathered them. Yet, he vehemently denied that you are his daughter. He said that if you are ten, he didn't know your mother that long."

I shrugged. "Maybe that's a good thing. I don't like Mr. Howard."

A small part of me wondered who my father was. But it mattered little. My family was Ma, Julian, and Josie. No father was there to help when we were hungry, cold, or sick.

Oli stared down at his knees. "I tried to persuade Verna and her husband to take you in. I hate that you are being separated from your brother and sister. But... they refused. Verna did promise to visit you with Julian and Josie."

I doubted Verna would keep her promise. The reassurance that the babies were healthy and wouldn't starve was enough for me. But the thought about visitors quickened my heartbeat.

"Would you visit me? You could sing me more songs."

He inclined his head. "I will while I'm studying at the university. But I only have six months of school left. Alan will likely stay at least another year if he gets the apprenticeship with Dr. Miller as he hopes. He could continue visiting you when I'm gone, but he'll leave eventually. He's too talented to stay here, in Dr. Miller's shadow." The last part he said more to himself than to me.

I sighed and closed my eyes.

"Abigail, you'll be alright." He bent toward me. "You will meet new people who'll care for you. You'll make friends. Look, this is it."

The carriage stopped by a gray building with a cross. It looked like a rundown old church. The cracks snaked across the façade. A couple of the windows were broken. Oli's mouth tightened.

"Please wait for a few minutes," he told the driver.

He led me to the railing. For a spell he was silent, viewing the dilapidated building and the empty yard.

"The place can use some upkeep, but it's the people inside it that matter," he finally said. "Let's wait and see if some children will come out."

Soon after he spoke, several children of various ages entered the yard. They strolled aimlessly, not skipping, or running, or starting any games. Their clothes were faded and patched. The girls' hair was unkempt, their aprons soiled. None of the children smiled.

My shoulders sank.

"Blimey, I thought only sick children look this miserable," Oli whispered.

A heavy woman with a flushed face came out, dragging a boy by his arm. The boy cried loudly; tears streaked his pale cheeks.

The woman grabbed him by the shoulders. "Tobby Hill, what were you doing in the kitchen? Empty your pockets."

The boy sobbed and dug out something from the pocket of his coat. "I'm hungry," he said in a soft voice.

The lady stared at the surrendered loot. The boy took a step to leave, but the woman grabbed his arm and slapped his cheek. Oli shuddered more than the child. None of the children reacted, clearly nothing unusual was happening.

"That bread is for the staff, you little thief," the woman said to the boy. "If I catch you in the kitchen again, you'll get a whipping of your life." She walked away with her back turned away from the crying boy.

I watched the scene with misery. Tomorrow or soon after, I might accidentally break a rule, and I'd be beaten, friendless. *Hungry.*

Oli fished out something from his sack and motioned for the boy to approach him. The boy stopped crying and narrowed his eyes.

"Here, take this. It's a currant scone." Oli passed the treat through the space in the railings and held a finger to his lips. The boy slipped the treat into his pocket. He tiptoed away with his head down.

"Tobby has something!" the largest boy yelled. In a flash, he and two more older children shoved the boy to the ground and climbed on top of him. Tobby screamed and struggled to push them off, but they held him down with their weight and ripped the pocket.

Oli clenched his fists. "Stop them! They can injure him," he yelled to the woman, who watched the scene with a passive expression.

"Children will be children," she said and sipped from her flask. "Don't give them things or they fight over them. What's your business here?" she asked, studying me.

My mouth went dry. I got hold of Oli's sleeve and pulled it to my cheek.

Oli said nothing. His eyes were on Tobby, who was slowly rising to his feet, his coat torn. A few steps away, his attackers were dividing the scone among them. When the boy staggered a few unsteady steps, Oli exhaled with relief.

"No business here, Madam. Must be the wrong address," he said to the lady and took my hand. "Let's go, Abigail."

With my mind muddled, my legs refused to move. "I'm not going there?"

"Not on my watch." Oli lifted and carried me to the coach.

He lowered me onto the seat and let me drink some water from his flask. Then he spoke to the driver, but I couldn't hear them properly. I imagined he inquired about other orphanages. My body and head ached as I leaned on my seat and closed my eyes.

When I opened them again, Oli's face was above mine. I was lying on his lap.

"Do you feel better after a nap?" he asked. "I tried to cushion you against the bumps."

I rose and looked in the window. We were next to a three-story house with pines growing in front. It was too quiet and tidy to be an orphanage. The hope I was afraid to believe grew in my chest.

The driver opened the door. Oli climbed out and gave me a hand.

"Is this where you live?" I clambered down.

He nodded. "I rent a room upstairs. You can eat and rest a bit while I pack a few things for the road."

I followed him inside, with my head more jumbled than before. *If he's renting a room here, why are we going somewhere else?*

He led me down to the kitchen. Several women crowded there, busy with various tasks: stirring a soup pot, cutting vegetables, washing the dishes and utensils. Oli greeted them and asked to make me something to eat.

The young woman who was cutting the vegetables lifted her head. "We have bean soup and our famous pork chops. The ones you always snub." Her grin seemed to say, 'I know something about you'.

Oli's face stayed passive. "Thank you, Kitty. Please bring her the soup with some bread. And please pack us some food for the road."

"For the road?" Kitty lowered her knife. Other women turned their heads and stared. "Are you leaving us, Mr. Higgins?"

"Going home to Chatham for the rest of the holiday. I'll be back next week."

"And the little girl? Is she going with you?"

Oli glanced at his clothes. "Yes, she's coming with me."

The women's eyes grew wide. They put their heads together, whispering.

Oli led me upstairs to the dining room. Our driver sat at the table, sipping a glass of wine.

"Eat and rest while I pack," Oli said. "We are going a long way, so eat well."

"Where are we going?"

Kitty appeared with a pitcher of water and a couple of rolls of warm bread. "The soup will be ready in a few minutes," she said, staring at me. I wondered if my face was dirty, but I couldn't wait to eat any longer. The aroma of fresh rolls lifted me into Heaven. I stuffed the crusty goodness into my mouth.

Oli smiled at me and climbed up to his room. Kitty watched him go and waited for the door to close behind him. Then she turned to me.

"Who are you to him?"

I almost choked on the bread. Kitty slapped me on the back and handed me a cup of water. When I stopped coughing, she spoke again in a low voice.

"Are you a Jew?"

"I am not!" I huffed. "Every day I pray to Our Lady."

"Then he's not your brother." She brought her face close to mine. "Why are you traveling with him? Where are your parents?"

The woman's reproachful stare bore into me. My heart hammered. "He... He means to adopt me," I blurted out. When I said it, I believed it.

Kitty nodded with satisfaction. "That's what we thought." She marched upstairs with her shoulders squared. Another woman brought me a steaming bowl of soup. Her eyes lingered on me a bit too long as she set it down.

When Oli entered with a valise in his hand, I was finishing my soup. I smiled at him, hoping he was about to tell me that he's adopting me. As if reading my mind, he approached me and touched my shoulder.

"Abigail, I want to tell you where we are going."

"Mr. Higgins." A woman in her fifties, wearing a black dress with a crisp white collar, descended the stairs. Kitty was on her heel, her cheeks flushed. "We also want to hear where you are going with this child. Why don't we speak in my office."

Oli raised his chin. "Mrs. Haley, is there a problem? Am I behind on my rent?"

The woman, who I understood to be the landlady, crossed her arms. "Unfortunately, there is a problem. Please come and bring the girl."

Sighing, Oli gave me a hand to rise. We followed Mrs. Haley to her office on the top floor.

Her office had little furniture, only a desk with a neat pile of papers and a chair. A crucifix adorned the wall. The landlady sat at the desk, leaving Oli, Kitty, and me to stand. Kitty closed the door. I fidgeted and glanced at Oli, who still held my hand.

"Mr. Higgins," the landlady began, looking straight at Oli, "you pay your rent without delay, and unlike some of your fellow students, never caused a complaint from the maids. Seeing that, I minded my business. When the kitchen staff gossiped that you never touch any foods prepared with pork or lard, I told them to mind their business. When maids noticed that early in the mornings or late in the evenings, you sometimes don't answer when called by your name, I told them to mind their business. But... I'm not a fool. You are a Hebrew. And you hide this because the university is for Christian men and does not allow Jewish students."

My eyes widened. This woman had to be wrong. A man who treats sick children, who made sure my brother and sister don't starve, who gave a scone to a hungry orphan. Surely Oli was a man of true faith. Jews were like Mrs. Levy, who took my mother's things and threw me out into the cold.

"He's a Christian," I blurted out. "He cared for me and many other children. A Jew would never be so kind. They are greedy, heartless people."

Oli released my hand. His cheeks grew a deep shade of red.

Mrs. Haley peered at me. "Children speak when spoken to." She shifted her gaze back to Oli. "What do you say to all this, Mr. Higgins? Please don't insult me with lies."

I raised my eyes to Oli, expecting to see him defiant and furious.

His face and voice stayed calm. "I'm not going to deny what you said." Oli rubbed his cheek. "If you wish me to leave my room for good, I will."

With her lips twisted, the landlady raised a pen from her desk and rolled it in her fingers.

"I don't think you understand my concern, Mr. Higgins. It's not about you as a tenant. It's about this child. She told Kitty that you plan to adopt her. She also told her that she's not Jewish and prays to the Virgin Mary. As a Christian woman, I must intervene. Where are you taking this girl? Do you mean to make her a Jew?"

Ice spread through my veins, making me shiver. My mind wanted to deny what my ears were hearing. *Oli would force me to become a Jew? To deny Jesus and Mary?*

His eyes blazed. "Her name is Abigail Jones. She's an orphan in need of a home. I appreciate your concern for her, especially when so few showed it for her fate. My family will take diligent care of her. And we will not, as you put it, make her a Jew. My people accept only voluntary conversion."

Mrs. Haley pursed her lips. "Does she have any Christian relatives?"

"None that want her. I have searched since the day she entered the hospital."

"What about an orphanage? St. Anne has a good reputation."

Oli's nostrils flared. "We just came from there. I'm outraged by what I saw. She will not last a month there. If she won't die of hunger or disease, the other children or possibly teachers will beat her to death."

"I see." The landlady inclined her head and studied me. "Abigail, I usually take girls that are older and sturdier. But under the circumstances... I'll make an exception. You will do light work. Eat meals with my staff. Attend church and school on Sundays." She paused and nodded at me. "Now is your turn to thank me."

My head swam, still working through what I learned about Oli. "You want to adopt me?" I asked her.

The woman grunted. "I'm offering you shelter and an honest employment. Kitty started here as a scullery maid when she was twelve." She looked at the young woman. "Kitty, have I treated you well?"

"You've been most kind, Madam." Kitty bobbed her head. Her smile, however, froze on her lips and did not reach her eyes.

"Good." Mrs. Haley stared at me. "What say you, Abigail? Think not only about the needs of your body but of your soul. Under this roof, you will grow up a hard-working Christian woman. If your mother were one, I'm sure she would approve."

I lowered my head. My ma would approve. She worked hard at the mill and attended church. She would expect the same from me. And yet, my heart grew heavy.

"Wait, Mrs. Haley." Oli fidgeted under the landlady's gaze. "I have not explained my offer."

He stooped to have his hazel eyes on the same level as mine. "Abigail, Mrs. Haley means well. But you are ten. You should not be working. You should be playing and learning. And you need a loving family."

I wanted a family. It was too hard and scary to be on my own.

"You met one Jewish person who was unkind to you. But my family is not like that woman. My mother and father will treat you as one of our own. My younger brother and sister will be your playmates. The children of my older sisters will be your cousins. You will be provided for and loved. Would you like to live with them?"

My throat dried and I couldn't speak. Overwhelmed, I gazed about. Kitty dabbed her eyes with the corner of her apron. Mrs. Haley stared at her hands; her expression had softened.

"Will your parents allow Abigail to attend church and a Christian school?" she asked, her eyes resting on the crucifix on the wall.

Oli straightened and gazed at her. "I consider you a friend, Mrs. Haley. And you, Kitty." He nodded to the maid. "I swear this oath in front of you. Abigail will never be forced to convert. I, and my family, will do all we can for her wellbeing. She will attend a Christian school and pray as she wishes."

I was reassured by the earnestness in his voice. He meant what he said.

Sobbing, Kitty crossed herself. "Don't ever break this oath. Our Lord hears everything."

"Why are you doing this?" Mrs. Haley clasped her hands. "You study to become a physician. Surely you can't save every orphan you meet."

He cracked a smile. "I wish I could. At least I'll save this one. She's a special child who sings beautiful songs." With his hands stretched toward me, he looked into my eyes and spoke with gentleness in his voice. "Abigail, please say if you want to come with me. My family lives in Chatham, near the sea. Our customs and foods are different from what you are used to. We speak a language called Yiddish among ourselves. But we will be your new family."

My tongue would not obey me. I could not form words about the feelings that birthed inside my heart.

"When I told you that children speak when spoken to, I didn't mean to make you a mute," Mrs. Haley said. "Few children get to decide their destiny. You need to state your choice. Stay here or go with Mr. Higgins."

"If it's hard to speak, just take my hand," Oli offered.

Chapter 5

"Let me tell you about my family," Oli said when we were back in the carriage, and his lodging disappeared from our view. He perched on the edge of his seat with a smile. I hadn't let go of his hand from the moment he asked me to take it. The rocking of the coach made me sleepy, but I forced my eyes to stay open.

"You will be the youngest child. Closest to your age is my brother Moishe, he's two years older than you. Then Shira is sixteen. She can be irritable, but I'm sure you'll get along. She has a friend Naomi, who spends much time with us because her mother is very ill. And I also have two older sisters, Miriam and Hannah. They are married with children of their own and live nearby."

"Is there enough food for everyone?" I blurted out.

"You and Mama will get along splendidly." He laughed. "She's always thinking about food."

He must have never been without it, I thought with envy.

Oli peered at my face and patted my hand. "Abigail, you won't be hungry again. My family had been poor when we came from Russia, but over time we've prospered in Chatham. It's a port city with a dockyard. My papa is a silversmith and a navy agent. He sells his goods to sailors and loans them money for their wage tickets."

I relaxed against his shoulder and listened to his voice. A family that has enough food every day. And I will be the youngest, without responsibilities for the little ones. With three older sisters, there would be plenty of hand-me-down clothes, maybe even in good condition. And Oli promised I could pray and attend church. He let my head lay on his lap so I could rest more comfortably. My eyes closed, but the bumps kept me awake.

"You remind me of my sister Rachel," he said after a few minutes. "She liked to sit with me and purr like a cat. I used to bring stray cats for her. We have one left, a black cat named Murka."

"How old is Rachel?" I murmured. I didn't remember her among the sisters he mentioned.

Oli sighed. "She died from the same disease that Amelia has. Consumption. There were also two babies who perished. And my friend Noah, who was like a brother to me. Their deaths, especially Noah's sudden end, made me choose medicine as my profession."

His voice quivered as he spoke. The family may have enough food, but they didn't escape sorrow.

I whispered a prayer to Mary, like I'd done in the hospital whenever a child died. When I finished, I peered at Oli to read his face. *Did he tell Mrs. Haley the truth? Would I be free to pray like my ma taught me?*

His hazel eyes brimmed with tears. "Did you just pray for my brothers and sisters?" he asked in a whisper.

"Our Lady would make sure they are in a good place." His sigh made my heart pinch.

Eventually, I dozed off until we stopped in some inn overnight. There, I was given a bed in a room with several young women. Their whispers and giggles interrupted my sleep.

In the morning, after washing my face and combing my hair, I stepped into the inn's dining room. People sat at plain tables with no tablecloths, drinking coffee and eating sausages and bacon. Oli waved me over and placed a plate with breakfast in front of me. The smell of greasy meats and onions made me nauseous. I forced down a few bites and winced from stomachache.

"Poor girl. You are exhausted and anxious." Oli offered me a glass of water. "We should be at Chatham by midday. Mama will care for you. By the Sabbath meal, you will be much better." He paid for the breakfast we barely touched, lifted his luggage, and led me to the coach.

The shaking of the coach was making me sicker. I was glad that I had little in my stomach. Questions swirled in my head. What if Oli's parents don't want me? What if they make me pray their Jewish prayers despite his promises? Would Ma approve of me living with them? I closed my eyes, hoping that a little more sleep would silence my mind.

"We are getting close," Oli said what seemed to be hours later. I raised my head to the window and saw the river under the bridge we were crossing. "Do you see the castle and the cathedral? That's Rochester."

The two buildings were proud and imposing. My gaze was glued to them. But soon the scene changed. Dirty streets were crowded with peddlers hawking old clothes and beggars pleading for coins. Drunk soldiers and sailors stumbled about, barely able to put one foot in front of another. One fell, yelling curses, and I jumped in my seat.

Oli shook his head. "All kinds of folks live and work here, and sailors stay while their ships are fixed at the dockyard. People in town sell them clothes, tobacco, as well as food and spirits. We also have watchmakers and jewelers to sell to richer customers. It's a booming town, but you should not explore it alone. There are pickpockets and ruffians about."

My ma kept me away from strangers. Even respectable-looking people could turn out to be rogues and thieves. My muscles tightened as I remembered her instructions and heeded Oli's warning.

He pointed out some more buildings. "The synagogue is further on High Street, near the St. Bartholomew's Hospital. There's Mr. Hyman's apothecary shop. That way is the market where we buy kosher meat. This is the home of Mr. Simons who runs a Hebrew school."

I was too tired to ask what those strange words, like kosher, Hebrew, or synagogue meant. But I noticed that this part of town was cleaner, and some folks were dressed better.

Our coach stopped in front of a two-story home built of brown bricks. Lace curtains covered the inside of every window.

Every muscle in my body was as heavy as lead and my head ached. When I stepped down from the coach, my knees buckled. Oli caught me.

"You look too tired to climb the stairs. Want me to carry you?"

The world spun in front of my eyes. I nodded. We ascended the stairs, with me nestled in Oli's arms. Someone was playing the fiddle; not a melody, but the notes from the lowest growl to the highest squeak. The instrument cried like it was hurting as badly as my head.

"It's David! *Vey iz mir*, what happened?" A woman's voice exclaimed when Oli opened the door.

"David is home?" A boy's voice rang, and the fiddle silenced to my relief. The stench of fried fish hit my nose, and my temples squeezed. I moaned softly.

"Ah, he found himself a bride and is carrying her over the threshold," a man with a deep voice said and chuckled. His black beard was down to his chest, and his eyes sparkled with laughter.

"Isaac, not a time for jokes," the woman huffed and wrung her hands. She was shorter and heavier than my Ma, and probably fifteen years older. A loose strand of graying hair peeked from under her headscarf. "David, is this child hurt? And why is your head uncovered?"

Oli grunted at the last question. He eased me onto a sofa. "She's exhausted from the journey. Mama, could you prepare a bed for her in Shira's room? I'll get my things from the coach," he said and walked out.

I glanced around, wincing from the throbbing in my head. The room boasted a long table with a spotless white tablecloth, fancy dishes, and silverware. I wondered if the family was preparing for a celebration, or this is how they ate every day.

"Who is this girl?" a boy asked.

I squinted to see his head peeking out from another room. He looked like Oli, with the same curly hair and dark eyes. I guessed him to be Moishe, and the man and the woman to be his parents.

"My intuition was right," the woman muttered as she threw open trunks and drawers, retrieving sheets and blankets. "Something told me we'll have guests for Sabbath. Good thing I sent Shira to the market for more vegetables."

"Is she going to sleep in Shira's room? Where would Naomi sleep when she stays over?" The boy queried, studying me.

"Why did you stop playing your violin, Moishe?" his father said sternly. "You have another twenty minutes."

"But I want to know what's happening!"

"I wish I knew what's happening," the man muttered, scratching his neck.

"Enough fiddling for today," the woman said as she retrieved a nightdress from a trunk. "This child is unwell. Look how she's cringing in pain. I bet her head hurts. And mine too," she added under her breath.

The man cleared his throat. "Leah, he's supposed to play scales for twenty more minutes. If we let him cut his practice short each time someone's head is hurting, how will he ever improve?"

"*Oy vey* Isaac! Next time you have a headache, I will play that fiddle over your head." She laid her warm hand on my forehead. "Come to the bedroom, child. I'll try to make you feel better."

She led me to a chamber with two beds. When I laid down on the crisp sheets that smelled of lavender, a black cat came out to sniff me. I tried to pet her, but she dashed under the bed across from me.

The woman's creased hands wiped my face with a wet cloth. "So thin and pale," she muttered. "Did David give you anything to eat?"

I heard the door open and guessed that Oli returned with his things.

"Why do you call him David?" I peered at the woman.

She gave me a puzzled look but then laughed. "My son took a Christian name so he could study in medical school. But his name is David Fridman. We named him after the great Jewish King. And what's your name?"

"Abigail."

"Ah, like one of King David's wives." She beamed at me. "The beautiful and wise Abigail."

I was neither beautiful nor wise. But I liked that my name was connected to King David and his namesake. I made a decision right there to call him David.

"What do I call you?"

"I'm Leah Fridman, but all children call me Mama. Even not my own. I visit children when they are sick. David may be studying in medical school, but I bet I know as much about measles and chickenpox as he does." She smiled before leaving me alone in the room with the small black cat eyeing me curiously.

"Mama," I whispered, listening for a sign from my ma. If she were angry with me for finding another mother, she would show it. But the word tasted sweet on my lips, like milk with honey. "Papa." I always envied the children who sat with their fathers in church. Bullies avoided picking on girls who had strong, well-respected fathers. A warm sensation spread through me.

Half-asleep, I listened to voices coming from the dining room through the door left half-open.

"Moishe, go play outside. Adults need to talk," Mama said.

"I want to hear about the girl. And to play chess with my brother."

"We will play later, I promise." David answered with affection in his voice. "And this time I won't go down so easily."

"If you don't want to play outside, you will read in your room," Papa said. "What will it be?"

The door banged shut.

Mama's voice was tense. "Son, what happened? Who is this child?"

I rubbed my eyes to keep myself awake.

"Abigail is an orphan in need of a home." David told them how he treated me in the hospital, and how he took me to the orphanage but couldn't leave me there. His parents sighed and gasped a few times throughout the story.

"Poor child who's suffered so much. Maybe she's Jewish?" Mama asked.

"Of course not, Mama." David groaned. "She prays to the Virgin Mary."

Papa chuckled. "Mary was a good Jewish woman."

I forced myself to sit up. If these people would not let me pray to my savior Mary, I wasn't sure what I would do. David swore an oath in front of me!

"That's nothing to make light of!" David's voice deepened. "Abigail's to worship as she likes. Her late mother taught her to pray. When I told her about Rachel and Noah, she prayed that

Mary would look after them. I almost burst out crying." David's voice quivered.

Mama sniffled. "What a sweet child. I love her already."

"We won't force our beliefs on her," Papa said. "But while living here, she will hear us pray and see us observe our holidays. Keeping her away would be ungracious."

"She shouldn't feel excluded," David answered after a pause. "But send her to a church school."

"Hmm, I saw well-dressed girls with books coming out from St. Margaret's. I'll see if that's a school she could attend."

I exhaled a sigh of relief and laid back.

"But... what will she eat?" Mama's voice pitched. "Do Gentile children eat gefilte fish?"

The men hooted and then Mama joined in with her ringing laugh. In their laughter, I heard 'Welcome'.

Chapter 6

After a rest and a good scrubbing, I felt like a new girl when I walked into the dining room. The table was covered with dishes, many of which I did not recognize. Pungent smell of fish tickled my nose. Papa sat down at the head of the long table, and the rest of the family took their seats. I found a spot between Mama and David, across from Shira, Naomi, and Moishe. The black cat, Murka, rubbed against David's feet.

My mouth watered as I inhaled the aromas of savory and sweet food. Yet, no one started eating. Shira, a thin and curly-haired girl around sixteen, scrutinized me. Her redheaded friend, Naomi, stared at her empty plate. Moishe fidgeted in his seat. He lost interest in me after learning that I couldn't play chess or musical instruments. Mama and Papa exchanged looks, as if unsure how to proceed. Only David seemed at ease.

"Abigail, why don't you say grace?" David said. "Then we'll light the candles and recite the Sabbath prayers."

In a voice just above whisper, I said grace. "Bless us, O Lord, and these, thy gifts, which we are about to receive from Thy bounty. Through Christ, our Lord. Amen."

The simple words were reassuring and calming. Repeating the familiar prayer was like walking into my old home and seeing Ma with the babies.

My world felt upside-down. People who were supposed to care for me turned me away. Jewish strangers I was taught to avoid sheltered me.

After I finished, Mama lit the two tall candles in silver candle-holders and waved her hands over them. "*Baruch Atah...,*" she started, and covered her eyes. Her intonation reminded me of the lullabies David sang. The family proceeded to say two more chants over the wine and the braided bread.

"I believe God accepted all our prayers," David said with a smile.

With her brow furrowed, Shira turned to Papa. "Is this what we'll do at every meal? She'll pray to Jesus in front of us?"

"Why doesn't she say the bracha with us?" Moishe leaned forward to study me.

I fidgeted and looked down at my lap.

Papa gave his children a stern stare. "When we left the Russian Empire and came here almost twenty years ago, we had nothing. Strangers shared food and shelter with us, including Christian people. Our fortune has turned around, and we are extending our home to Abigail. Under this roof, she can pray however she wishes." He smiled at me then drank from his cup.

Shira cringed but didn't persist in arguing. She clenched Naomi's hand and whispered in her ear, but I caught one of the things she said. "Mama will use her as free help rather than hire a servant." Naomi caressed Shira's shoulder.

After Papa reached for the bread, the family filled their plates. Mama hovered over me, asking what I wanted. "Do you eat herring? Will you try blinis? Do you like tzimmes?"

Eager to try everything, I nodded to whatever she offered and filled my mouth with the variety of foods, new but delicious. David explained that blinis were Russian pancakes and tzimmes was carrots and honey. I was too busy chewing to fully listen. My stomach hummed with pleasure. Mama beamed at my appetite and kept offering more.

"You'll make her sick," David warned when Mama filled my plate with more oily blinis. "Her body needs to get used to such feasts after years of undereating."

"What do you know about hunger?" Mama countered. "You were still a baby when we came to England with nothing but the clothes on our backs and your father's violin. Your older sisters were all skin and bone, just like this child." She patted my head. "Eat as much as you want, dear," she whispered into my ear. I nodded and bit into a scone, the most delicious of the foods I've tasted at the dinner. Maybe the best one I'd had in my life.

I wouldn't regret gorging on those scones even if they gave me a bellyache later.

"What do I care about what happened all those years ago?" Shira lowered her cup with a bang and fired an angry gaze at Mama. "She's wearing my old dress. She took Naomi's bed. Now Naomi can't stay overnight."

"It's all right," Naomi whispered, staring at her untouched plate. "My mother has been sleeping better lately, and I get decent respite as well. You were right, Mrs. Fridman. She's calmer since my marriage has been arranged."

Shira squeezed her friend's hand and glared at Mama. "Should I expect that you'll find me a marriage match as well? You now have a new daughter." She pointed at me.

My mouth dried. If Shira disliked me, I may find myself homeless again. *Hungry.* My hand reached for another scone. I wrapped it into a napkin so I could eat it later, when my stomach would growl from emptiness.

Mama rubbed my back and gave her daughter a fierce stare. "Don't upset the child with your wicked tongue. And show some respect to your elders."

Shira huffed and rolled her eyes.

My gaze dashed between the mother and the daughter as I sipped water to wash down the food. David, who was feeding Murka a piece of fish, bent his head to me. "I'm sorry that my sister is being rude. She's not always like this. When she's in good spirits, she bakes delicious cakes. Those scones you were enjoying are her specialty."

I marveled that the mean girl was so good with her baking.

Papa put his fork down. "Shira, I'm ashamed of your behavior. You will apologize to your mother and to Abigail. Our Lord commanded us to obey our elders and to help others in need. I repeat, Abigail is to live with us and to be treated like family."

Shira reddened and lowered her eyes as she apologized.

I held my breath. This must be what it was like to have a father. Someone to take charge, to set things right but without yelling or beating. Never had I such a man in my life. And this man was inviting me to join his family. "Thank you," I whispered to Papa.

"I hope you will be happy with us, Abigail," he replied.

Mama hugged my shoulders. David watched me, smiling. Murka jumped into his lap and cocked her head at me.

When most plates were clear, Naomi rose with her gaze downward. "Thank you for dinner. I must go home and give my mother her medicines. Good Sabbath."

David turned to her. "Perhaps I could stop by in the morning and examine your mother?"

"She's had enough doctors." Naomi averted her eyes. "I appreciate your offer, but it's cancer of women's parts, and those exams are not dignified. She suffered in silence for years rather than calling for Dr. Kaplan."

Shira raised her head. "There should be women doctors."

"I wholeheartedly agree." David nodded. "It's a shame women are not permitted to enroll in medical schools. As well as Jews." He clenched his napkin.

"Women studying in schools with men. Whoever heard of such a thing." Mama waved her hand dismissively. "Women teach women how to care for their families, passing experience from one generation to the next. If only the young would listen."

Naomi's eyes dulled. "With my mother beyond medical help, I don't have a choice."

Wearing an understanding smile, Mama gathered some food into a sack and offered it to the sad-looking girl. "Naomi, dear. I'm doing what's best for you. It will be a relief to your mother to see you wed to a good man."

Naomi accepted the bag with a curt thanks.

"Take some soup for your mother. And I'll come in the morning to help you wash her," Mama called after Naomi, but the girl walked out without a reply.

"Poor girl. But soon she'll see it was all for the best. A good man, like the one I found her, will provide for her and make her happy." Mama returned to her seat with a sigh.

At least Naomi wasn't forced to work at the mill or beg. A marriage seemed like an excellent alternative. Ma's friends, Lulu and Mabel, dreamed of husbands who would have enough money to support them. Lost in thought, I bit into another scone but a wave of nausea made me leave the rest of it on my plate.

"What you've done is cruel. She hardly knows her match. And he's ten years older than her," Shira hissed at Mama.

"Nothing wrong with all that." Mama shrugged. "Lots of women marry older men. He's twenty-seven, and she's seventeen. It's a good age for both. With *Hashem's* blessing, they'll be fruitful. As for not knowing him, just ask your sisters. One look is all it took. *Bashert*. Soulmates. And look how happy they are with their husbands and children."

Shira lowered her head. "It won't be so simple for her," she whispered. "Or for me."

My very full belly ached mildly. My eyes began to close on their own.

"Did Abigail eat all those scones?" Moishe asked. "How did they all fit into her?"

Suddenly, there was silence. I opened my eyes to see everyone watching me. "They were so good," I whispered.

"Are you feeling all right?" David studied me with concern.

I rubbed my swollen belly. "I've never been this full before. I feel... strange. And sleepy."

Mama walked me to the bedroom, helped me get ready for bed, and kissed me goodnight. When she left, I said my prayers to Our Lady. I thanked her for sending me to this kind family that had plenty of food. They were Jews, and yet they were kind.

As my body relaxed on the clean sheets, I wondered if I should ask my new family about taking in Julian and Josie. Ma would have wanted us to stay together. But if my brother and sister were to come here, I'd have to help with them. There would be soiled clothes and sleepless nights all over again.

"No. They should stay with Verna," I murmured to myself. "It's her job to care for them now."

Chapter 7

Murka sprawled on the rug between Shira's and my beds, shifting her green eyes from the older girl to me. Lately she preferred to cuddle on my blanket, staying away from Shira's foul moods. Judging from my new sister's jerky movements as she donned her night dress and combed her hair, tonight something made her especially cross. The cat waited for us to climb into our beds and scrambled onto my legs.

Shira and I shared the bedroom for four months now, but there was an invisible wall between us. In a half-hearted attempt to break that wall, I made a habit of speaking about my day, even though Shira rarely replied.

"Today I polished silverware with Mama," I said, smiling to myself. "She showed me how to make it shine so clearly that I could see my reflection in the spoons."

"I don't understand why you adore Mama so much." Shira grunted after a pause. "All she wants for her daughters is to marry and have babies. Like we don't have minds or can't learn a trade."

Glad to hear Shira speak but outraged by her lack of esteem for Mama, I petted Murka's soft fur. "You don't know how lucky you are," I repeated the phrase Mama often said to Shira. *How many other families could boast a set of silverware for special holidays?*

The girl punched her pillow, making poor Murka scurry under my bed. "You are the lucky one. You are simple. All you need is a full belly."

I hugged my knees. "That's not true. I like school and get good marks." Since I started at St. Margaret's School for Girls, I worked hard to catch up to my classmates.

"A lot of good that will do for you. When I finished school at the age of twelve, I begged Papa to hire me a tutor so I could continue learning. Papa almost agreed, but Mama said that a daughter of a Jewish silversmith doesn't need to paint or study French."

Mama's reason made sense to me. *Why spend money on something not useful?* But I liked that Shira was talking to me.

I turned to face her. "Why do you want to study French?"

"Because... because when David showed interest in German, Papa bought him books. When I opened those books, Mama said I was being idle and gave me mending to do. *Hashem* forbid I become too clever. A girl with little education has fewer choices. And marriage becomes the best option." She growled.

"I heard Mama say you will learn to love your husband. Like she loves Papa."

Silence for a while, then Shira spoke. "Mama arranged Naomi's marriage so Naomi's mother could die happy. And now my dearest friend is miserable, and so is her husband. She can't learn to love him. And if I marry some man Mama finds for me, I'll be unhappy as well."

Shira turned her back to me and pulled the blanket over her head. Muffled sobs broke the peace of the cool April night. To lull myself to sleep, I hummed one of David's lullabies. He left soon after bringing me to Chatham. I missed him singing to me.

The song reminded me of Julian and Josie. *Does Verna sing to them? Does she comfort them when they cry?* My heart pinched, but I told myself they were where they should be, cared for by their godmother, a hard but honest Christian woman. My chest heavied, as if a stone lodged inside it. But my ache for my brother and sister dulled.

Soon after the Easter break, I came home from school with my knees trembling and my heart in my throat. Mama gasped as I stumbled into the kitchen.

"Abigail, you are trembling like a rabbit. Who frightened you?"

I opened my mouth but couldn't speak. She wiped her hands on her apron and touched my shoulder. "I knew I shouldn't let you walk alone. Are you hurt?"

I shook my head. The knock on the door made us flinch.

"Don't open, Mama," I whispered.

Her eyes widened and her grip on me hardened. "Talk to me, Abigail. I need to decide if we should run or scream for help. Everyone is out, but the neighbors will hear us. How many of them are there?"

"Three."

"Big men?" She grabbed the carving knife from the counter.

"No," I whispered. "They are ladies."

Mama gaped and returned the knife to its place. "What ladies?"

"From my school."

She doubled-over laughing. "You made me think some ruffians are coming for us. Well, I better see what they need. Don't you worry, child. I can take on louts, and I can handle proper ladies."

Chuckling, she went to open the door. I followed, even though I preferred to hide under the bed. Three women and a girl from my class stood on the threshold, all wearing hats and gloves. I recognized Mrs. Willowby and Mrs. Franklin with her daughter, Beatrice. My classmate looked down at her feet. A lady I didn't know held a fancy Bible under her arm.

Mama plastered a smile on her face. "What do I owe the pleasure to?"

Mrs. Willowby frowned. "Didn't Abigail tell you?"

The ladies studied me with stern expressions. I wanted to sink through the floor.

"Abigail," Mrs. Willowby said. "I asked you to tell Mrs. Fridman about our proposal. You've put us in an uncomfortable position."

Mama stared her down despite the disadvantage in height. "Don't use the child as a go-between. You have something to say, then say it to me."

Mrs. Willowby forced a smile. "It's all right. We are the heads of the Mothers' Committee. We came to tell you that we all appreciate that you not only gave Abigail shelter but sent her to a proper religious school. When our group learned of her circumstances, however, we became concerned."

"Why?" Mama cocked her head.

"This household is not appropriate for Abigail," the lady with the Bible exclaimed. "This is not a Christian home."

Chills traveled through my blood. I could hardly breathe.

Mama scoffed. "Is Abigail not fed, not clothed, not loved? She was barely alive when my son carried her in here four months ago. Look at her now. She is as healthy as any girl I've seen. Healthier than this one," she pointed at Beatrice, "with liver spots and a slouched back. You need to teach her to walk with a book on her head and feed her cod oil."

Mrs. Franklin gaped and peered at her daughter's face and stature as if noticing the issues for the first time. Beatrice hid behind her mother's skirt.

"Abigail's body may be healthy, but her soul is in peril," Mrs. Willowby said. "Your home is not the proper environment for a child to grow up Christian. Abigail is picking up your customs and baffling her classmates. She refuses to do her homework on Saturdays. Sings songs in an outlandish language. A couple of weeks ago, she brought this flat, brittle bread instead of a roll for her lunch. When Beatrice generously offered to share her own sandwich, Abigail refused, saying she doesn't eat leavened bread for Passover."

Mama patted my head. "So much ado over a piece of matzah."

Mrs. Willowby went on as if she did not hear. "Fortunately, Mrs. Quincy," she indicated the lady with the Bible, "has connections at Our Lady of Divine Suffering, a very fine boarding school for girls. We already contacted the headmistress, and she agreed to severely discount the price of admission and boarding. Our committee will use the money raised from donations to pay the rest of the sum. It's an opportunity not to be missed."

"Generally, the term starts in the autumn, but the headmistress is inviting Abigail for the summer. She will work with a teacher to improve her reading and writing and to clear up her... confusion," Mrs. Quincy added.

"Mama, no," I cried. "Don't make me go." I would be among strangers. Not see Mama, Papa, Moishe for months... and David even longer between his visits. Tears filled my eyes.

"Ah, darling," Mama turned to me with a smile. "Do you really think I will let these women take you away from me?"

I hugged her waist and buried my face in her skirt.

"Maybe you don't understand what opportunity this school offers. My husband and I would send Beatrice if we could afford it," Mrs. Franklin said.

"Well, aren't you lucky, child." Mama stepped forward and took Beatrice's hand. "Now there's money to send *you* because Abigail won't be going. Run home and pack. Your mother can't wait for you to leave. And let's hope there will be someone at the school to comfort you when your liver hurts and when the other girls call you a hunchback."

Wide-eyed, Beatrice crouched even lower. "I want to go home, Mother," she mumbled.

"Don't talk to my daughter like that!" Mrs. Franklin shouted.

Mama crossed her arms. "You talk to mine. You show up here, giving no thought to all she's been through. I won't allow you to terrify her."

Mrs. Willowby raised her hand. "I hoped it would not come to this, but I'm afraid we have no choice. We can't have Abigail confusing our children with the Jewish rituals. If she doesn't go to the boarding school, we'll start a petition to have her dismissed from St. Margaret's."

"Well, I'm sure frightened of your petition." Mama laughed as the women's faces reddened. Then she threw her shoulders back and her face tensed. "I escaped from my village when the mob burned Jewish homes. I buried three children. You think you can scare me with a piece of paper? I'm Abigail's mama, and I've decided that your school is not good enough for her. You won't see her there anymore."

She slammed the door in their faces. Then she turned to me and inhaled a long breath. "I'm sorry, Abigail," she said, hugging me. "David was a dreamer to believe you could live here and attend a church school. I won't allow these people make you miserable."

Mama loves me and won't ever let me go. That thought comforted me like a blanket over my trembling shoulders. The price for that love was my schooling. Deep in my heart, I dreamed of growing up educated. Make a better life for myself than Ma and her friends who worked at the mill. *A girl with little education has fewer choices,* Shira said. I wanted to have choices.

Chapter 8

Trembling, I entered Moishe's and David's bedroom. An imposing bookcase and a writing desk were crammed in there. Moishe's violin, sheet music, and school papers were scattered on top of one of the narrow beds. This room was to study in, rest with minimum comfort, and study more. The bedroom Shira and I shared had softer beds, drawers for our clothes, a vanity with a mirror, and baskets for sewing. Even though Shira was literate, there was no bookcase or writing desk. I started to understand Shira's frustration.

My heart was pulled in different ways. Relief of not having to leave my new family. Love for my fierce Mama. Confusion over why sons and daughters were taught differently. The disappointment in myself for muddling my Ma's beliefs with Judaism. Because I could not keep my Christian teaching straight, I would grow up unschooled and dim.

With my fingers shaking, I grabbed a random book from the bookcase. Reading Moishe's books would prove that I'm not a dimwit. But the dusty volume was in a foreign language. I grabbed another. It was in English, but I didn't know half the words in the first paragraph.

Frustrated, I threw the book on the bed and stormed out of the room. After aimlessly wandering from one place into another, I found myself in the music room. It had only two pieces of furniture: a bookcase and a black pianoforte. I suspected the room had other uses before Papa bought the giant instrument years ago from another family. Moishe played it every day and never let me touch the keys. But I heard that the oldest sisters, Miriam and Hannah, used to play in their younger years.

I sat down on the bench and banged the white and black keys with all my might. The instrument screamed as disjointly as the feelings inside me. I banged some more, and each whine and boom released something in my clenched chest.

Pacified, I used one finger to press on every key, one by one, and I was shocked with the logic of this giant box. The placement of the keys was not random. It had perfect order, the same seven notes over and over, but arranged from the deepest sounds, which resembled the growl of a bear, to the highest, like the raindrops against the roof.

I played all keys in order, from lowest to highest pitch and back. Then, with one trembling finger, I played the notes of the lullaby David sang to me at the hospital. Even played by such a poor pianist, the music was sweet and fragile. I played it over and over, at least ten times, until my finger found the keys with no pauses. When the sound flowed and my soul was as peaceful as the song, I laid my arms and head on the keys, exhausted.

The applause made me bolt upright and gaze around. My family stood on the threshold, clapping. Shira and Moishe stared wide-eyed, while Mama's eyes pooled with tears.

"When there's music in you, it finds its way out. Congratulations!" Papa said as he approached to hug me.

Shira hid her face behind her hands and ran out of the room.

Papa patted my shoulder and sighed. "Poor Shira. She is the only child in our family who is not gifted in music. Her name means 'a song', yet she can't sing nor play. But music takes other forms. Someday, she'll discover the kind of music she's meant for." He kissed me on the top of my head. "You, however, just found yours."

"Isaac, we must discuss Abigail's schooling," Mama said, wiping her eyes. "She needs to study at home. And she should have music lessons."

"We'll hire her an excellent tutor. And I will teach her pianoforte." Papa pulled my cheek and left with Mama to talk in another room.

I stared at Moishe, trying to read his face. He was the musical star of the family. *Does he resent my newfound talent?*

His face was thoughtful as he repeatedly nodded and whispered to himself. Then he plopped down next to me and played the same lullaby using all his dexterous fingers, pressing keys faster than my eyes could follow. The flourish of his performance was an entirely different level from my playing. After he finished, he played the melody with the right hand only, using all his fingers, but slow enough for me to follow.

"You had it almost right. It's C flat instead of C. Still good, since you never had lessons... and you are a girl."

I jabbed his side with my elbow, pushing him off the bench. He got up laughing.

When I was getting into my bed with Murka purring on my pillow, Shira studied me. "So, you are not just a stomach on legs. Papa went through your school papers and said you've made remarkable progress in a short time. Now you'll have piano lessons as well. While I... Can you keep a secret?"

I ran my finger over my lips. "I won't tell a soul."

She came to sit by me. Her hand reached for Murka, but the cat jumped off and hid in the corner. "Soon, I will run away to London. Every week, I bake a cake for Mr. Stein, and he pays me for it. In three months, I will have enough money saved for my trip. I don't know how I will make a living in London, but I expect in a big city a girl can find a way."

Her eyes sparkled in the dark as she spoke, but my throat closed from a painful lump. Even I could foresee a disaster. My mind showed me Mama's eyes, full of tears and worry. Papa's quiet despair. David leaving his studies to search for his sister. If Shira ran away, my new family would become unhappy.

And Shira ... would she find whatever she's searching for in London?

I met her eyes. "When my ma died, and I was looking for somewhere to sleep, I met this girl just a little older than you, Amelia. She had wealthy parents, but she ran away to London to become an actress."

My hand on hers, I told Shira all I remembered about Amelia. Her being mistreated and robbed, catching illness, begging for food. My eyes brimmed with tears because I was sure Amelia perished. The only consolation I had was that her mother found her and hopefully comforted her daughter in the end.

Shira listened as if she was drinking in every word. When I finished, she was quiet for a long time. Murka found enough courage to climb back onto the bed. When Shira extended her hand, the cat rubbed her nose against the girl's fingers.

"You are good at telling stories," Shira said finally. "Do you have a favorite pastry?"

This was a sisterly gesture, and I took it, beaming at her. "Scones."

She rolled her eyes. "I'll bake some tomorrow." In Shira's world, this was the highest honor.

A month later, we received a letter from David saying was coming home after his exams. If all went well, he'd be awarded his medical degree. We threw ourselves in a fury of chores for the celebration. Shira's spirits improved as she tried various recipes for cakes and pastries.

"Will David open a practice here at Chatham?" Shira asked Mama as they stood in the basement kitchen, making the shopping list. I heard them from the pantry where I worked with Murka running between my feet. Shira's question made me stop counting the jars of sour cherries and turn to the two women.

Mama clicked her tongue. "People are unlikely to leave Dr. Kaplan, who served our community for twenty years. They would see David as young and inexperienced. It would be better if David worked with Dr. Kaplan and gained trust."

"Would he agree?" Shira rubbed her cheek. "He was so angry at the doctor after Noah's death."

I remembered that on our way to Chatham, David mentioned that Noah was like a brother to him.

A shadow crossed Mama's face. "That poor boy. His death was a shock for everyone. But Dr. Kaplan did all he could, and I'm sure David understands that now. I say we invite the doctor to our celebration." Mama winked, and Shira cocked her head.

I was eager to show David how much I'd grown and learned. Thanks to him, I had a full belly and new clothes, a patient tutor for my schooling, and the joy of music with Papa. David gave me the greatest gift: a loving family. My heart was full of gratitude. And he ensured that my brother and sister had all they needed. I didn't have to worry about them.

After many tries, Shira had managed to talk Mama into hiring a kitchen help, but the washerwoman was sacked that morning, on her second day of work.

"What kind of fool mixes up the *fleishik* dishes with the *milchig* ones?" Mama waved her hands as she complained to Shira after the washerwoman left. Sighing, she gestured at the piles of dishes by the kitchen basin. "She almost washed them all with one tablecloth. A Jewish girl who doesn't know how a kosher kitchen operates! This is what happens when our people forget their ways in this country and don't teach their children. Well, not my daughters. Even Abigail can wash the dishes and put them away in the right places."

"Yes I can, Mama." I started washing the dishes, pleased with myself for using the correct washcloth. *Fleishik* dishes and utensils were for meat, while *milchig* was for dairy. Meat and dairy were never eaten together. I knew which drawers and shelves Mama used for meat, dairy, or even the special set for Passover.

Mama beamed at me. "What a good helper." She bent down to wash the dishes with me.

Shira scoffed. "Of course. Why hire help when you have daughters as free servants?"

"You may think me tightfisted, Shira, but you'll remember my lessons," Mama said. "Someday, when you are married, you'll be thankful for the practice I gave you. And you'll learn to save for a rainy day."

"How many times do I have to say I don't want to be married!" Shira yelled and stormed out.

Mama sighed. "I've never had trouble with my older daughters, born in Russia. At her age, they were dreaming of handsome husbands. Girls get strange ideas in this country. Education. Travel. Men's work. They forget that a woman's mission is marriage and family."

I peered at her. "But my ma had no husband and worked at the mill."

"She had tough luck." Mama leaned back and shook her head. "If she had a husband, she and you would be provided for. Naomi cries to Shira how unhappy she is, but she has food on her plate and a warm bed to sleep in. If not for me, she'd have to work somewhere for a meager wage. She has no reason to complain."

I nodded. "You are right, Mama. You did a good thing, finding Naomi a husband."

Mama draped her arm around me. "My clever girl. You make me so happy." She pulled me close and kissed my cheek. I beamed at her. Every hug warmed me from the inside, gradually filling the deep hole in my soul.

When Moishe and I finished our chores, we worked on the entertainment for the family concert. I was perfecting the lullaby under Papa's instruction. Moishe composed an upbeat piece he called a 'Rondo in B major' and practiced it for hours. Sometimes, Mama would watch us rehearse together and smile to herself.

After supper, the family gathered in the music room to listen to Moishe and me play. They stood around the pianoforte as I sat on the bench. I warmed up with a couple of exercises. Readied, I took a few calming breaths and played the lullaby. Despite my hands sweating under everyone's gaze, I played my piece with no mistakes.

Happy to be done, I basked in praise from Mama and Papa. Even Shira smiled. Next, Moishe played his composition on the pianoforte, his fingers darting all over the keys. He finished with a flourish.

"Bravo!" Mama exclaimed. "You are getting better and better."

"Terrific, son," Papa said and scratched his beard. "Now, how does that piece sound on the violin?"

Moishe frowned and stared at his knees. "Not very well."

"In that case, I expect you will practice until it does," Papa replied with a twinkle in his eyes.

"No." Moishe rose from the bench, his face flushed. "I will not play the violin anymore. You are good at it, but I hate it."

"Isaac, maybe piano is enough ..." Mama began, but Papa raised his hand to halt her. The laughing sparkle in his eyes replaced by a blaze we rarely saw.

"I don't ask much of Moishe. While he's living under our roof, he's to study in the Hebrew school and to play the violin. If he chooses medicine or another demanding profession, I can overlook the second requirement, but for now, he's to master the instrument." Papa's nostrils flared. He stormed out of the room followed by our wide-eyed gazes.

We froze and stared at each other, until Shira reminded Mama that they needed to iron the sheets for David's bed. They left to do their work.

Moishe and I remained in the bedroom, both of us stunned by Papa's outburst. I pretended to read the titles of the books in the bookcase, looking at Moishe over my shoulder. With his eyes full of loathing, Moishe picked up the violin and the bow from his bed, but then laid them down.

"Why is the pianoforte not good enough for him?" he muttered to himself. "I'm ten times better at it than the violin. I would be even better if I spent my free time practicing it and not wasting an hour a day trying to extract music out of this piece of rubbish."

"Have you asked why?" I made a small step toward him.

"He doesn't say." Moishe shrugged. "He just tells me to keep practicing."

I found that hard to believe. Whenever I asked Papa a question, he explained with patience and vigor until I understood the meaning.

I took Moishe by the hand and brought him to Papa, who was hiding his face behind the newspaper.

"Papa," I said, "please tell us why Moishe must play the violin."

He lowered the paper. With his eyes clouded, he spoke in a soft voice.

"Because he can't bring the pianoforte with him. Not when an angry mob has gathered to take their troubles of disease and hunger out on the Jews. Not when the houses nearby are aflame and the next one could be yours. When trouble comes, as it always does, you order the children who can walk to hold each other's hands. You carry your screaming newborn. Then you grab all you think you will need to survive: money, wedding rings or watches to sell, food, blankets, medicines, water. And a few books, because we are the people of the book, and leaving them to burn is like betraying your friends."

He glanced at his son. "Finally, when you are on the threshold, you would run back for the violin case. And you," he looked at me, although I was not sure if he saw *me* at that moment, "would yell, 'What are you doing, you lunatic? We must go now, or we die! Who needs your violin at a time like this?'"

He paused to catch his breath. We stood still, holding ours. "You wouldn't know why you went back for the violin that frustrated you so much. Yet, you bring it with you through the trials that follow. One evening, your family is huddled in a corner by a dying fire. Your daughters are crying because they can't sleep with hunger gnawing in their bellies. Your wife is wailing because, in her anxiety, her milk dried up. You are empty and defeated, and yet your fingers burn to touch the bow. And the song would be there, the song of anguish, fear, despair, and then of hope. Because when you find yourself at the bottom, the only way left is up."

Papa held up his hands as if he were lifting an imaginary violin. His voice rang louder. "With your song, your girls will stop crying and fall asleep holding each other, and your wife will gasp and bring the baby to her breast. Someone will hear you play and spare a few coins, enough for your family to make it through another day. And you will understand that it was a divine power that guided you in the moment when you saved your violin."

Moishe blinked rapidly. "And after, you decided to move to England?"

Papa nodded. "Yes. We lost our home and my silver shop. Several Jewish villages were burned. But when I was a boy, thousands of Jews were massacred in Uman with my uncle among them. I wanted security for my family. We marveled at the stories of Jews thriving in England, like the Goldsmids and the Rothschilds. To scrape up for the ship fare, I played the violin on the streets. All through the difficult voyage, the harrowing storms, the deadly illnesses that spread through the ship, I played to give hope and strength to myself and the people around me. We arrived at Chatham and built a life here. Our family expanded and eventually prospered. One fine morning, we bought the pianoforte because the horrors we lived through seemed a distant past."

He paused and studied us. His jaw was set. "But I cannot forget how we survived. So after I told you all that, son, is it too much for you to practice one hour a day?"

Moishe stared at his shoes. Then he grunted and sped to his room. The screechy cry of the violin echoed from there.

"Abigail," Papa said, smiling at me. "Do you know that your name means 'father's joy'? You embody that name. Thank you for teaching my son how to ask questions."

With my heart so full it threatened to burst, I wrapped my arms around Papa.

We were all asleep before Moishe finished practicing his violin that night.

Chapter 9

The next day, David arrived. His hands were full of gifts for everyone in the family. As he crossed the threshold, Papa blocked his way.

"Do we have a doctor in our *mishpacha*?"

"Can't you tell by his smile?" Mama made a beeline to hug her son.

"This says I can treat patients." David set down the wrapped boxes, removed the expensive-looking paper from his case and passed it over. While Papa studied the document by the window, Mama and Shira hastened to the kitchen to finish preparations for dinner.

"Who is this beautiful girl?" David grinned at me. "You look so much healthier. Mama must be happy that you are eating well."

My heart danced. His praise made me want to spin and twirl around the room.

At dinnertime, the oldest daughters, Hannah and Miriam, arrived with their husbands and children. Aromas of the goose, roasted with plums and apples, the crispy vegetables, and freshly baked bread, all mixed together into the heavenly smell. Murka jumped onto David's lap, anticipating bites from his plate. We were seated and more than ready to eat, but we waited for the last guest to arrive.

The doorbell chimed, and Moishe rushed to let in Dr. Kaplan. The doctor touched the *mezuzah* on the doorframe and kissed his fingers, a custom that blessed and protected the inhabitants of the home and their guests. He was a thin man in his sixties, with gray sidelocks showing from under his hat. His eyes scanned the table, and he grinned. "What a feast! And a rare occasion when I'm invited to indulge and not to work."

When he sat, Mama filled his plate with the best pieces of the goose, and Papa poured the wine. As usual, I said grace first, and then everyone else said the *bracha* for the food we were about to enjoy.

"I have quite a story to tell," David said as we dug into the meal. Everyone at the table looked up to listen. "My friend Alan Parker turned out to be a girl called Ella. Top student of my class, my tutor and study partner, a brilliant young woman." It was obvious from his tone that he admired Ella.

I remembered Alan, who found me begging with Amelia and carried me to the hospital. This was six months ago, but now it seemed like another lifetime. With a pinch in my chest, I realized weeks had passed since I last thought about Julian and Josie. They probably forgot me already.

"A woman surgeon?" Dr. Kaplan asked when David said that Ella intended on treating the wounded aboard a warship. "I doubt the sailors will welcome her."

"Not at first, but Ella is incredibly determined and intelligent." David's eyes sparkled.

"This Ella, she's not Jewish, is she?" Mama asked, with forced casualness in her voice.

"No." David rolled his eyes. "She's from a noble British family."

Frowning, Mama bunched her napkin. "You seem to be taken with this girl."

Shira jumped to her feet. Her cheeks flushed. "David is right to admire her. She showed her teachers that a woman could be a surgeon, not just a wife and a mother."

"What's so wrong with being *just* a wife and a mother? Keeps me busy enough," Hannah scoffed.

"Wait till you have a husband and children, Shira." Miriam said. "It's hard work to care for your family. But it's a labor of love," she added, smiling at her husband.

Shira stomped her foot. "You don't understand. This woman will have a profession, respect, pride in her achievements. That's what I need!"

"Calm yourself, please," Papa said. "I don't want Dr. Kaplan to think that my children are ill-mannered."

Shira sat and hid her face in her hands. I longed to hug her even though she would not welcome affection from me. Ever since I discovered my musical talent, I felt a spark inside me that grew each time I played. *What if Shira has the same spark but does not know how to make it grow?*

David placed his hand on Shira's shoulder. "I didn't mean to rile you, sister. But Ella's not only talented. She had the best tutors since she was little. I don't think you could succeed in a university with the education you received."

"Yes, all I've learned is domestic work." Shira let out a heavy sigh. "And I despise it."

I remembered Ma teaching me to wash the floor when I was four. *Was domestic work something to enjoy or despise? It just had to be done.*

"Mmm. The bread is wonderful, Shira." Papa bit a piece and closed his eyes. "Crusty with the soft middle. It's better each time you bake it."

"But didn't you hear me? I need..." Shira groaned and threw up her hands.

"Why don't you go check on the cake, Shira?" Mama suggested. "And as you walk, take a moment to think about the blessings you have."

After Shira stomped out, an uncomfortable silence followed. Dr. Kaplan said he needed to visit a patient, but Mama refilled his plate with another cut of the goose. "You must stay for Shira's cake," she added. "That girl may have vinegar on her tongue, but her baking is heavenly sweet."

"Son, why don't you tell us about the things you've learned in medical school?" Papa suggested. Dr. Kaplan stopped chewing and whipped his head to listen.

"My thesis was about hygiene. Surgeons and midwives must wash their hands and instruments. When they touch one patient after another with no handwashing in between, they spread disease." David lowered his head. "My ideas were not well received."

"Jewish doctors have known this for centuries." Dr. Kaplan grinned. "I learned to wash my hands thoroughly from Jewish healers in Germany. But I doubt you'll sway the British medical men. What else have you learned?"

David chewed his lip and put Murka down. He spoke after a minute of contemplation. "Some surgeons are making great strides. I watched Dr. Miller operate on a child with appendicitis. She made a full recovery."

A pregnant pause hung in the air. "Well, that's wonderful," Mama muttered. "Hopefully this malady will be conquered."

Keeping his eyes on the guest, David paused. "What do you think of that?"

"Are you still angry about Noah?" Dr. Kaplan cringed and leaned back. "Surely after medical school you can understand that I could not save him. The surgery you witnessed must've been the first of its kind. Only the famous Dr. Miller could take on such a risk and not fear for his reputation. It will be years before other surgeons attempt the same feat."

Shira returned and placed the honey cake in the center of the table, but no one gave it attention. We all forgot our food, listening to the discussion.

"I intend to master the procedure." David sipped his wine. "There are many risks, but it can save lives. Dr. Miller is planning a series of lectures on the subject. Will you attend?" He gazed at the doctor with a challenge in his eyes.

"Leave my patients? Impossible." Dr. Kaplan waved his hand.

"I'll tend to your patients while you are gone."

Mama lifted a knife to slice the cake. "That's a splendid idea. David could—"

"No." Dr. Kaplan shook his head. "My patients are used to my ways and will feel uncomfortable with someone so young. And frankly, I doubt I could learn a surgery of such complexity. For the last ten years, I've only picked up the blade to remove warts and hang nails."

David clasped his hands together and set his jaw. "Then, the next time, you will be as helpless as you were with Noah. Because you refuse to learn, another patient may die. How can you live with that thought?"

His parents gasped at the same time. Dr. Kaplan's face reddened to the shade of the beet soup. He slowly rose and headed for the door.

"I'm sorry about my son's behavior. Please wait," Papa exclaimed and leaned across the table to David. "Apologize, son. This is not how we treat guests."

Mama drew a sharp breath. "Go after him and apologize. You need him to find your footing in this town." When David shook his head in answer, she hurried to Dr. Kaplan on the threshold. "I'm so sorry. David is tired after exams. When he's in better spirits he'll come to you and apologize. You have much to teach him."

The doctor shrugged and shook his finger at David. "You speak like that because you have little experience. I hoped to work with you and become your mentor, but your attitude makes it unfeasible."

David rose and approached the doctor. "I can't have a mentor who isn't willing to learn. And I have no desire to practice in Chatham. I will volunteer for the army. The war with Napoleonic France is in a critical moment, and there's a shortage of surgeons."

Paled, Mama shrieked as if she saw a ghost. Hannah and Miriam grabbed each other's arms. My heart dropped into the pit of my stomach. I breathed hard to keep sickness down.

"Son, no!" Mama cried with her hands on her head. "You'll get yourself killed."

"Are you *meshugener*?" Papa asked, rising.

Dr. Kaplan clicked his tongue. "Young man, listen to your parents. Don't risk your life foolishly."

David tossed his head back. "This is important not just for my career, but for all British Jews. We are outsiders in England. We are barred from universities and many professions. Joining a patriotic cause would demonstrate our loyalty to the King and country."

"Am I old enough to join?" Moishe asked, but his sisters shushed him.

"What good will it do if you are dead?" Mama's voice trembled.

"You are a dreamer to think that your sacrifice would count for anything," Papa said. "You will break our hearts, and nothing will change."

A cold chill seized my body. Every fiber of it screamed with a horrible premonition. *If David goes to war, he won't come back.* I was certain.

With sobs convulsing my throat, I ran to David and threw myself on my knees. My short arms hugged David's legs.

"Abigail don't cry. I will be all right," he said, patting my head. "I won't be fighting. I'll be safe, treating the wounded." There were false notes in his soothing tone.

"Look what you are doing to the poor child," Mama said, wiping her tears. "If you have no pity for your parents, think of your brothers and sisters."

"Abigail, please let go of my legs. I brought you a new doll. Let me go so I can show it to you." David tried to free himself, but I only held him harder.

"Son," Papa spoke. "You don't need to enlist to treat the wounded. Naval hospitals receive the injured seamen. I'll use my connections in the navy to get you a job. You may need to continue using your Christian name, but you'll see all the battle wounds you desire."

I squeezed my eyes shut and silently begged Our Lady to make David listen.

After a minute, he loosened his posture. "Fine. I will work in the naval hospital if you get me a position."

The sigh of relief came from everyone at once. I let my hands drop. Dr. Kaplan tipped his hat and left. The older sisters and their husbands rose and said goodbyes, while Papa summoned David to his room for a talk. Mama, Shira, and I gathered the dishes to the cries of Moishe's violin. Our concert was postponed, but Moishe never skipped a practice.

"My heart is still heavy," Mama confessed as we descended to the kitchen. "I prayed that David would return to our community. And this Gentile woman, Ella. Did you see how excited he was when he spoke about her? I don't like it."

Shira filled a basin with water from a jug, avoiding Mama's gaze. "He said they are friends."

Mama rested her hand on her bosom. "A mother's heart feels trouble before it comes. If David falls in love with a Christian... it would be as bad as him dying in the war."

"But why?" I interjected. I didn't want David to fall in love with Ella, but Mama's statement shocked me. *I am a Christian too.*

Shira wiped her palms on her apron and lowered her head.

Mama studied me and spoke slowly, as if she chose her words with care. "Abigail, you may be too little to understand. Ella sounds like a wonderful person. I remember she was the one who brought you to the hospital when you were ill. But Jews are commanded to marry within our faith. If a Jewish man takes a Gentile wife, his parents must disown him and mourn him as if he died. We'd sit *shiva* for a week, crying and grieving. For the rest of our lives, we'd never acknowledge that we have a living son."

"This happened in our family before." Shira swallowed hard. "We never speak of Papa's cousin."

"Never." Mama shook her head. "That's why it's very important that David meets a good Jewish woman and takes her as a wife."

Black dots danced in front of my eyes. My insights twisted, and the contents of my full stomach rose up my throat.

"Are you all right?" Mama bent down to me. "What's wrong, Abigail?"

"My belly," I grabbed my middle. "I think I'm going to be—"

I ran outside, but instead of dashing to the privy, I crouched in the bushes. Fresh air helped me keep my food down. My head was muddled with the strangest thoughts as I tried to make sense of them.

David saved me and gave me a wonderful life with his family. I was so grateful. When he was away, I missed him. But the notion that he would find a wife, whether Gentile or Jewish, made me ill. I couldn't understand why.

Part 2

Part 2

Chapter 10

*B*right light assaults my eyes.

"She's alive! Turn her on her side!"

The water pours from my mouth and nose. Someone is hitting my back. My chest contracts. I cough, spitting out more water. Air rushes into my lungs. Heavy towels cover my quivering body.

"Why? Why did you do this?" a woman's voice demands. Her face is a blur. My mind is too sluggish to place her voice.

I speak between the coughing fits. "I love David... Always have... Wanted to marry him."

Bitter water rushes into my mouth and I vomit. Then I tumble back into my memories.

Two Years Earlier

Mama unwrapped Sarah's infant and inspected the red spots on his legs and belly. Then she used a finger to pry his mouth open. "It's chickenpox," she said with confidence. "Give him a cool bath with oatmeal and do your best to feed him and give him water. There's also an ointment you can buy from the apothecary to ease the itch."

Under the weight of our purchases from the market I fidgeted, my arms were heavy. At fifteen, I was taller and stronger than Mama and carried most of our shopping. Still trying to be a perfect daughter, I accompanied her on her errands, which often included unexpected visits like this one. A woman at the market remarked that Rabbi Cohen prayed for his grandson to get better, and Mama rushed over to check on the sick baby.

Usually, I didn't mind. Helping Mama at home and watching her care for children would make me a good wife and mother one day. Mama impressed on me that schooling and music were luxuries for young women, but mastery of domestic work was a must. This morning, however, my back and head throbbed.

Sarah, the rabbi's daughter, adjusted her robe. Mama's early visit caught her off-guard. "I thought that's what it was, but with the smallpox outbreak, I was worried. They say St. Bartholomew's Hospital is overrun with patients."

The baby fussed; Mama's deft hands massaged his belly, carefully avoiding the lesions. Watching her burp the infant reminded me how my brother and sister, Julian and Josie, twisted and whimpered at times. Not knowing how to help them, I sang to them instead of turning them on their bellies. It was good that they were with Verna, who was much more able to care for them than me. Except... they were now six and five, and no longer needed help burping. It was strange to imagine them as children who could run and play. *Do they even know about Ma or me?*

"Such a shame." Mama shook her head, returning the quelled infant to his mother. "All my family is inoculated from smallpox. I hope yours is as well. David says that's one disease we don't have to worry about catching. He is a doctor, you know." Her cheeks pinked with pride as she spoke of her son. Then she gasped. "By the way, is your younger sister unattached?"

"Rivka?" Sarah raised an eyebrow. "She is. Mother is thinking of talking to the matchmaker."

"David is a modern man and wouldn't agree to a matchmaker." Mama twisted the wedding ring on her finger. "But it's high time he takes a wife. He lives away at Plymouth, near the naval hospital where he works. I so want him to marry and return to Chatham. He should meet Rivka. She's such a lovely girl."

The load in my arms turned to lead. I suppressed a groan.

"But how would they meet?" Sarah asked. "Our parents are strict."

Mama gave her a cunning smile. "There are ways even the Rabbi won't object to. Abigail and I will go to the apothecary and purchase the ointment for your little one. Then, around noon, send Rivka to our home for the remedy. David happens to be visiting this week. If *bashert*, one look will be enough."

On the way to the apothecary, I confronted Mama. "What are you planning? David would not like you pushing him to marry. He's busy with his patients in the hospital."

Mama rested her hand on her forehead with a deep sigh. "I must do what I must. This British air is making young people uncontrollable. The most important thing for a Jewish person is to marry and start a family. And what are my children doing? David still writes to that *shiksa* Ella. Shira declared that she'll never marry. I bid more time for Shira to come to her senses, but I will not rest until David meets every eligible Jewish girl in Chatham."

My head swam. This morning, when David complimented me on my piano playing, I thought that he *saw* me. Perhaps saw how pretty and clever I was becoming. Noticed how much more intelligent my speech sounded thanks to all the books I'd read to impress him. Acknowledged how much I grew up since that day almost five years ago when he brought me into his family. And now, Mama was charging ahead with plans to get him married.

We were passing by the synagogue, a modest building built on the grounds of St. Bartholomew's Hospital, situated near the river. Mama gazed at the graveyard next to it. "Let's visit Rachel," she said. "Her birthday is coming."

She picked a round pebble from the ground and walked over to the gray headstone. There was a name 'Rachel Fridman' and the years of birth and death. Twelve short years.

After we pulled a couple of weeds from the grave, Mama placed the pebble on the headstone, a ritual to pay homage to the deceased and drive away evil spirits. There were many pebbles on Rachel's headstone already. Mama visited the graveyard at least once a week, and other family members stopped by as well.

My hand ran over the cool headstone. *Does Verna care for my ma's grave? I wonder if Julian and Josie visit it.* More than a year since the last letter from Verna. Her letters were short—she barely could write—and biting. In each letter she berated me for living with the Jews. She said I sold my Christian soul for their food and money. Yet, she did not invite me to live with her.

"My dear little girl, how I miss you," Mama began speaking. She always spoke to Rachel as if she were there to hear her. "As I told you last week, Hannah birthed a healthy boy. Miriam's youngest is now walking. David is visiting for the first time this year. He's been busy with his patients at the hospital. I hope to find him a bride. Moishe is doing well with his music. Abigail makes us all proud with her learning and piano. She's always helping me at home." Mama smiled at me. "And Shira... Shira..."

Mama paused and choked out, "will drive me into an early grave."

I clenched my teeth. "Stop it, Mama. There's nothing wrong with opening a bakery."

Papa and I were proud of Shira. First Jewish woman in town to own a shop. Papa loaned her the money and wrote his name on official documents but let Shira make all decisions concerning the business. He said that Shira finally found her song.

Mama's eyebrows rose. "You've grown up, Abigail. You are learning to speak your mind. But there are things you don't understand. I would approve if Shira sold some cakes at the market. But no, she had to have a shop on High Street and call it Shira's Kosher Bakery. Why draw attention like this? She's asking for trouble." Mama swallowed hard. "And you don't know the latest. Shira has hired Naomi permanently and is moving in with her."

I gasped from the sudden chill. Naomi's husband killed himself a year ago. People said it was Naomi's fault. Whenever the redheaded woman headed our way, Mama crossed the street.

Mama watched me jerk back and nodded in satisfaction. "Yes, now you see. David insists I make peace with Shira. Made me invite Naomi to dinner." She clutched her chest. "If my suspicions are correct, I may die of shame on the spot."

"Is it shameful for two women to live together?" I asked. "There are two spinsters who share a room in the house next to ours."

"There are things that you are too young to understand." Mama patted my head. "I just hope I'm wrong this time. But I'm rarely wrong."

You are wrong about me, I thought. I could never tell her that I loved David, that I dreamed of marrying him despite our differences in religion and age.

After Mama said goodbye to Rachel, we walked to Mr. Hyman's apothecary shop to buy the ointment. My head grew heavy, and I shivered despite the summer heat. I wondered if I caught a cold.

As we stepped into the shop, my nose wrinkled from the smells of potent herbs. Jars and vials of all sizes and colors filled the shelves. There were a few customers gazing around, waiting their turn. A woman was showing Mr. Hyman, the apothecary, an angry burn on her arm. He clicked his tongue as he carefully measured out ingredients for the remedy.

The lady in front of us wrung her hands and fidgeted. "May I be next?" she called to Mr. Hyman, but he ignored her question.

"Golda?" Mama called the woman, and she turned.

"Leah! Oh, hello Abigail. It's good to see you both," she said, although her face expressed slight annoyance rather than delight.

"What a coincidence!" Mama exclaimed. "Last night, I saw your Ester in a dream. She and my David were walking hand in hand in this beautiful rose garden. It was a vision to behold."

A dream, indeed. I suppressed an urge to roll my eyes.

Golda gaped and her eyes bulged. "Ester and David?"

"I've had prophetic dreams before." Mama gave her a knowing smile.

The woman bobbed her head. "It must be true," she whispered and clenched Mama's hand. "I had the same dream last week."

I groaned; people turned their heads to me. I pretended to cough.

Mama's grin stayed on her lips. "Visit us with Ester tomorrow for dinner. I'll make sure that David will be home. If it's *bashert*..."

"A dinner would be lovely. I just hope Ester's bellyache passes." Golda chewed her lip.

"Bellyache?" Mama's smile disappeared and her eyes grew keen. "Any fever? Vomiting? How does her tongue look?"

Golda fidgeted more with each question. "It's probably just the fish she ate. I'm sure she'll be all right after taking whatever Mr. Hyman prescribes."

"Fish?" Mama gasped. "Spoiled fish could make her terribly ill. You better fetch Dr. Kaplan."

"Oh, it's nothing that serious." Golda wiped a bead of sweat off her forehead. "We all ate that fish and only Ester got sick. Her stomach is a little... sensitive."

"Why don't I stop by?" Mama leaned in and lowered her voice. "I've treated all kinds of bellyaches. One time Hannah had closed bowels for five days—"

"Next!" The apothecary called, saving me and Golda from a story that would surely go into unpleasant details.

Golda put her hand on Mama's shoulder. "I insist you go before me. Abigail looks tired. And no need to worry about Ester. I'm sure she'll be fine by tomorrow."

Mama tried to argue, but I stepped up to Mr. Hyman's counter and asked for the chickenpox ointment. After he dispensed it to us, Mama wanted to stay and hear what remedy he would suggest for Ester's bellyache.

I grabbed her arm and led her away, eager to be home. My head was hurting. We were almost by our house when Mama turned to a side street.

"Where are we going now?" I whined. My whole body ached like I carried stones.

"This will only take a minute. It's Wednesday, almost noon. Dr. Kaplan will be drinking tea with Mr. Simons, the Hebrew teacher. I should let the doctor know about Ester. I'd send David, but with Ester it may not be... appropriate. It may be *bashert*, but I don't think he should see her undressed just yet."

I rolled my eyes. "Mama, why do you meddle? It's up to the family to send for the doctor. Her mother said it's just some bad fish she ate."

"I doubt that because no one else became sick. Golda will thank me later." She rang the bell.

Mrs. Simons, an older woman with her hair covered by a black headscarf, opened the door and grinned. "Mrs. Fridman!

Oh, Abigail has grown since I've seen her." She patted my cheek and glanced at Mama. "Are your sons well? My husband often says how proud he is of David."

Mama touched the *mezuzah* and kissed her hand. "My family is well, but I need to speak to Dr. Kaplan. Is he here?"

"Yes, he brought us some delicious rugelach from your daughter's bakery. I may have to visit and see what else she makes."

Mama frowned but then raised her chin. "She learned it from me."

The woman led us into a small room, where Dr. Kaplan and the gray-bearded Mr. Simons drank tea at a table.

Mr. Simons rose with difficulty and gestured at two empty chairs. "Please join us."

Heading for the table, I hoped to rest my feet and relieve my thirst, but Mama waved her hand. "Thank you, but next time. This will be quick."

"Hello Mrs. Fridman. I will need new clothes if I keep eating Shira's rugelach, but I can't stop myself." Dr. Kaplan patted his stomach and shoved another piece into his mouth.

I was shivering. Maybe I caught a summer cold after all.

He shifted his eyes to me. "Is Abigail sick?"

"Abigail and the rest of the family are fine, thank *Hashem*," Mama answered. "David is visiting. He gave us all thorough exams. But I have a concern that hopefully you can allay. I'm worried about Ester Rosenbaum. Golda said it's the fish the family ate, but only Ester came down with a bellyache. It makes no sense. I hoped you might check on her."

The doctor shook his head. "Ah, Mrs. Fridman. You sure like to make other people's aches your own problem."

I smirked despite my tiredness. Mama frowned at me.

"Doctor." Mama placed her hand on her heart. "I have intuition. My gift is telling me you should check on Ester. If it's all a misunderstanding, blame it on me. But please examine her. And if she prefers a woman to give her an enema, I'm happy to help."

Mr. Simons winced and lowered his fork. Heat rushed to my cheeks and spread to my neck. I was unsure if I was embarrassed or feverish.

Dr. Kaplan sipped his tea. "All right. I have a couple of patients to visit, and then I'll see Ester." He checked his pocket watch and rose. Mrs. Simons walked him out.

The schoolteacher waited for the doctor to leave and turned to Mama. "Please tell David I'm proud of him. He was one of my brightest students, and he chose a noble profession. I wish he would spend more time in Chatham. Dr. Kaplan is an old friend, but his salves are doing nothing for my knee pain."

"That's because there's no cure for old age," his wife said, walking in.

Mama's eyes took on a dreamy expression. "It's my heart's desire for David to open a practice here. And it's time for him to marry. Say, are there suitable young women in your family?"

Sparks danced in front of my eyes. Like a child, I burst out crying.

Chapter 11

At home, I threw the shopping baskets on the floor. My face in my hands, I curled into a fetal position on the dining room sofa. Murka snuggled next to me.

Mama harrumphed. "What's gotten into you?"

"Leave me alone." My arms and back itched like I was bitten by mosquitos as I rubbed at the ache in my head. I was thankful Moishe was not home practicing his violin.

Mama winced and shifted her feet. Then she shuffled down to the kitchen. She returned a short while later with a cup of malodorous tea for monthly bleeds. I read in her eyes, *Look how well I know you.*

You don't, I screamed in my head. Yet, I sat up to drink the tea.

David walked in from the bedroom. "I'm going to post a letter," he said and sped past Mama toward the door. His hand on the knob, he turned his head to me. "Are you all right, Abigail? You look a bit flushed."

My forehead felt hot.

"She's fine," Mama said before I could answer. "Just a little... woman trouble."

My cheeks went from hot to burning. I sipped tea to relieve my thirst.

"You said something about a letter?" Mama raised her eyebrow. "A letter for who?"

David pivoted and faced her. "Does it matter?"

"I'm only curious." Mama crossed her arms. "When you were away in medical school, I received four letters from you. And now, I see you writing every other day. May I find out who inspires all those letters?"

"She's a friend." David kept his face even. "I prefer not to discuss this further."

He is writing to Ella, and more often than before, I thought. *Mama is observant and is often right. Except when it comes to me.*

The doorbell chimed, and David jerked his head. "Are we expecting anyone? Shira and Naomi can't be this early."

Mama straightened her skirt. "Rivka Cohen was going to stop by to pick up an ointment. Her nephew has chickenpox. Have you met her?"

David shrugged. "I don't remember."

"Why don't you invite her in while I fetch the ointment?"

While David sped down, I wished with fervor that Rivka would turn out to be extremely tall or have a couple of teeth missing.

"Dr. Kaplan! What brings you here?" David's voice came from the door.

The older doctor walked in with his case in hand, and his face tense. David followed, frowning in confusion.

Mama rushed over to the doctor. "Is this about Ester? Does she need me?"

"Your intuition left an impression on me." Dr. Kaplan spoke while scratching his chin. "I decided to see Ester before my other patients." He shifted his gaze to David. "Were you serious when you said you can perform an appendectomy?"

David stiffened. "I've practiced on cadavers. Why?"

"Ester Rosenbaum..." Dr. Kaplan stooped. "I am afraid she has appendicitis."

I shifted on my seat remembering the tense conversation between David and the older doctor.

Mama gasped and clutched at her chest. "*Vey iz mir.*" When David glanced at her, she added. "You know Ester. The jeweler's oldest daughter. She was friends with Shira."

David shook his head and peered at Dr. Kaplan. "Are you sure?"

"I would give anything to be wrong, but her symptoms are the same as what Noah had. Sharp pain on the right side of the abdomen, fever, vomiting. I gave her some laudanum. She was in terrible pain."

David paled and bit his lip. "Does she and her family consent to me performing the surgery?"

The doctor nodded. "Yes. They understand that this may be her only chance."

David pulled on his boots. "Where will we operate? I don't have an admission to St. Bartholomew's."

"I thought about that. The large table in their dining room should serve the purpose. Do you have your instruments?"

Despite my headache, I found myself speeding to David's room to fetch his case.

"Is this all you need?" I asked, trying to catch his eye as he checked the contents.

"Thank you, everything is here." His eyes moved past me to the older doctor. "I will require you to assist. And obey me without question."

Dr. Kaplan bobbed his head. "Anything you need of me."

"What is the patient's medical history?" His brow creased in concern. "Any complications you foresee?"

The older doctor stepped toward the stairs. "We can discuss on the way." David followed without a glance back to Mama or me.

Mama stood rooted in her spot for a few heartbeats, then staggered to her bedroom. Behind the door, her voice sang a melodic prayer in Hebrew, interrupted by sighs and gasps.

The doorbell chimed again, and I went to open. A young woman with a long braid stood there.

She gave me a shy smile. "Hello, I'm Rivka. I'm here to pick up the ointment for my nephew."

I kept my face poised. "Wait here. I'll fetch it for you."

The girl frowned, then nodded. I dashed to the table and grabbed the ointment jar Mama left there.

"Here you are. Good day!" I said, handing her the jar.

The girl accepted the ointment with a thank you, but the corners of her mouth turned down. She kept looking over my shoulder.

I stepped closer. The smell of lavender soap tickled my nose. She must've bathed before this errand. "You are too late. David is taken," I whispered in her ear.

Her jaw dropped to her chin. With a sob, she stepped back and flew down the path. For a moment, I stood watching her retreat.

Mama was leafing through the prayer book when I entered her bedroom. I told her that Rivka picked up the ointment, but she spoke as if she did not hear me.

"Abigail, let's pray, however you can. Poor Ester, she will endure a dreadful operation. Even with laudanum, it will hurt terribly." She opened the book to a worn page and whispered the words of the prayer in Hebrew. Her body rocked back and forth to the rhythm of her prayer.

I tried praying to Our Lady, but a terrible thought distracted me. *What if Ester recovers and David falls in love with her?* I chided myself for my lack of compassion. Still, as I kneeled, prayer refused to roll off my tongue.

When Mama finished, she gave me a searching look.

"Sorry, prayer is not on my mind right now."

She nodded. "It may be because you don't know Ester. Or how it happened with Noah, David's dear friend. David will be thinking of him when he operates."

"He told me once that losing Noah fledged his choice of profession."

Her eyes welled with tears. "Yes. I was holding Noah's hand, together with his mother, when he died. I thought my heart would break. Only a month after Rachel perished."

I wrapped my arms around her waist.

Mama leaned into me, letting me support her. "When I came home, I told David, fifteen years old at that time, that Noah was dead. He slammed the door to his room. I heard him shout and throw things. After that, he came out and demanded that I explain what killed his friend. Kept asking, 'How does a healthy boy die from a bellyache?' Since I couldn't answer, he donned his coat and stormed out."

My heart pinched. "Where did he go?"

"He never told me." Mama wiped her face on her sleeve. "My poor boy returned a few hours later, white as a sheet. He vomited his supper. I'm guessing he saw Dr. Kaplan. And pried the answers he needed from him."

Bile burned my throat. "Poor David," I whispered.

Her chin trembled. "He stayed in his room for days. Then, one morning, he came to breakfast and told Papa and me that he will study medicine. Not to apprentice with the local surgeon or apothecary but to find a way to enter a medical school, even if it did not admit Jews."

David turned his pain into a drive to learn medicine and save lives. My breast swelled with admiration for him.

"This will be a difficult surgery for David," Mama said, hugging herself. "He may have the education and able hands, but I know his heart. It's tender and full of compassion, especially for women and children. If he fails to save Ester, the loss will be hard on him."

She opened another page of her prayer book. I stared at the Hebrew letters that peppered the page. I desperately wanted to pray, but I could not do it alone.

"My head is muddled," I said. "Can I repeat your prayer after you?"

"But..." She touched her face. "If you wish. A prayer has more power if people say it together. Let's recite *Mi Sheberach*, the prayer for the sick."

She spoke each line with incantation, rocking her body back and forth. I repeated the foreign words, imitating her rhythm and pitch. My mind was on David, on the strength he would need to master his emotions and perform a successful operation. Mama might've been praying for Ester, but I was praying for David.

The fury inside me calmed. I welcomed this peaceful sensation, the reassurance that all will be well. Some days, I had the same feeling when praying to Mary for my Ma.

After finishing the prayer, Mama caressed my arm. "This was beautiful, Abigail. You are so sweet to pray with me, my dear girl."

I smiled at her. "I feel better too." I did feel better, but not entirely. My skin itched and my throat felt parched.

"I should make dinner to bring to Rosenbaums." Mama tapped her foot. "Oxtail soup. Stuffed kishka. Potato kugel. They need to keep up their strength."

My body was achy, and I craved rest, but Mama's energy was spreading to me. "What do you want me to do?"

She shook her finger in thought. "Go to the docks and find Papa. Tell him about Ester's illness. He'll gather the men to pray in the synagogue for her recovery. Like I told you, a prayer has more power when people say it together."

David needs their prayers to succeed. For him, I'll run the whole way.

Mama gasped. "Oh, before that, would you stop by the bakery and tell Shira that we must cancel tonight's plans? At least, I don't have to deal with Naomi and her just yet." She curled her lip but then her eyes blinked from welled up tears. "Tell Shira about Ester's illness. They are friends."

Although I felt unwell, I would persevere for David. He would need everyone's prayers to succeed. After drinking a cup of cool water, I staggered toward the bakery.

Chapter 12

By the time I reached the bakery, I was covered with sweat, and my heart hammered. I stopped by the door to catch my breath. A woman in a large hat decorated with flowers sauntered out of the shop. With surprise, I recognized Mrs. Franklin, one of the mothers from St. Margaret's who wanted to send me to the boarding school. Her hand flew to her mouth when she saw me.

"Oh, Abigail, hello. Beatrice insisted I order her birthday cake from this place. I was unsure, but I've just sampled their honey cake. It's simply divine! If the birthday cake is just as good, I'm only going to order from this bakery. Although the women working there gave me funny looks when I asked about hot cross buns."

I rubbed my throbbing forehead. "That's because it's a Jewish bakery. My sister runs the shop."

"Oh. I didn't realize..." Her mouth hung open. "Well, I see no harm in patronizing a Jewish shop, if it belongs to your family. They educated you and allowed you to grow up Christian, right?"

"Yes." I stiffened my spine. "I had an excellent tutor for secular subjects. I read the Bible on my own and go to church." Although lately, I'd been going on holidays only. The churchgoers asked too many questions about my family and why they didn't attend the services with me.

Mrs. Franklin touched my shoulder. "I admire your strength, Abigail. But you must be on guard. Some Jews are cunning. They used to be nothing but beggars, but now they own shops and banks, getting rich on loans to Christians in need. A few have even married Christian women." She gave me a meaningful look.

"That's not possible," I said. My pulse beat in my ears. "The Jews don't—"

"Oh, it's becoming more common, unfortunately. Usually, the Jews become baptized. They commit the sacred ritual to improve their place in society." She stroked her throat and grimaced. "But sometimes, Christians undergo Jewish rituals and convert. When you enter a marriageable age, *beware*. Better you marry a pauper, but a Christian."

My knees trembled. Jumbled thoughts sped through my head.

Why didn't anyone tell me that I could convert to Judaism? If I convert, will I have a chance of David marrying me one day?

Mrs. Franklin patted my arm and walked away.

My mind raced as I leaned on the wall for support. *David can have any Jewish girl in this town, even though he shows no interest in the ones Mama introduced him to. I am better educated than most, but an orphan with no dowry is not a catch. Still, it's something to consider.*

Then ice ran through my veins, and I shook myself. *Did I dare to think I could betray my Ma's beliefs? Turn away from my protector, Our Lady?* I was ready to drop to my knees and beg the Virgin for forgiveness.

I waited till the world stopped spinning before my eyes. Then I drew a deep breath and entered the bakery.

The aromas of cinnamon, nutmeg, and vanilla floated around the shop. Naomi, with her red hair pulled up into a tight bun, arranged the various breads on the counter. Shira stood at the other end, jotting something down in a thick book. Her brow was furrowed as she wrote.

My sister lifted her head and beamed at me. "Abigail! Please tell me you know what hot cross buns are."

"People bake them for Good Friday and other church holidays."

Naomi shook her head. "Why did we accept the order if we've never prepared them?"

"Because we will learn." Shira squared her shoulders. "This was our first order from a Gentile, and we will deliver. This woman will get the grandest birthday cake in town for her daughter and the best hot cross buns she's ever tasted."

The two women grinned at each other in a conspiratorial way. Shira's eyes shined. I'd never seen her this happy at home.

She stared at me, and her smile faded. "Abigail, why is your face so red? Are you sick?"

My cheek felt burning hot to the touch.

Naomi fetched me a cup of water. When I brought it to my lips, she gasped. "There are red spots on your hands. Did you have chickenpox when you were younger?"

"I don't know."

Shira rushed over and felt my forehead. "Hot enough to bake a cake! I can't believe Mama sent you here when you are burning with a fever. What happened?"

While Naomi fetched me a chair, I told them about Ester's surgery. It was needless to add that today's dinner was canceled.

"For once, Mama's meddling did some good," Shira said wide-eyed. "God-willing, David will save Ester."

"I have to go," I stammered. My teeth chattered despite me feeling hot. "I'm supposed to tell Papa so he would gather the people to pray for Ester."

"I'll take care of that," Shira said. "I will bring Moishe, as well as Miriam and Hannah with their husbands." She frowned at me, and then her eyes darted to Naomi. "Would you walk Abigail home? Bring the cakes we baked for dinner."

"I don't need Naomi to walk me home," I protested. The young widow scared me. Her husband took his life because of her wickedness.

"You are not fit to walk alone." Shira grabbed a 'Closed' sign. Just as she sped to the door to hang it, Mrs. Simons entered the shop.

"Shalom, ladies," the Hebrew teacher's wife said. "My husband and I fell in love with your rugelach. He sent me for more." She gave Shira a smile and Naomi a hesitant glance.

"I'm sorry, Mrs. Simons," Shira said, hanging the sign. "We are closing early. Ester Rosenbaum is terribly ill. My brother is trying to save her life. I'm going to find my Papa and help him gather the congregation for prayer."

Mrs. Simons straightened and raised her chin. "Our community comes together in a crisis. I will call everyone to join us." She grabbed Shira's hand, and they marched out onto the street like two soldiers on a mission.

Naomi gathered a basket full of cakes and ushered me outside. We walked at a slow pace. Every step required effort for my achy muscles. She offered me a hand for support. "Don't be scared," she said with a wry smile when I declined her hand. "My misfortunes don't transfer by touch. And not everything people say about me is true."

My legs weakened. Afraid to fall, I held on to her arm. We ambled in silence until we were in front of my house. At the door, Naomi sighed. "I miss this home."

"The day I came here was your last visit," I remembered.

She nodded. "This place was my escape. My mother was wasting away from cancer. When I was too tired and sad to care for her, I came here."

I recalled how Mama arranged Naomi's marriage and assured that she would be well with her husband. But the marriage ended with her husband's death at his own hand.

Mama, wearing a stained apron, opened the door for us. "Abigail, you are back already?" Her eyes bulged when she glanced at my companion. "What are you doing here?"

"Abigail has a fever," Naomi answered. "And red blisters on her hands."

Mama grabbed my arm and rushed me inside. Naomi followed.

"You've never had chickenpox?" Mama asked me as she led me to the window for better light.

I shrugged. "I don't remember."

"Well, everyone gets it sooner or later." She unbuttoned the front of my dress.

Naomi averted her eyes and placed the basket with cakes on the table. She fidgeted, looking between the door and Mama.

"Yes, there are blisters on your neck and chest too. And some on your face. There will be more." Mama made a clucking noise with her tongue.

"On my face?" I touched my cheeks and found little bumps. "Will they stay?"

"Don't scratch them!" Mama warned. "I'll get you the ointment from the apothecary. This malady sure catches like wildfire."

I fetched a hand mirror from my room and sat on the sofa to study my face. Red blisters with a clear fluid inside them marred my forehead and chin.

"I will go, Mrs. Fridman," Naomi said. Her eyes were sorrowful as she glanced around the room. "Just like I remembered it," she muttered.

Mama raised her head. "Thank you for walking Abigail home. You are looking well. Did you finally start using the cream I recommended all those years ago?"

The young woman drew a sharp breath, but then burst into a laugh. "You have not changed, Mrs. Fridman. Yes, you were right about the cream. It cleared my pimples."

"People think I'm a meddler, but I don't care." Mama gave her a smug look. "When I see a child with a problem that will only get worse if nothing's done, I refuse to keep my mouth shut."

Naomi's shoulders dropped. "You saved Ester's life."

"We don't know that yet. I am only glad that my intuition was right." Mama clenched her hands. "But I am wrong sometimes. My intuition told me that your husband was a good man. I made a grave mistake. I am sorry I pushed you to marry."

"You were not wrong about *him.*" Naomi's eyes brimmed with tears. "He was a good man and he loved me. But he had an illness of the mind. Despite the doctors' advice, I could not bear to place him into a mental asylum."

My back and shoulders slouched. Naomi's situation was much more complicated than I knew, yet I judged her harshly. I wanted to apologize to her for all those times I didn't greet her when passing by.

"The rumors people spread about you... It's shameful." Mama made a disapproving noise with her tongue. "I'll have a word with the busybodies who still talk about you and your husband. But about you and Shira..." She gave me a glance, approached Naomi, and whispered in her ear.

The young woman froze. Her chest rose and dropped as she stood paralyzed. Then she raised her chin.

"Mrs. Fridman, your meddling might've saved Ester. But it serves no good purpose for Shira and me. We are grown women and can make our own choices." Her eyes rested on me. "Get well soon, Abigail."

She turned on her heel and showed herself out.

For the next few hours, Mama nursed my fever and washed the blisters with soft rags dipped in cool water. I burned all over my body. The bitter taste in my mouth and parched throat gave me an unquenchable thirst.

"Try to relax and fall asleep," Mama said when I told her that my head was ready to burst. "I don't remember my other children being this sick. I suppose I can bring Golda that dinner tomorrow." She sighed and wetted another cloth. Much needed sleep took me.

A door squeaked, and I pried my eyes open. The sun must have set while I slumbered. Mama hastened out of the room. Because no voices reached me, I forced myself to stagger out of bed and threw a robe over my nightdress. Knowing that Mama would send me back to bed if she noticed me, I stayed in the dark corridor to observe.

David paced the dining room. His face pale and tense, and his mouth tight. His eyes darted across the room and stopped on a wine bottle Mama bought at the market. He poured himself a glass.

"Don't drink on an empty stomach," Mama chided, approaching him. Her hands wrinkled her apron. "Sit. I kept the soup warm for you."

He collapsed on the chair and rested his head in his hands. A deep sigh escaped his lips. I longed to drape my arms around his shoulders to comfort him.

Panting, Mama returned from the kitchen and placed a bowl of golden broth with noodles in front of him. He whispered a thank you and took careful sips. I willed him to speak, but he kept eating with small sips, keeping his eyes on his plate.

Mama placed one of Naomi's cakes by him. "David, please tell me what happened. Is Ester... dead?"

He closed his eyes and took a deep breath. "She's alive, if barely. Her fever holds. Pulse is weak. As for her baby... I can't say anything yet."

"Ester's pregnant?" Mama gasped. "But... Who is the father?"

David raised his eyebrows. "That was the least of my concerns. But she's three months along."

A tremor shot through me. I reached for the wall to keep myself upright. Despite my fever and body aches, I understood the most important thing. *Ester will not be David's wife.*

"Golda had some nerve," Mama muttered. "'I had the same dream.' She wanted to find Ester a husband before the baby would come. What a fraud!"

"Mama, do you understand?" David rubbed his forehead with his fist. His voice cracked. "I thought I was prepared. I studied medical drawings, I dissected cadavers. But none of it was for a surgery on a pregnant woman. I don't know if the laudanum will hurt the baby. I don't know if the baby will survive the mother's fever. There is so much I don't know, and my helplessness is driving me insane. Dr. Kaplan insisted that I get a few hours of rest, but I won't be able to sleep."

"Oh, my boy." Mama patted his head and kissed it. "You've done all you could. Now, it's up to God. Our community is praying for Ester to pull through."

He sagged deeper into the chair; his head dropped. Aching for him, I tiptoed to him and hugged his shoulders. He glanced up at me with a weak smile, but it froze on his face and his eyes widened. "Abigail, are you sick?"

"She caught chickenpox," Mama said. "Not to worry. I'm experienced with treating the itches and the fever. She will be well in a week or two."

David's eyes narrowed. He lifted a candle and brought it closer. "It can't be," he murmured as he examined the blisters on my hands. His head jerked to Mama. "This is not chickenpox. Chickenpox lesions vary in size and develop over time." David's voice quivered. "Her lesions are circular and firm, and so many came at once. This is much worse. Smallpox."

My heart hammered against my ribs. *Smallpox.* My legs grew weak.

Mama threw her arms around me and held me to her chest. "*Vey iz mir!* One trouble after another."

"Put her to bed," David ordered. "I'll mix the medicine for the fever."

Mama studied him. "Make the medicine then get some rest. It would do no good for you to fall off your feet. I'll stay up with Abigail."

David opened his mouth to object, but Mama raised her hand to halt him.

"You will rest and then tend to Abigail. You did what you could for Ester. Now her family and Dr. Kaplan will take over. We will nurse Abigail day and night until she's well again."

She led me back to bed. When I lay down, she covered me with two blankets.

"I'm scared, Mama," I whispered. "I will die. Or I will have ugly scars for the rest of my life."

"You will live, child," she said, patting my head. "And you will always be beautiful."

David entered, holding a cup. Mama stepped away. Bending down to me, David checked my forehead, and bit his lip. "Drink to the bottom," he said, handing me the medicine. "It should bring your fever down and help you sleep."

"Did you mix in laudanum?" Mama asked.

"Yes," he replied. "Better that she dozes through much of what's to come."

As I sipped, I winced at the bitter taste. A small smile appeared on his lips. "Do you still like raisins after taking your medicine?"

I stared into his red-rimmed eyes, dull from exhaustion. They were full of concern and kindness. I felt scared that I might be seeing them for the last time in this world.

"David, I love you," I whispered.

He took my hand. "I love you too, little sister. We all love you." He eased me down onto my pillow.

You don't understand, I tried to say, but my tongue did not obey.

"Moishe should stay with Miriam or Hannah while Abigail is ill." Mama paced the room. "He shouldn't bother her with his music. How could Abigail catch smallpox? Wasn't she in-oculated?"

My eyes closed and I did not hear David's reply.

The next few days and nights were hell. My body burned all over. I tossed in bed from pain and fever. My mouth was dry as a desert but swallowing hurt and even cool water tasted bitter. Most of the time I was suspended in darkness. Darkness did not hurt. But it scared me. I was falling into it and would be falling forever. All alone in it. Neither Mary nor Ma appeared to save me and guide me to Heaven. The faces I did see between those black gaps were Papa's, Mama's, and David's.

Sharp pain brought me out of my dreamless sleep. I gasped and opened my eyes. The scarlet light of the sunset reflected in the jars and glasses on my nightstand. The air was hot with the windows closed and thick with the stink of the greasy ointment that did little to cool my skin.

Murka's paw touched my arm. In a sweet attempt to comfort me, her claws scratched my lesions. Hurting, I brushed her off me.

Another twinge came from my leg. I raised my head to see David sitting at the foot of my bed. His hands were tugging at my tender wounds. Sweat trickled down his cheek. *Or is it a tear?* I wanted to say something nice, to thank him for tending to me, but the first word that escaped my lips was "Ouch".

He raised his head. His face was pale and eyes red-rimmed. "Did I wake you? Sorry. I'm cleaning out the puss. If that's too painful, I'll give you something to fall back asleep."

The treatment hurt, but I was glad to feel something that kept me awake. I refused to go back into insensate darkness. If I were dying, I wanted to know what would happen.

"David," I whispered, "if I die, would I be buried next to Rachel?"

He stared at me. "What did you say?"

"I want to be buried next to her, like one of the family."

His breath shuddered. "Don't upset yourself with those things. Try to think of something nice. For example... What would you like to do after you get better?"

I forced myself to sit up. David rushed to stand by my side. "No, don't get up," he warned. "You are too weak."

My head spun, and I grabbed his arm. "If I live, I want to marry you. Promise me."

His mouth gaped. He averted his eyes, refusing to meet my gaze.

Tears ran down my cheeks and I sobbed. "That's all I dream of. Promise."

He touched my forehead. "Your fever is back," he muttered and eased my head onto the pillow. "You need to calm yourself."

I wrapped my hands around his neck. "David, if you promise, I'll live. I will become Jewish so we can marry someday."

He untangled himself from my arms and measured out a dose of the medicine from my nightstand. "Agitation is harmful to you. You need to go back to sleep."

"Promise me. If you won't, I'd rather die."

His hands shook and he spilled the medicine. Cursing under his breath, he poured it again. "I promise. Just drink the medicine, all right?"

Despite the pain all over my body, I beamed at him. The smile stayed on my lips as I downed the foul-tasting remedy.

Mama shuffled into the room. "Abigail, how are you feeling?" she asked, coming closer.

"She got herself worked up and her fever returned," David said. "She's been talking, but I don't think she knows what she's saying."

"That's not true," I murmured.

"Abigail, please don't waste your energy on talking." David smoothed my blanket. "You need it to fight the fever."

"No, I need to say it." My speech was slurred from the medicine. "Mama, I..." My mind struggled with what I wanted to ask of her. Darkness creeped on me. I willed myself to fight against it. "I want to be Jewish."

"No, I vowed that you will not be forced to convert." David clenched my arm to count my pulse. His grip was unusually tight.

My vision blurred. Mama's voice sounded far away. "This is not about you, David. Abigail told us what she wants. And so it will be."

Chapter 13

With David's and Mama's promises on my mind, I clang to life. Drank Mama's broth even when had no desire to eat. Endured pain when David squeezed out the pus from my blisters. Despite the treatments and my will to get better, the illness worsened, spreading to my eyes. The lesions in them burned and blistered, making me rip at them with my nails. At times, I woke up with my hands tied behind my back, preventing me from damaging my eyes more.

The ointments David applied were of little help. There were days I hurt so much that I welcomed the darkness. It became familiar, even comforting. But I refused to stay in it.

One morning, the scent of dew hit my nose, so fresh and invigorating, I could taste the coolness of it. I stretched my legs and wiggled my toes. The attack of pain didn't come. Murka rubbed against my arm; her smooth fur felt pleasant and didn't irritate my skin. I opened my eyes and looked through the haze. Vague silhouettes of David and Mama stood by my bed, facing each other.

"What do you mean you didn't give her laudanum?" David rasped. "I prepared the dose."

Mama's voice was even. "I've been around sick people enough to recognize when the doctor is giving too much of the sleep drugs."

"I don't want Abigail suffering!"

"In *Hashem's* mercy, she's over the worst of this illness. Now she needs to be awake more and start eating more than broth."

"But her eyes—"

"It's all right. I think I'm better," I interjected.

"You are not in pain?" David asked.

"Nothing like before."

He exhaled a long breath.

"Abigail, you need to drink," Mama said. She lifted my head and placed a cup to my lips. Cool water ran down my chin as I drank in small sips.

She moved to let David examine me. He counted my pulse, felt my forehead, and had me stick out my tongue. "You are better," he said, bent down to me. "Now tell me, do you see me clearly?"

My breath caught. "I... I see you up close, but farther... like I'm looking at your reflection in the water."

"Could you close your right eye and tell me what you see?"

I did as he asked. "Nothing changed."

"And now open it and close your left."

"Same."

David straightened and uttered an oath.

"Get a hold of yourself!" Mama exclaimed. "She's not blind like you've feared. This is a blessing."

"Will my eyes stay foggy?" I swallowed. "Spectacles won't help?"

He did not answer, but his breath shuddered like he suppressed a sob.

Autumn would come, but I won't see the veins on the leaves or the drops on the windows. My world would remain a haze.

"It's all my fault. Her eyes... Her face..." David's voice trembled.

My face. I ran my fingers over my cheeks, chin, and forehead. Instead of the blisters, I found pits.

"You are upsetting Abigail when she just started improving." Mama pushed him away from the bed. "The lack of sleep caught up with you. Get some rest."

He pressed a palm over his mouth and hastened out of the room.

I sat up quickly. My head spun. "Glass. I want to see myself."

"The scars will fade over time," Mama said. "Don't look now. Will you have some porridge? You need to eat."

"Mama, let me see my face!"

She threw up her hands and brought me a hand mirror. I almost touched it with my nose to see my reflection in detail. Hideous scabs and pits marked my face, neck, and shoulders.

My eyes were red and cloudy. I was ugly. With a scream from my very soul, I threw the mirror to the floor.

The next four days I lay in my bed, my thoughts murkier than my vision. Living the rest of my life with clouded sight and a pitted face was a miserable prospect. But while my mind reeled from the shock and gloom, my body started to heal.

My hearing had become sharper. I noticed the smallest sounds. And I could often sense people's moods: the raised eyebrows, the frowns, the smiles, even when I could not see their faces clearly.

Mama busied herself in the kitchen, making special meals to help my recovery. The house smelled of chicken stock and fresh herbs. The food returned strength to my body, but I found no reason to rise from the bed. No pursuit that occupied me before seemed possible now. With such poor vision, I couldn't imagine myself reading, sewing, or playing piano.

David checked on my scars, washed away the pus, and asked if I was in pain. When speaking to me, his head was turned away. Even though his face was blurred, I sensed his discomfort.

"You've suffered so much already. It's unfair. I'm so sorry," he kept saying. I told him he had nothing to be sorry for. It was my misfortune, and he and Mama saved my life. *But how will I live after this disease ruined my face and eyes?*

On the fifth day of my recovery, Papa attempted to distract me from my gloom by reading to me. I feigned sleep. Papa's chair screeched, and I heard him tiptoe out. Then his paper rustled from the dining room. The window creaked as someone opened it. "Moishe," Mama yelled. "I told you before, don't shout from the yard. What do you want?"

"I want Abigail to hear this!"

A melody drifted into my sickroom. It was upbeat and stimulating. A fighting song.

Gingerly, I swung my legs over the edge of my bed and stood up holding on to the wall. Lightheadedness eased after a minute. In the fog of my vision, one careful step after another, I walked to the dining room like a baby making their first steps.

I stopped near the sofa. It took me a moment to orient myself, but everything was in a familiar place. The long table and chairs used for large gatherings, the cupboard with the silver wine cups and candlesticks. The world didn't change, only I did.

Mama, standing by the window, spoke. Even though I could not see her face, there was a smile in her voice.

"Abigail, won't you come closer? Moishe composed this music for you. He was staying with his older sisters while you were ill, but he came by every day to ask about you."

David rushed in from his room and halted at the threshold. "Careful. You are still weak." He walked over and offered his arm.

"No. I feel strong enough." I waited for him to withdraw. If this was my new life, I could start by learning how to cross the room with no assistance.

On my weakened legs, step by step, I made my way to the table. There, I rewarded myself by touching the silky roses in the vase. Their perfume was enchanting, almost unreal.

"Moishe brought those when you were sleeping." Mama threw a shawl over my shoulders. "Some rare sort that's especially fragrant."

With increasing confidence, I walked to the chair, where Papa waited for me. I locked my arms around his neck.

"I did it! I walked across the room." A weak laugh escaped my throat.

"You did so much more than that." He patted my back. "How I missed your hugs, Abigail. Your recovery means the world to me."

I sighed. "But... my eyes... and my scars."

He caressed my cheeks. "Maybe my eyes went bad too because I see no scars. I see my brave and beautiful daughter."

"Oh Papa..." was all I could say.

Moishe's melody became louder and grander.

"Isaac, you were right to make Moishe stick with the violin," Mama said. "He wouldn't be able to drag the pianoforte to the yard."

"Is Abigail coming?" Moishe shouted, still playing.

Mama draped her hand around my shoulder. "Come to the window, Abigail. Not every girl gets to be serenaded like this. I know why you asked to become Jewish. You are in love with my son. Mama's heart can tell. You and Moishe are young, but someday you could make a lovely couple."

She was right and wrong. I was in love, and I loved her son. Just not the one she thought.

Over my shoulder, I turned back to look at David. His head was bent down, avoiding my gaze.

Mama ushered me to the open window, and the summer breeze played with my hair. The scents of the sea, the wildflowers, and the horse manure mixed into an aroma of late summer. The bouquet was not all roses and lilies, but it was full of life.

"There you are, finally!" Moishe yelled, still playing. "Do you like my composition?"

"Not bad for a boy!"

I don't know how clearly he saw my face in the window, but his fingers didn't miss a beat.

That evening, he moved back home. As if the clocks turned back a month, the next day began like any day before my illness. We ate breakfast of meat pies and potato perogies as a family.

After draining two cups of tea, Papa left for the docks to sell his goods and offer loans to sailors. David went to check on Ester, who was making a successful recovery under Dr. Kaplan's care. A bit later, Mama hurried to the market to buy eggs and milk and then to visit someone's colicky baby.

Mama told me to rest, but when everyone left Moishe dragged me to the music room.

"When was the last time you played?" he asked as he seated me onto the piano bench.

The white and the black keys were covered with a fog. The notes in the propped up book were indiscernible scribbles. "It doesn't matter. I can't play anymore. The keys are all blurry."

He snorted. "You don't need to *see* the keys to play. They are at the same place every time. Watch."

He plopped next to me, retrieved a black handkerchief from his pocket, and tied it over his eyes.

"Now I'm more blind than you are," he boasted.

"That's not funny."

He pressed a few keys, then positioned his fingers. Nodding to himself, he played the opening of Mozart's Eine Kleine Nachtmusik, one of the pieces I was practicing before I got sick. The music poured into me, tugging at my memories, creating pictures in my mind.

"I imagine the keys in my head, and the fingers remember." He played another piece, his own composition. His fingers found the right keys in every chord, never stumbling. When he finished, he removed the blindfold.

"At the synagogue, I practiced playing blindfold on the pianoforte. Playing an instrument that's out of tune was worse than not seeing the keys." He chuckled. "Did you know that Mozart performed blindfolded when he was six?"

"Well, I'm no Mozart."

He scoffed. "Obviously, but your talent is still worth honing. What else are you doing all day?"

I shrugged. "Sleeping."

"That's what nights are for. Find the middle C," he commanded.

My fingers touched various keys until I recognized the familiar note.

"That's your center. Once you find it, you know where all the other keys are. Play the scales."

Tilting my head, I played the scales as I did during my first lessons with Papa. Then I played them again, with more confidence. My fingers remembered, like Moishe said. I did not have to see the keys to play them.

"You understand? With enough practice, your fingers will remember any melody."

"I'll never play as well as you do."

"No, you won't. But you can play the accompaniment when I play the violin. We could give concerts."

My mouth gaped wide. "You are joking."

"No. A couple more years of training, and I will start my music career. You could perform with me and travel the world."

"Who would want to see an ugly girl with bad eyes playing pianoforte?" I turned to him, letting him see my features up close.

"Anyone who appreciates music. Anyone who has their own scars. Anyone who overcame something life threw at them."

He wrapped his arm over my shoulder and spoke into my ear. "Stop calling yourself ugly. You are pretty with pox scars and all. And you can play despite your vision problems. The blind pianist Maria Theresia von Paradis toured Europe and performed for royalty."

I shrugged. "She sounds much more talented than me."

"But you have something special as well when you play. Are you going to convert to Judaism?"

Part of me still wrestled with this decision. Ma taught me to worship Our Lady when I was a little girl. I'd have to stop calling on my protector and praying for my Ma.

"I don't know yet." I frowned. "What's it to you?"

His fingers intertwined with mine. "If you become Jewish, someday you could marry a Jewish man."

Stunned by Moishe guessing my secret, I went still. "David wouldn't have me otherwise," I chocked out after a pause.

He jerked and let go of my hand. "You want David? He's an ass."

I recoiled like he hit me. "Don't speak like that. He cared for me day and night."

Moishe rose and stepped away from me. "He didn't look at you the whole time we had breakfast."

Even though I couldn't see David's eyes across the breakfast table, I suspected that he wasn't looking at me. The meaning of his behavior sank in. My face repulsed him. And he was likely thinking of asking me to release him of his promise.

"I need to lie down," I muttered.

Moishe gave me a hand to stand. "After you rest, the pianoforte will be here for you. And so will I."

Chapter 14

The last day before David's departure for Plymouth, the men in the family attended the service at the synagogue.

In their absence I practiced piano with Murka keeping me company. Mama was in the kitchen packing up food she had prepared earlier. I imagined it was for some family that had a new baby or someone unwell.

"Abigail, we have a surprise for you," Papa said when he returned with his sons. "Please put on your best clothes, and we all will go back to the synagogue for a celebration."

"Is it a special holiday?" I asked, rising from the bench.

"It is. The whole community is overjoyed with your and Ester's recovery. David treated both of you, but we believe our prayers helped as well."

I fidgeted, unsure how people from the town would react to my marred face. *They will have to see me some time*, I told myself. And many of them prayed for me despite me being Christian. "I'd like to thank them for their kindness."

"You can thank them at the celebration."

In my bedroom, Mama helped me into a dress she sewed for me, rose-colored with mother-of-pearl buttons. The fabric was soft and light to my skin. Like all my clothes, it covered my neck, arms, and legs for modesty. The dress hung on my thinned waist, but Mama adjusted it with pins.

I entered the dining room and approached David and Moishe, trying to read their expressions. David's eyes studied my dress. Moishe was next to him, grinning at me.

"You look nice," Moishe said. Seeing that I was staring at his brother, he nudged him.

"Don't overtire yourself," David said. "If you feel unwell, let me know right away."

David sounded like a caring brother and a diligent doctor. I bit the inside of my cheek. The promise I pleaded him to make churned my chest. Although it helped me overcome my illness, now it seemed forced and unfair to David.

"Come, Abigail." Papa offered me a hand. "We'll go slowly and stop to rest whenever you need to."

With that, we proceeded to the synagogue, a modest wooden building located on High Street. The men in my family prayed there daily, while Mama joined for important occasions. Her priority was to make hearty meals and to tidy up the home for their return.

A month indoors made me forget how much I enjoyed walking around the town. While my vision distorted the details, I heard birds chirping and smelled the apples being baked. By the time we reached our destination, I was winded but exhilarated. Papa opened the heavy doors, and I followed my family inside.

The room in the back was prepared for a gathering. People sat at decorated tables or chatted in small groups. The long table was covered with platters of assorted sizes. Shira and Naomi sped back and forth, arranging the mouthwatering dishes. Mama joined them, unwrapping the food she brought. Moishe snuck away to fill his plate with cakes, while an older gentleman whisked David away to complain about his rheumatism.

Upon seeing me, Shira ran over and threw her hands around my neck. "Abigail! Naomi and I are so happy to throw this celebration for you!" Bouncing on her toes with the energy of a child, she showed no reaction to my marred face.

"You prepared all that food yourselves?" I marveled, scanning the table covered with dishes.

"The knishes and desserts are ours. Other folks contributed, especially Ester's family. It's their celebration as well."

Papa approached and extended his arms to Shira. "You and Naomi have outdone yourselves. The dessert table is fit for royalty."

Shira gave Papa a kiss on the cheek. "We received orders for Rosh Hashanah and for a wedding. I'm so happy, Papa."

"Congratulations, Shira. Your song was waiting for you in the cake batter. Now you are sharing your talent with all of us." Papa's voice was warm like a summer day.

I beamed at her. This happy, fulfilled Shira was so much more pleasant than the old one.

Mama also complimented her daughter on the scrumptious desserts and led me to meet the guests. "Mrs. Cohen, the rabbi's wife, sent us meat stews and fish pies," she told me as we shuffled across the room. "Mrs. Solomon brought a mixture of medical herbs that's supposed to cure every disease. David forbade me from giving it to you, but it is the thought that counts."

I grinned at the women Mama introduced and thanked them for their kindness. I could not see faces clearly, but I knew they were smiling at me. Their cheerful mood reassured me that no one was here to gawk or pity me. Leaning toward them, I shared how my family cared for me.

Mrs. Cohen, the Rabbi's wife, put her hand on my shoulder. "Mrs. Fridman told us that you are as much of a daughter to her as any of her other children. Our women's group prayed for your recovery daily. That's what a community does for each other. *Hashem* heard us and saved you, as well as Ester."

My heart warmed at her words. "Thank you. May the good Lord protect you."

A group of women chatted nearby, some of them nibbling on cakes. Their ringing voices interfered with our pleasant conversation.

"I'm shocked at Golda," a woman wearing a red headscarf said. "A pregnant daughter with no husband must be sent away. I'm glad she survived, but celebrating her is improper. And

Naomi dares to show her face here after what she did to her husband."

Their tone contrasted with the joyous mood of the room. My spirits dampened.

A woman in a blue shawl, who stood with her back to Mama, nodded in agreement. "Our young women are losing their way in this country. Just look at the two who opened the bakery. Not only they are running a business, like men, but I hear they are not *just* friends."

A couple of women gasped. "I'm not sure I know what you mean," another said but no one volunteered to explain.

Heat rushed to my face. I didn't know what she meant either, but hearing these women discuss Shira and Naomi while enjoying the dessert they prepared made my blood boil.

"They also accept orders from Gentiles. Something called hot cross buns," a large woman said while stuffing cake into her mouth.

Mama advanced on the group like an enraged bull. "This is my daughter about whom you are talking. As well as a widow who lost her husband less than a year ago."

The woman who chewed cake doubled-over coughing. Mama rushed over and hit her on the back. When the woman recovered, Mama scanned the group. "Eating sweets while spitting out vile rumors is bad for your health, ladies. I suggest you get some air. Please return when you are ready to celebrate and not gossip."

The women cowered before her stare. "We were just leaving anyway," one of them said and marched away. The rest of her companions followed, except for one who rushed to grab another pastry before fleeing the room.

Mama returned to me, chortling with satisfaction.

"That was good, Mama," I said. "Shira and Naomi did not deserve such treatment. And neither did Ester."

"I will always protect my children." She held me to her chest. "No matter what."

"By the way," Mrs. Solomon said, "does anyone know who the father of Ester's baby is? I suspect it's her father's apprentice."

"I heard it's a Gentile," another woman countered. "A sailor who came to pawn a watch."

"Ladies, do I need to send you outside as well?" Mama answered. "So much curiosity leads to indigestion." When the ladies lowered their eyes and changed the subject, Mama turned to me. "You've been on your feet too long. Let's find you a chair and some food."

She filled a plate with blinis and fish pies and led me to a table where Golda sat with a dark-haired young woman, I presumed to be Ester.

"Mrs. Fridman!" Ester exclaimed. She winced and grabbed her stomach as she rose to greet Mama.

"Don't get up, dear!" Mama protested. "Are you still hurting?"

Ester rubbed her belly. "Not from the surgery. The baby kicked. My child and I are alive thanks to you and David."

Teary-eyed, she embraced Mama. Then she opened her arms to give me a sisterly hug.

Golda clutched Mama's hands and kissed them. "Bless you, Leah. I was such a fool that day at the apothecary's. I suspected Ester's belly pain was from her pregnancy and I did not want you to know. Thank you for sending over Dr. Kaplan."

"No need to thank me, Golda, but you have something to come clean about." Mama clicked her tongue. "Remember your supposed dream? Did you think you could deceive my son—a doctor—or me?"

"Mother, what dream?" Ester exclaimed, releasing me. "What did you say to Mrs. Fridman?"

Golda covered her face. "I was desperate to find Ester a husband before her condition became obvious. What a *schlemiel* I was."

I concealed a laugh while biting into a crusty pie. There was something satisfying in this failed matchmaking.

Mama touched Golda's shoulder. "As a mother, I understand. God willing, the baby will be born healthy, and a good Jewish man will marry Ester one day. I may even know someone for her."

"They don't give up, do they?" Ester murmured to me.

"Speaking of matchmaking," Mama continued, "is that your niece standing over there?" She pointed toward a petite young woman wearing a colorful shawl.

Golda nodded. "Yes, that's my niece Talia. My sister's oldest."

"Ah, I remember her as a child. She caught colds often. Talia!" she called the girl over.

"Mama, what are you doing?" I muttered.

She ignored me and addressed the girl who dashed over. "Do you want to meet my son David? He's the doctor who saved your cousin's life."

The girl bounced on her heels. "It would be an honor."

Golda's fingers drummed on the table. "Not here, Leah. People will talk."

Mama snorted and turned back to Talia. "David is the shorter one standing there in the circle, listening to the men complain about their aches and pains. You would do him a favor by giving him an excuse to get away." She handed Talia a handkerchief from her pocket. "Walk by him and drop this, as if by accident. When he picks it up, say something nice and smile. Go!"

With her cheeks burning red, the girl hastened towards the group of men. Ester whispered that she needed to go to the privy, and Golda gave her a hand to rise.

When they walked away, I crossed my arms. "Mama, are you playing Cupid again?"

She giggled. "Cupid is a babe compared to a Jewish mother. I stopped with the matchmaking when you were ill, but I'm resuming tonight, before David leaves. There is no time to lose. When I cleaned David's room, I found piles of torn and crumpled letters."

My heart skipped a beat. "Love letters?"

"I did not read them, but he obviously put a lot of effort into them. There was one very long one, and I accidentally saw his signature, 'Oli Higgins'. Whoever he writes to likely doesn't know he's Jewish." She bolted from her chair. "Confound it, another man picked up Talia's handkerchief. I must intervene."

She wedged her way into the crowd. Left alone, I dug into my food, but an older man with gray hair and a long beard, dressed in all black, approached me, accompanied by Papa.

"Abigail, I'm Rabbi Cohen," the man said in a kind voice.

Unsure how to behave, I rose, but he bid me to sit and pulled up a chair. Papa stood behind him.

"I'm delighted to express how happy and relieved we all are about your recovery. Our community came together to pray for you and Ester with great fervor, and God answered our prayers. I also heard that during your illness you expressed a wish to convert to Judaism."

My mind was made up. In my delirium or drugged sleep, I did not see Ma or Our Lady. Meanwhile, the Jews prayed for me, and I survived.

And David... There were so many reasons why my chances of marrying David were minuscule, but at least my faith would not be an obstacle. He promised that I would never be forced to convert, but I could make my own choices. I needed David to see how much I would do for him.

"Yes, I choose to convert." When the words left my tongue, I held my breath, waiting for something terrible to happen. For Ma to appear and curse me. Or lightning to strike me dead.

Instead, Papa's smile beamed like a rainbow after the rain. The atmosphere in the room remained cheerful. The storm lived only inside me, undetectable to anyone else.

Rabbi Cohen tilted his head. "I understand that you revealed that wish when you were in danger of dying. Are you still firm in your desire after you've recovered? There is no shame in changing your mind."

"Yes. I want to be Jewish. I want to be like my family in every way. To pray with this community."

"Our tradition says that the converts are wanderers led by the Lord back into our fold." The rabbi raised a finger. "I see evidence of this in your story. Of all the desolate children David treated in the hospital, he chose you to rescue from poverty and a bleak future. From the first days in Chatham, you fit into the Fridman family like one of their own."

"Abigail is a loving daughter and a good influence on our other children. Always helpful to my wife. And she's been working diligently with her tutor and shows wonderful musical talent," Papa confirmed.

The Rabbi nodded. "Our laws consider you old enough to choose conversion to Judaism. By tradition, I am supposed to reject your request three times before accepting it, but since you lived in the community for years, I will omit that requirement. Some converts choose a new name, but Abigail is a Hebrew name, possibly another sign from *Hashem* that you were meant to be Jewish all along. What I will require of you is to spend three afternoons a week with me learning the commandments and the prayers. My wife will talk to you about the woman's role in the family. When you master our lessons, you will immerse yourself in the *mikvah*, a ritual bath, and your conversion will be completed."

I gave my voice firmness. "I will do all you ask." *Forgive me Ma, but you did not come when I was ill. I need family and love. David's love.*

"This is truly a great day." Rabbi Cohen clapped his hands. "I rejoice at the prospect of adding you to our number. Now, if you will excuse me, I will greet Ester and her mother."

As soon as the Rabbi left us, we became surrounded by people congratulating me on my recovery. Already someone spread the word that I was converting, and more people gathered to talk to Papa and me. Soon I was exhausted from chatting. When the crowd thinned, Papa went to help with distributing the leftover food and putting away the furniture.

David collapsed on the chair next to me. "I can't suffer Mama's games anymore. She introduced me to every unmarried girl at this gathering." He wiped his flushed face with his sweaty hands.

"Did you at least look at those girls when you spoke to them?" I asked with a hard edge in my voice and my arms crossed.

His back stiffened. "Did I offend you in some way?"

"You did."

He glanced around. "Why don't we talk outside."

I followed him out of the building. He brought me to a large oak that gave off generous shade. We were a good distance away from anyone.

"I'm sorry, but what did I do?" He stared down at the ground as he spoke.

I pointed to my face. "You are a physician. You must've seen pox marks before. Am I so ugly that you can't stand to look at me?"

David gasped and raised his head. "Oh, blimey. I didn't realize. I just feel so guilty seeing those lesions on you. They are my fault."

"I don't understand. Why do you blame yourself for my illness?"

He inhaled a deep breath. "I should've inoculated you against smallpox. It was my duty. I did not do it in the hospital or soon after because you were so small and weak. And later..." His shoulders slumped. "I vividly remember comforting a little girl who was weeping after receiving the inoculation Dr. Kaplan administered."

I frowned, trying to recall this. "I don't..."

"I thought it was you. But later, I realized it was Rachel. You fit in so perfectly with my family that my memories of you and her became jumbled. You could've died because of my mistake. And you are now scarred by it."

My chest squeezed tight. "You must hate me for making you vow to marry me."

He shook his head. "You were deadly ill. I'd promise you the moon to make you better. Abigail, you are a lovely, gentle, and talented girl. But you are significantly younger than me. You've seen almost nothing of the world."

"I don't need to see the world. Everyone I care about is here in Chatham, except for you, because you are often away for work." A pinch in my chest reminded me that I forgot my brother and sister, Julian and Josie, who were in Churcham. But I heard nothing of them for so long.

David fidgeted. "You are too young to know what you want."

"That's not true. You were my age when you decided to be a doctor. Just now, I told the rabbi that I want to become Jewish."

"Why?" David touched his face. "You loved praying to the Virgin Mary. I vowed you will not be forced to convert."

I raised my chin. "No one forced me. I want to fully join the community and your family." I paused, mustering courage to say the words. Better I speak than forever regret silence. "What I desire more than anything is to be your loving wife someday."

My heart was on a platter before him. I begged him to take it. But he leaned away from me.

When silence grew heavy, my hands fell to my sides. "Of course you don't fancy me. Do you intend to marry someone else? Perhaps the woman you've been writing to?"

He swallowed. "How did you know?"

"Mama found your torn letters."

He flinched. "She read them?"

"No. But she thought you made a great effort since you tore up so much paper."

With a sigh, he combed his fingers through his hair. "It was a difficult letter to write. I was saying goodbye."

Saying goodbye. His dulled voice and slumped posture told me that this goodbye was heart-wrenching for him. Compassion and relief competed inside me.

I grabbed his wrists. My heart fluttered like a bird's wing. "I will not hold you to your promise. But I am here. I will become Jewish like you. And I love you."

He stepped back, his eyes downcast. After a few moments, he said, "Abigail, I very much want your happiness. But let's revisit this conversation in five years."

"Two." I planted my feet wider. "Mama was seventeen when she married Papa."

"It worked for them, but still..." he sighed. "Please promise you will make friends your own age and pursue various interests. In two years, you may feel differently about me."

He wanted more time, but he did not ask me to release him from his promise.

Chapter 15

I *should not be breathing. Air should not be swishing through my lungs, my chest should not be rising and falling.*

"Abigail, can you speak? Can you tell me where we are?"

I recognize the nightstand next to me, the curtains on the windows. I want to answer that I'm on the bed in my room. Instead, I gasp from the pain shooting through my back and limbs.

"Mrs. Fridman, I'm going to bleed her to get the fever down."

Mama's voice quivers. "Are you sure, Doctor? David doesn't approve of bloodletting."

"Since he's not here, I'm in charge. Trust me, it's the best thing to do."

I want to yell 'No' but my tongue is too listless to obey. I moan something inaudible.

A blade slices into my arm. I gasp as the warm wetness pours. The room is swallowed by the fog.

One Year Earlier

I stared into the translucent water of the *mikvah*, taking in the significance of the moment. My studies with Rabbi Cohen lasted a year. I insisted on learning Hebrew to understand the prayers, not simply memorize them. Because of my poor eyesight, the Rabbi read to me or copied the most important passages by writing with large letters.

In preparation for the *mikvah*, I washed myself at home. Then the attendant, a jolly middle-aged woman named Ditza, scrubbed me with a harsh brush till my skin reddened. With my body clean, I was ready to cleanse my soul.

Ditza removed my robe, leaving me naked, and pointed at the stairs in the water. "Can you see the steps? I can hold your hand."

"I'm fine." Water enlarged everything, and I felt no fear of falling as I descended. When my feet found the bottom of the pool, my body shivered from the cool water. The depth was enough for only my head and shoulders to show above the surface.

"I'm excited," Ditza said. "You are my first convert. This ritual links you to all Jewish women who came to *mikvah* since Biblical times. My ancestors will be your ancestors as well. When you are ready, dive in. Every strand of your hair must be underwater."

Frightened by stories of people drowning in the sea, I was nervous about submerging. Pushing my fears away, I filled my lungs with air and plunged below the surface for the first time in my life. Bubbles escaped my lips. Water poured into my ears; an unpleasant sensation I did not expect. When I emerged, I could barely hear Ditza say *Baruch Ata.*

She recited a blessing with me and asked me to dive again. I did so, grabbing my knees. After rising and catching my breath, I chanted another blessing.

"One last time," Ditza said. "Then you will recite *Shema* to affirm your belief in One God."

Eager, I dove, water splashing over my head. My brisk submersion made my head spin. It took me a few seconds to steady my breath when I emerged. In my full voice, I sang, "Sh'ma Yisrael." *Hear O Israel, The Eternal Our God, The Eternal is One!*

"Amen!" Ditza cried in answer.

My feet found the steps, and I ascended to the edge of the mikvah. Ditza threw the towel over my shoulders. The metamorphosis was complete.

I am a sixteen-year-old Jewish woman. No more calling on Our Lady for protection. My Hebrew prayers would have to satisfy my ma.

"The next time I will see you here will be before your wedding day," Ditza said with a laugh.

My heart fluttered. Someday, I would return here to cleanse myself for the wedding night. In my innermost fantasies, I pictured David as the groom.

As a married woman, I would return every month, seven days after my menses. Purified by *mikvah*, I would be ready to receive my husband and fulfill God's command to be fruitful and multiply.

After dressing, I stepped out of the inconspicuous building behind the synagogue. Cool wind reminded me that summer was still on its way. Chilled, I covered my damp hair with a scarf Mama knitted for me.

Shira paced by the door, waiting. Because of my poor eyesight, my family escorted me everywhere.

"It's done," I said. "Now I'm truly your sister."

She kissed me on both cheeks. "You always were. And always will be."

Hand in hand, we strolled on High Street, as the town started another day. More shops had appeared since I came to Chatham six years ago. There was a new tailor next to the apothecary, and a new wine merchant across from Shira's bakery. The street packed with shoppers, including some Gentile men with their heads uncovered. Coaches and wagons rushed by on the cobbled road, raising dirt and leaving a stench of manure.

A queue had formed outside of Shira's bakery. I recognized the women I often saw at the synagogue. Behind them, there was a group of chatting girls in uniform dresses, the students from St. Margaret's school I once attended. Two ladies in large hats with feathers, Gentiles by my guess, fidgeted as they waited for Naomi and another worker to open the doors.

"Business is booming," I remarked.

"Yes. The new menu is popular." Shira waved to Naomi, but the redheaded young woman turned her back on her. Shira grunted. "Naomi is upset with me. We had a fight last night. Again."

"About what?"

"I don't even know. When I'm at work, everything is all right with the world. At home, something is missing for me. I get irritable and hurt Naomi's feelings. She then thinks that I'm unhappy. She's ... afraid I'll leave her and marry."

My hand squeezed hers. "You may be ill-tempered because you must hide your secret about Naomi and you. It's a heavy burden to carry."

"Ah, you would know." She gave me a light shove. "Are you still pining for David?"

I bit the inside of my cheek. "Is it so obvious?"

"Maybe I inherited Mama's famous intuition." Shira giggled. "Any time we receive David's letters, your face becomes dreamy."

Busy with work, David had not visited the family all year. At times, I wondered if he stayed away because of Mama's matchmaking or because of me. His letters were addressed to the whole family and contained only accounts of his work and regrets that he had to miss holidays and birthdays. As an attentive son and brother, he sent thoughtful gifts. For my sixteenth birthday, he sent me a compass. "So you always know your way," his letter said.

Moishe said he never saw a stranger gift for a girl, but I loved it. I only regretted that the giver did not congratulate me in person.

Shira attempted to help me up the stairs of our home but I shooed her away. The familiar stairs were no trouble even for my blurred eyesight. When she pushed the door, her voice rang, "*Mazel Tov!* Say hello to our new Abigail!"

No answer came. No excited chatter from Mama or the boom of Papa's laugh. Full of a dire premonition, I clenched Shira's arm as we walked into the dining room. There Papa stood slumped, staring down. Sobbing, Mama leaned on him, as if she had no strength to stand. Moishe rubbed her back, speaking softly to her. A letter lay on the floor next to them.

Chapter 16

I knew at once that the unhappy news in the letter was about David. My mind conjured images of him gravely ill or injured. My chest tightened. I couldn't breathe. The room spun in front of me.

When I opened my eyes, I found myself lying on the sofa with my clothing loosened and my feet on a pillow. Mama was waving smelling salts under my nose. Shira slapped my cheeks.

"Ouch," I moaned.

"Sorry, I didn't mean to hurt you." Shira sat next to me.

"Is she all right?" Moishe's voice came from another room. I silently thanked Mama and Shira for preserving my modesty and sending the men away while undressing me. Papa's voice was chanting the prayer for the sick.

"She's awake." Mama stroked my head. "My poor girl, we should be celebrating today. Oh, David…"

I grabbed Mama's hand. "What's wrong with him? Please tell me."

"I'll make some strong tea. That will make you feel better."

"Mama, I asked you about David."

Shira groaned. "David is fine. Mama made too much drama."

Mama placed her hands on her hips. "Watch your tongue, Shira."

"You let Abigail and me think the worst."

David was alive and unhurt, and that was all that mattered. Only one other thing I could imagine that would upset Mama this much. I braced myself for the answer. "Did he ... marry a Gentile woman?"

If he chose to be baptized to marry a Gentile, we would mourn him as if he died. We would never see him again. My heart was breaking into pieces.

Shira fanned me with her palm. "Your face, Abigail. Calm yourself. David... took another job."

Mama huffed. "I'm sure Ella Parker had much to do with this."

They were going to kill me with their elusiveness. "Please, tell me what's happening."

My sister patted my arm. "David got into some trouble at the hospital and was sacked. Instead of returning home, he took a posting as a surgeon on a warship called *Southern Star*. Papa says the ship has a bad reputation because of her ruthless captain and treacherous voyages to remote places. David may be gone for a year and unable to send letters."

I closed my eyes. A year of not knowing whether David would be safe, whether we would see him again. A year to dream of him drowning, succumbing to an illness, or dying from wounds. Mama didn't exaggerate the misery that was coming; she was understating it.

Mama's reddened eyes loomed over me. "Dear one, you understand. Of all my children, you are the most like me. We will endure, Abigail, like many other families who await their loved ones."

Mama and Shira helped me dress and called the men. The five of us joined hands.

Papa spoke. "We will support each other, and we will put our faith in God. We'll pray that David will evade danger and return to us."

Moishe led us in reciting the words of *Tefilat HaDerech*, the Traveler's Prayer. For the next year, my lips repeated that prayer before my head touched the pillow and as soon as my eyes looked upon dawn.

One time, I've had a dream about Ma. We were in our old church, seated at the pew together.

"Abigail, you don't pray for me anymore. Why?" There was an accusation in her eyes.

"David needs all my prayers," I said, shaking my head.

Her face crumbled, and she stared down. "If he means that much to you, I will pray for him as well."

In my mind, I composed my next letter. "*Dear David. It's been a whole year without you. We made it our routine to say prayers for you, to stock extra food in case you return. The rumors in town are worrisome, but we keep faith that you are coming home.*"

Moishe touched my arm. "Abigail, where are your thoughts? It's your move."

Squinting at the chessboard, I bit my lip. My position was precarious. Moishe had a two-pawn advantage and positioned all his light pieces ready for attack. I still had a bishop stuck behind my pawns.

I shifted on my knees. Mama would not approve of us sitting on the floor and wrinkling our clothes, but it reminded me of my younger days, when I used to curl up on this rug and play with dolls. This rainy April day was good for piano and chess.

The only clever move I could find was advancing the knight. It would add some pressure on Moishe's pawns. "Knight C3 to D5."

He snickered. "You are so predictable."

I itched to smack him. At nineteen, he acted like he knew more than anyone. "You know, you don't have to play blindfolded. I can see the pieces." I had to squint to distinguish between them, and I couldn't see the letters on the board. Moishe let me play white and wore a blindfold to even our chances, but I had yet to beat him.

"I don't need to see the board. It's in my head. Bishop E6 to G4."

I moved the piece for him. "How old were you when you beat David for the first time?"

He rubbed his cheek. "Before he left for medical school. I was eleven. He's not that hard to beat. As a player, he's clever but very emotional. He can't get over small mistakes and makes bigger ones."

I fiddled with my rook. "He's like that in everything."

More than a year since David's last letter. Papa and Moishe scoured every naval paper for the news of *Southern Star,* but the official reports gave little information. The sailors from other ships told wild stories: the ship was caught in a storm, it was captured by pirates, it was recovered but most of the crew didn't survive. Papa urged us not to believe the seamen's yarns.

Mama came up from the kitchen. She clicked her tongue like she wanted to chide us but chose not to. I guessed that she liked seeing us play together.

"I'm going to visit Hannah," she announced. "I saw her at the synagogue this morning, and her face looked greenish. I'll bring her some chamomile."

I cocked my head. "In other words, you want to learn if you should expect another grandchild. Why not wait for her to tell you?"

"If my children didn't keep secrets, I wouldn't have to play tricks." Mama sighed.

"It's raining," Moishe warned.

Mama threw on her coat. "I won't be long. And I'll carry an umbrella."

After she left, Moishe reminded me to make my move. Without thinking, I advanced my center pawn. My head was not in the game anymore. I yearned to write to David.

My letter would say, "*I attend the synagogue regularly with Mama or Shira, and we pray for your safe return. At the Passover seder, we added an extra chair and a cup of wine for the Prophet Elijah. But, the whole time, I hoped you would arrive to sit in that chair and drink the wine.*"

Moishe touched my arm. "What were you thinking? You fell right into my trap. Now you'll lose your rook or your queen."

I shrugged and laid down my king. "I resign. May I dictate you a letter for David?"

He removed his blindfold. "Splendid. Just what I wanted to do. We don't even know if he's receiving our letters."

"If he is, he needs to hear that we love him and pray for his return." I threw my shoulders back and stood.

Moishe rose, shaking his head. He still resembled his brother but grew to be much taller than him. "David knew that before he left. When I see him, I'll punch his teeth for putting us through this worry."

None of us acknowledged that we may never see David again. Moishe was angry, but worried about him as much as we all did.

"If you don't want to play another game, why don't you practice pianoforte?"

I listened to the raindrops tapping on the window. The rain was strengthening. "I already played for two hours this morning."

"You think two hours of practice a day is enough to play professionally?"

My hands clenched. "For the last time, I'm not going to be a musician. I play for myself, for my family. Someday I'll give private lessons to children." I already started teaching Miriam's oldest daughter. When her little fingers grasped the lesson, and her gleeful laugh mixed with the melody, my chest would swell with pride. Those lessons were often the brightest part of my day.

Moishe pushed the board with his foot, making the pieces topple. "That's not enough. You have talent. Your ability to play despite poor sight makes you special. The war with France and Napoleon is finally over. We can travel around Europe, even tour the world. And we won't hide that we are Jews. I will insist on Kosher food and no concerts on the Sabbath."

"Ha! Good luck." I turned away to go to my bedroom.

I was determined to write that letter to David, with or without Moishe's help. I would be bold and finally ask the questions that kept me awake at night.

"David, what drove you away from your home? Was it Mama's matchmaking? Or was it me? I'll release you from your promise if you ask. Please, return and don't leave again."

"Abigail, please, listen to me," Moishe pleaded.

I pivoted. "What?"

"There's a great arts patron in Rochester, Lord Linden. He could help me get started and connect me with the right people. I'm going to write to him. If he invites me to play, will you come with me to the audition?"

My stomach clenched at the thought of playing for a stranger. "No. I'll get nervous and spoil everything."

"I don't care." Moishe pulled me close to him. His fingers touched my face. "I want to play ... with *you*."

"Why? I'm not that good. You should look for a professional accompanist." I turned my head away from him. "I need to write to David."

Moishe sighed. "Abigail, I'm trying to tell you... that I love you."

How could he toy with a word like that? My head snapped back in anger. "You know I love David. You aspire to win me from him? Is this a chess game to you?"

Moishe's arms let go of me. "That's not true!"

Before I could respond, the door opened, and David staggered in. He leaned on the wall for support. If thunder had roared at that moment, I wouldn't have noticed.

"Sorry if I frightened you. The door was open," he said, breathing heavily.

I rushed to him, tears welling in my eyes. He had no coat on. Shirt and breeches were wet from the rain. Even with my poor eyes, I could see that he was gaunt and unkempt. His overgrown hair was stricken with gray. His back slumped as he caught his breath. I grabbed his trembling hands to warm them.

"Don't punch him!" I yelled to Moishe, remembering his promise.

"No, a punch would knock him dead." Moishe circled his arm around David, helping him straighten.

"Well, thanks for that. I'm sure I deserve a good thrashing," David said with a chuckle.

"You look like hell," Moishe said. "Are you hurt?"

"Thankfully, no, only exhausted. Nothing Mama's meals won't cure. Where's she?"

"Visiting Hannah. Do you want me to fetch her? Or Dr. Kaplan?"

I silently agreed with Moishe that fetching the doctor would be a good idea. David's face was bloodless. His hands were like ice despite my efforts to warm them.

"I just need some rest. A glass of brandy wouldn't hurt either." His teeth chattered as he spoke.

My lips tightened. "We don't keep spirits in the house."

The brothers burst out laughing.

"There's a bottle behind the thickest book in Papa's room," Moishe said. "Papa's hiding place."

David exhaled a long breath. "Ah, it's good to be home. Nothing changes here."

"Let's get you to bed." Moishe let his brother lean on him. "Hold me so you don't fall."

He walked David to their bedroom, while I scurried to check behind Papa's books. To my surprise, I found a half-full bottle that gave off a strong whiff of alcohol. With my heart in my throat, I brought it to Moishe.

David was stretched out on his old bed while Moishe helped him unbutton his soaked shirt. Averting my eyes, I handed Moishe the bottle and dashed into the kitchen.

My hands were trembling. The kitchen was Mama's domain, although I kept it clean and organized for kashrut. I wanted to help with the cooking more, but after a couple of ruined meals, I was not trusted with cutting vegetables or measuring ingredients. Anxious about David, I needed to busy myself with something useful. I grabbed a knife and started peeling and cutting the onions for a broth. Tears poured from my eyes as I worked the knife. Twice, I almost cut myself.

"What are you doing?" Mama's voice startled me.

I gestured at the mutilated onion slices that lay before me in a pile.

"If you were hungry, you could've grabbed an apple before dinner. I got held up by that nasty rain. But it was worth it. Hannah *is* expecting."

I turned to face her, tears from the onion and worry running down my cheeks. "Mama, David is home. He's unwell."

She clutched at her chest and hurried up the stairs. I trailed behind as she flew into her sons' bedroom.

"What have you done with yourself?" she cried.

"Mama, let him sleep." Moishe led her out of the room and closed the door behind him.

"What's wrong with him?" I asked.

Moishe shrugged. "He said he is recovering from an illness. He was too tired to tell me more."

"Whatever it is, we'll get him back on his feet," Mama said. "Abigail, you made a mess of the onions. Let's slice them together."

We worked late into the evening, making nourishing foods for David. It felt good to be useful in his recovery. When Papa came home, we whispered the news to him. He tiptoed to the bedroom to get a long-awaited look at his son.

"He's home with all his limbs intact. He's luckier than many of the men who've sailed," Papa said after seeing him.

When I finally climbed into bed, sleep refused to come. My gladness about David's return mixed with worry about his health and anxiety over his feelings for me. In my letters, I'd shared my deepest fears and hopes.

Once, I described how I imagined our life as a husband and wife. I would get up early in the morning, make him breakfast and pack food for his lunch. In my own kitchen, I would learn to cook without anyone's help. While he would visit patients, I would take care of our babies and clean the house. Then, while our older children would go to Hebrew school, students would come for my piano lessons.

In the evening, we would dine together, extending our table to Mama and Papa, and all our family. Our home would be a place of love, a refuge for my husband after a busy workday.

At times, I wondered if David would want me to help with patients, but I wasn't sure what that would entail. Tossing and turning, I decided to let David bring up the subject of my letters first.

A moan, and then a scream pierced the night. I jumped out of bed and looked for my robe. Running into the furniture on my way, I found David's bedroom. Mama blocked my way at the door. "Go back to sleep, Abigail. David had a bad dream."

She walked me back to my room and kissed me goodnight. I shivered under my blanket, wondering what nightmares tortured David and if he experienced them when he was awake.

In the morning, David did not rise for breakfast. When Moishe staggered to the table, Mama jumped on him with questions.

The younger son yawned and rubbed his eyes. "He had a nightmare about a ship battle. He was sorry he disturbed everyone."

"Poor dear," Mama said as she poured the tea. "He must have been through a terrible ordeal."

Papa drummed his fingers on the table. "I'll ask Dr. Kaplan to stop by when he can. David may not be fond of him, but it doesn't hurt to hear his opinion." He donned his coat and left.

David slept through much of the day. Whenever I crept by the bedroom door, I listened for his deep breaths. To avoid disturbing his brother, Moishe went to practice his violin at Miriam's. He asked me to come with him, but I refused. Music was the last thing on my mind.

At dinnertime, Mama arranged a tray with oxtail soup, slices of beef, vegetables, and rye bread. I volunteered to bring it to David.

"Make sure he eats everything," she instructed me.

With a fluttering sensation in my stomach, I knocked on his door. "David, I brought you dinner."

"Please give me ten minutes," was his reply. Beyond the closed door, I heard water splash. When he bid me to come in, he sat at the desk.

"Are you feeling better?" I placed the tray next to him, noticing that he had shaved and wore a fresh shirt. Murka flew in and jumped onto David's lap, ready to share his meal.

He scratched behind the cat's ear. "A little better. It may take me some time to feel like myself. But I'm glad to see you looking so lovely. All grown up."

My cheeks heated at his compliment. I believed he was sincere. In his absence, my pox marks faded. My body turned womanly, with wide shoulders, curvy hips, and a sizable bosom. Mama recently remarked that I was built to bear babies. I hoped David noticed all those changes.

He sighed. "Does Mama expect me to eat all this?"

"I'm afraid so. She'll check for empty plates."

"I doubt I can manage such a portion," he said after taking a couple of sips of the soup. "The meals on the ship were modest." He tore off a piece of meat for Murka.

"Will you tell us what happened on your voyage?"

"Eventually. Let's just say the life of sea adventures did not turn out well."

"I'm sorry. We were so worried about you."

He looked away. When silence became uncomfortable, he said, "I can't finish all that food. Eat something so Mama doesn't scold me."

I placed my hands on my hips. "At least finish the soup. I cut the onions for it."

"Well, thank you. It's very good." He chuckled, making my heart sing. "What else have you been doing besides cooking with Mama?"

"I joined the women's prayer group. Tomorrow, we will visit Mrs. Katz because the walk to the synagogue is too hard at her age. And I play the pianoforte and give lessons. Sometimes, I play accompaniment for Moishe. He aspires to be a professional musician."

"He has the talent and the resolve for it. What about Shira?"

"The bakery is a success with Jewish *and* Gentile patrons. Sometimes she gets orders for weddings and parties."

"That's wonderful." There was warmth in his voice. "How are Mama and Papa? Are they in good health?"

"Yes, except they have more gray hair on your account." I gave him an accusing look.

He sighed and brushed his hand across his hair. "I received my share of gray as well. It's nice to know that little has changed here. You've changed the most."

I beamed at him. My heart sped up, anticipating a confession of some sort.

"You are now Jewish. You have no regrets about converting?"

"Oh. No." My spirits wilted. "I like worshiping with the rest of the family."

He swallowed the last spoonful of the soup. "That's good. I hated to think that you were coerced in any way."

I raised my chin. "It was all my decision. I studied with Rabbi Cohen for a year before converting. The Chatham Jewish community is my family."

"I'm glad. I wanted a family for you."

While I tried to be patient, the suspense was too much for me. I allowed myself one question. "You are part of this family. Will you remain in Chatham?"

He cleared his throat and grew quiet. "I'm sorry, but I'm getting tired. I'd like to go back to bed. Let's talk later."

"Of course." I picked up the tray and staggered out of the room.

Our chat echoed over and over in my mind all day. As I readied to say my bedtime prayers, the realization hit me. He ended the conversation when I asked him about staying in Chatham. He didn't want to stay. *He prefers being far away from me.* My pillow was drenched with tears by morning.

Chapter 17

The next day, David joined us for breakfast. Despite Mama's coaxing, he ate little. The parents' voices rang with joy; their prodigal son had returned. I couldn't help but wonder for how long.

After breakfast, Papa left to sell his goods at the docks, and Moishe went out to procure some paper for his music compositions. Mama and I inspected David's clothes for laundry and mending. Some shirts and trousers we could restore to their former glory, but many were beyond saving. When I asked David permission to discard the tattered garments, he was slumped on the sofa, holding Murka to his chest.

"Do what you will with them," he said with a lifeless tone.

My jaw tensed. "David, what's wrong?"

"Nothing. I'm only tired."

"But you just got out of bed." I paced a small circle through the dining room, then stopped in front of him. "You need a doctor."

He grunted. "Dr. Kaplan will not know how to help."

The doorbell chimed. Murka dashed into the corner. Mama's voice pitched as she exchanged pleasantries with the visitor.

"Did someone already send for the doctor?" David grunted. "That's a waste of time."

"What's that, David?" Dr. Kaplan asked, waking in. "Did you say you don't need a doctor? We cannot treat ourselves, you know."

I brought a chair for the physician and retreated into a corner to stand with Mama. She wrapped her arm around me.

David let Dr. Kaplan count his pulse and listen to his chest. "I imagine you've never had a patient with malaria," he said after the doctor finished prodding him.

Mama clenched my arm as I leaned on her for strength. Malaria sounded ominous and foreign.

Dr. Kaplan cocked his head to the side. "You underestimate me as usual, young man. In my youth, I organized a hospital in Bombay. I'm well familiar with the nasty malady you caught in the tropics. Are you still having fevers?"

"No, not since I arrived to England. The last bout on the voyage back almost did me in. I couldn't make it out of bed for days."

My hand went up to my mouth. "Is he going to be all right?"

Dr. Kaplan turned to us. "I'm sure you and your Mama will nurse this patient back to health. Fresh fruit and nuts will aid his recovery. In India, I noticed that patients who ate oranges and figs were most likely to improve."

I made mental notes for the next shopping trip.

"I didn't know that," David said. There was humbleness in his voice.

Mama nodded. "Thank you, Doctor. I'll buy any fruit I can find."

The doctor stood. "You take care, David."

"Please wait." David rose as well. "I owe you an apology."

"You owe me nothing." Dr. Kaplan waved his hand.

"Yes, I do, for how I spoke to you when I came back from medical school... I'm sorry for what I said that day."

Dr. Kaplan touched David's shoulder. "You were harsh but not wrong. I should try harder to keep up with the medical advances. Ever since I've opened my practice, I've been extremely busy caring for my patients. While most days I only treat colds and closed bowels, I need to be better prepared to handle an emergency. That day, when you operated on Ester, you taught me a great deal."

David ran his hand through his hair. "You assisted on that very well. And you took diligent care of the patient post-surgery."

"I was honored to be of help. Earlier this year, I published about your surgery in Medical Essays and Observations. I used the name 'Dr. Oliver Higgins' to avoid attention to your background, but that story created some noise among medical men. You are the first to perform a successful appendectomy besides Dr. Miller, and this was the first case of a pregnant patient."

David gasped. "That's brilliant. Thank you. I will look for the publication."

A grin spread on my face as I bounced on my toes from pride for him. "That's wonderful, David."

Dr. Kaplan tipped his hat. "I need to see my next patient. Ester's little girl has a sore throat and an earache."

"Ester's little girl?" David echoed. "The baby she was pregnant with when we operated on her?"

"Well, Dina is hardly a baby now." Dr. Kaplan chuckled. "But yes, that's her."

"Didn't I mention her in my letters?" Mama said. "Everyone was worried about Ester giving birth after her surgery, but all went well. The child developed slowly and did not start speaking until recently, but she's catching up."

David's voice regained vigor as he addressed the older doctor. "I'd love to see her. May I come with you?"

"You need rest," Mama interjected.

"It's all right, Mrs. Fridman," Dr. Kaplan said. "A little excursion may do him some good. We won't be long."

While David was gone, Mama and I visited the market and purchased a variety of fresh fruit and nuts. I rejoiced at doing something useful for his recovery.

After we returned, I practiced my part in the duet Moishe composed. Whenever we played it together, it didn't go well, mostly because of the mistakes I made. Seated on the piano bench, I ran my fingers over the keys, pondering what I was doing wrong.

The music Moishe wrote was so daunting to me. It was all technique. When I asked him what this duet meant, he said it was to show our abilities as musicians. He loved the challenge of a difficult piece—as if music was something to conquer. My fingers longed for melodies that were simple but gave me quiet joy or cleansing tears.

What made me want to play piano when I was a child? I discovered my talent finding the notes of the lullaby David sang to me at the hospital. The Yiddish cradle song opened hidden doors in my growing mind. Hearing the emotion in the lullaby helped me sleep despite fears of the constable and the orphanage. Music connected people in their trials, whether it was me singing Ma's songs to Julian and Josie before we were separated, or Papa playing violin for his half-starved children as their ship sailed to England.

My arms relaxed, and the music of the lullaby flowed effortlessly through my fingertips. When I finished, I sat with my eyes closed, savoring the pleasure.

"You play very well," David said behind me. "That song took me back to that night in the hospital when I sang it for the dying boy. Then you prayed for him, and I thought, 'I can't let this girl go to the orphanage where no one will care about her.'"

I spun around on the bench. "I didn't hear you come in. Are you all right? I hope the visit didn't tire you."

"Not at all. I needed to feel like I can be of help." Notes of regret sounded in his voice.

"You saved many lives as a doctor." I stood up and approached him. "The wounded sailors at the hospital—"

"Too many of them die from festered wounds." He shook his head. "I tried so hard to convince the hospital management to enforce hygiene, but they refused to listen. When I lost my job, Ella's success as a ship surgeon inspired me to follow in her path. But the tropical fever spread, and I was afraid I would die alongside my patients."

My hands rested on his shoulders. "That was my biggest fear. I prayed so much that you would come home."

"Your letters meant a lot to me. When I was delirious with fever, a friend read them to me, and I would see you here, making dinner with Mama or playing the piano. I told myself that someday I would be back to the safety of this home."

I released a breath I held too long. "I hoped our family's love would protect you. That's why I wrote so much."

His hands took mine. "Your words were a beacon in a storm. Did you know you saved my life once before, when I was going to leave for the army? My military posting was almost arranged, but when you stopped me from going, another surgeon took my place. He died in battle, along with everyone in his unit, only a week after they set foot in France."

My stomach lurched. "A premonition told me that if you enlisted, you would be killed. David, why do you keep trying to leave us? What's driving you away?"

He let go of my hands and walked to the window. "My ambitions as a physician. My frustrations with living a double life—a Jew here and a Christian everywhere else. My belief that my absence would benefit you. And... other reasons."

My arms went limp. "Will you leave us again because of all those reasons?"

Still staring into the window, he hung his head. I tiptoed to him and put my hand on his elbow. I wished my body could absorb the pain that weighed down his shoulders.

"Abigail!" Moishe barged in holding a letter. "This just came from Lord Linden. The audition..." He froze, then put his letter away. "I'll tell you another time."

"You are invited to an audition?" David pivoted. "I'd love to hear about this."

I put on a bright smile. "That's exciting. Why don't you tell David about it while I help Mama with dinner? We bought oranges for dessert, but I also made the honey cake, and I dare to say, it's almost as good as Shira's."

"I think my appetite is improving already." David turned to his brother. "What will you play?"

I sped out of the room. My heart was fluttering like a bird as I heard David's voice in my ears, speaking of my letters.

At dinner, David was animated when he spoke of his visit. "Ester's little girl is a dear. She does not hear well, but overall, she is a healthy child. And Ester was sweet and gracious."

Mama placed a bowl of fruit in front of him. "Well, of course. She and her daughter owe you their lives."

I didn't need to see David's face to know he was smiling.

"Then as we were walking back, a maid spied our medical bags and called us to help her mistress. The lady suffered from abdominal pain after overindulging on cake from Shira's bakery. Dr. Kaplan joked that Shira's treats must come with a warning," he said with a chuckle and tossed a grape into his mouth.

He was coming alive. His easy laugh and energetic gestures spoke of it. I wanted to throw my arms around him and not let go.

The next few days David took walks in the morning and rested in the afternoon. His appetite improved to Mama's joy. Whenever I practiced piano, he listened and complimented me. I asked him to sing with me, but he declined. I longed to resume our conversation, but I commanded myself to be patient as he recovered.

One morning, Papa, Mama, and Moishe went to the synagogue. I feigned a slight cold to stay home with David. While he sprawled on the sofa and read a medical journal, I considered asking him how physicians' wives help their husbands with their work. The thought came to me when visiting the apothecary to purchase a tonic Dr. Kaplan prescribed for David. Mama and

I met Mrs. Kaplan there, requesting a whole list of medicinal herbs.

The doorbell sounded, and I went to see who it was. The Hebrew teacher, Mr. Simons, stood at the door. A redheaded boy of three was with him. I led them into the dining room.

"David... I'm sorry... Dr. Fridman, do you have a minute?" Mr. Simons asked with his head bent. The boy twirled, examining his surroundings.

David threw down the paper and stood. "For my beloved Hebrew teacher? Anytime. And please call me David. What can I help you with?"

Mr. Simons' knees cracked as lowered himself onto a chair I brought him. I set his cane in the corner.

The elderly man rubbed his face. "I'm sorry to occupy your precious time, but we've been terribly concerned. I even heard my daughter-in-law cry at night."

"Why?" There was tension in David's voice.

I looked for an excuse to stay in the room and listen. Mr. Simons was a kind man, lending me Hebrew books. Hoping that nothing awful had happened to him or his family, I busied myself with searching for a suitable toy for the little boy.

"You see, my grandson Nathan swallowed a plum pit yesterday. And after what happened with Noah and Ester... we are beside ourselves with worry."

"Has he complained of a bellyache?"

"No, but..."

"Then it's nothing to be concerned about." David invited the boy to lie down on the sofa. "Nathan, did Grandpa teach you the Hebrew letters?" he asked the boy as he palpated his belly.

Nathan giggled. "*Alef, Bet, Vet...*"

"That's great. Does it hurt when I press here?"

The boy laughed. "It tickles."

David helped the boy sit up and addressed the grandfather. "You have a terrific grandson. Almost certainly the pit will come out in a couple of days and all will be well."

With my arms full of my old rag dolls, I knelt by the boy. Nathan examined them with interest and asked for their names.

The grandfather stared at the floor. "You said, 'almost'. So, there's some chance..."

David waved his hand dismissively. "Please don't worry and tell your children to calm themselves. Yes, there's a remote chance the pit may get stuck in his appendix, however, it's not likely. Many children swallow pits, but seldom does anyone become ill."

The man bowed his head. "We'll have to hope for the best. Ester was lucky that you were home that terrible day. Such luck may not occur twice. Last year, Haim, one of my students, was run over by a coach and broke his leg. Dr. Kaplan said he could not treat such a bad break. We carried the poor child to St. Bartholomew's as he was screaming and moaning. When we reached the hospital, there was a long queue, twenty people at least. I pleaded for someone to help him ahead of others, but the orderly did not budge. If Haim received help sooner, he would have avoided the amputation."

David shivered. "A child lost a leg?"

"Yes. And he's still not walking. The wooden peg the hospital surgeon fitted is causing him pain. Maybe you could sort out what's wrong?"

"Of course. I've helped many wounded sailors adjust to artificial limbs."

"I'm sure Haim's parents will be grateful." Mr. Simons placed his hand on his chest. "David, I had such high hopes when you received your degree. Fine medical men are in short supply everywhere, but please think of us, your neighbors and friends. We need you."

Nathan looked up from the dolls I was holding out for him. "Grandpa, I like this doctor. Can we come again?"

I couldn't help but smile at him. My mind was already conjuring dreams of having a little boy of my own one day. With dark, intelligent eyes like David's.

Mr. Simons shook his finger. "Nathan, you need to stay quiet when adults talk."

David ruffled the boy's hair. "I want to help, but ... I will be leaving soon."

Silence hung in the air. My throat convulsed. After a terrible year of worrying about David's voyage, we'd have to endure another absence.

"I was afraid that might be the case." Mr. Simons sighed. "You never stay here long."

Years ago, I may have talked David out of going to war. Now, I silently prayed to find the words to persuade him to stay. He cared about the people in this town, and he loved his family. I would play whatever role he wanted of me if he agreed to stay.

I rose from my knees and touched his arm. "David, don't you see how much you are needed here? When trouble comes, your neighbors and your own family rely on you. The hospital is too crowded. Dr. Kaplan can't treat the diseases and injuries that you can. The patients look to you because of your skill, your compassion, and your bond with the community. Please stop seeking distant places for your work when people in your hometown depend on you with their lives."

Mr. Simons rose from his chair. "I couldn't have said it better."

David stood in silence, staring down at the floor. Then he glanced at the boy. "I... I will organize a private practice."

The Hebrew teacher made a gleeful sound as he took his grandson by his hand. "May *Hashem* help you."

When they left, David collapsed on the sofa, resting his chin on his hands. I perched next to him. "David, what's wrong?"

"It's just... so much to think through. The location, the logistics, the finances. I dreamed of starting a medical practice, but not just yet. I had... other plans."

"You intended to leave again?" Tears welled in the corners of my eyes. "David, we've spent a terrible year, not knowing if you are dead or alive. Why don't you stay?"

His shoulders tensed and he looked away.

"It's because of me, isn't it? I pushed too hard, pleading for a promise of marriage. You stayed away from your home and then sailed on a dangerous voyage to avoid me. Did you expect my love to quell while we were apart?"

He turned to me and took my hand. "It wasn't the only reason. My own heart needed to heal as well. Abigail, in your letters, you opened up your soul with such trust. I was deeply touched. But you deserve someone who will burn with passion for you."

My body and voice shook from tears. "I won't speak of love if you don't want me to. Please stay here for your family, for the patients who need you. I will release you from your promise of marriage... Even if it breaks me."

He pulled me to his chest and kissed me on the top of my head. "Abigail, that letter where you described how you imagine our lives together. Don't you dream of something bigger for yourself than days full of household chores and marriage to a man who is not in love with you?"

I swallowed tears. "I would be glad to perform any chore for you. It does not matter if you don't love me just yet. My love is strong enough for both of us."

He stayed silent for a while, stroking me as I cried. "Fine. Let's have it your way."

Fearing that I misheard him, I asked, "You wish to marry me?"

"If you are sure that's what you want. When I brought you to my family, I became responsible for your wellbeing. Twice, your love saved my life. Making you happy is very important to me. I will be a kind and patient husband. Hopefully, I will learn to love you the way you deserve."

My heart was ready to burst with happiness. I wanted to dance and spin around the room. In my mind, I was thanking *Hashem* for this miracle. *This is the best day of my life!*

"Abigail, did you hear me?"

I beamed at David. "Yes. You said that you want to make me happy. And you did."

"Yes, but first I need to leave. Just for a little while."

My spine tensed. "Why?"

He clasped his knees together. "I promised someone a visit."

My bliss was short-lived. A premonition pricked like needles in my belly. "You don't sound happy to visit this person."

He hung his head. "It's not going to be a pleasant meeting. I owe someone an explanation why I broke contact with her."

My chest squeezed, and I rose to my feet. "The woman you used to write to?"

"Yes. Her brother assisted me during my voyage. He also made me promise I'd speak to her."

I paced around the room. "When will you go?"

"When I will be well enough for the journey to Seatown, in Dorset. I won't stay long."

My arms crossed my chest. "Can't you write her a letter?"

"I must keep my word. There's no reason for you to worry. She and I... can't be together."

There was heartache in his voice when he said the last three words. I stopped pacing and stared at him.

"Why? Is she...?"

"Yes. She's a Gentile. Outside of Chatham I pretend to be a Christian man, Oliver Higgins. But I will not convert. I need to tell her that was the reason for my abrupt goodbye."

My head hung. "You've been away so long. And we just decided on our future."

He rose and cupped my face. "When I return, we'll announce our plans to marry."

I closed my eyes and nodded. "I'll be waiting."

Chapter 18

Moishe ordered the driver to hurry and promised a generous tip. The coach shook on the cobbled road, making my insides, already twisted from anxiety, hurt even more. Moishe clutched the violin case on his lap, protecting it from bumps.

"What will we say to Mama and Papa? They will be furious with us," I fretted.

Sitting across from me, Moishe tossed his head back. "I'm an adult and can spend an evening outside of home. And, when it's appropriate, I can bring you along."

"We should've asked permission."

He snorted. "Since you came to Chatham, you haven't been beyond the town boundary, which is only five streets from our house. Aren't you curious to see how the rich lords and ladies live? Where is your sense of adventure?"

"I don't have one." I rolled my eyes. "Remember in what state David came back after his ship voyage? That should be enough for anyone to stop wishing for an adventure."

"Yet, he left as soon as he could stand another journey." Moishe gave a bitter laugh.

My stomach squeezed so tight I almost became sick. "He had to keep a promise. And a holiday at the seaside will restore his health."

"Well, I hope he's enjoying his sunbathing. It's been two months."

Sixty days of agony for me. Sixty nights of imagining David in the embrace of another woman.

Moishe tugged on my sleeve. "Come now, you are acting like I'm whisking you away to the West Indies. We are only going to Rochester for an audition."

He said it so calmly. His musical career could be decided tonight, and he broke no sweat. I had no intention of being his accompanist beyond tonight, yet I couldn't take a full breath.

"Do you think we are dressed appropriately?" I asked, smoothing the dress Mama made me for the celebration after I recovered from smallpox. Pearls buttoned up to my throat. I envisioned marrying David in it.

Moishe shrugged. "We are wearing our best clothes. And Lord Linden wants to hear our music, not gawk at us."

"I mean, we look... like Jews." Moishe was dressed in all black and wore his skull cap and tzitzit. My dress was lovely, but distinctly different from styles the Gentile women wore.

"I'm not hiding who I am. I'm not like David, ready to toss away everything I value the moment I cross the town border. Wherever I go in life, I will be a Jew first."

I wished I had half as much confidence as him.

The coach stopped near a palace; I had no other word to describe that immense mansion that stretched for half a block, with marble columns and enormous windows. My legs shook.

"Now, that's what I call a house," Moishe said with a laugh.

I buried my face in my hands. "Please, let me wait for you inside the coach. I can't do this."

He took my arm, pulling my hands away from my face. "Are you mad? This could be an evening we'll be describing to our grandchildren."

He jumped out of the coach and offered me a hand. I walked with an unsteady gait, leaning on him. A servant in livery and a white wig stepped forward. "Are you the kitchen help? The backdoor is this way." He pointed.

Moishe grunted. "We are guests of Lord Linden. Moishe Fridman and Abigail Jones."

"Ah, the musicians. Go through the backdoor."

"Absolutely not. We will go through the front."

The valet stepped back. "This is ... insolence. Who do you think you are?"

I tugged on Moishe's arm. "Please, let's go through the back. Who are we to argue?" I preferred a more discreet entrance anyway. Maybe I could find a dark closet to hide in.

"Nonsense. Man, your master is a patron of the arts. Does he ask all performers who visit his home to enter through the back?"

"Well, the famous ones, like the tenor we had last week, enter through the front of course, but you..." the valet shrugged.

"Then you should be leading us through the front and learning our names, so such folly wouldn't happen again. Now, let's go. You don't want to keep Lord Linden waiting."

In what school did Moishe pick up such self-assurance? I marveled with my mouth open.

The servant jerked his shoulders and bowed. "I'm sorry. Your clothing confused me. I do recall now that I was instructed to lead you through the front doors. Please forgive my mistake and follow me."

We entered through the gold-decorated doors, greeted by more servants. A lanky butler asked for our names. A vast hall, lit by a grand chandelier was before us. A man in a fine ebony jacket and a woman in an emerald ball gown descended from a marble staircase.

"They are so young! How charming!" the woman exclaimed and turned to the man. "Darling, this will work marvelously."

When she approached, the scent of her jasmine perfume wafted in the air. "I'm Lady Margaret Linden, and this is Lord Linden."

Moishe bowed his head. I did the same, but he nudged me. "What?" I whispered.

"Ladies curtsy," he said under his breath.

Untrained, I performed a clumsy curtsy.

The lady threw her head back, laughing. "You will have to work on that. Oh, but such innocence… so refreshing after that puffed-up tenor who could barely fit through the doors."

She rested her arm on mine like we were old friends. "My dears, it's a brilliant coincidence that you are here tonight. Upstairs, I have a ballroom full of guests who came to watch a Russian dancer. Alas, she sprained her famous ankle. What a relief it was to learn that my husband was expecting young musicians. Instead of your audition, would you be my heroes and save my reputation as a hostess? Please treat us to a musical evening." She folded her hands into a praying position.

Lord Linden, a tall gentleman in his sixties, tilted his head. "I hope you don't mind. Our guests are music lovers. I trust their opinions about the arts."

They expected me to play for wealthy, sophisticated people. I envied the dancer who sprained her ankle. *Is it too late to injure my fingers?*

Moishe put his hand on his chest. "It's a great honor, we happily accept."

"Splendid. Except… oh, we will fix this in a jiffy." Lady Linden snapped her fingers, and the butler rushed to her. "Find something stylish to wear for the young man. Then please have the waiters serve champagne."

"I won't remove my kippah or my tzitzit," Moishe protested.

The hostess made a "hmm" sound in her throat. "I have no idea what you said, but your clothes are more suitable for a funeral than for a party. Please change."

Moishe followed the butler, who as he walked, gave orders to the small army of waiters. Lord Linden wished me luck and went to mingle with the guests. His wife waved over a strict-looking lady in spectacles. "Madam Turner, please dress her for a performance."

I followed Madam Turner, who held her back so stiff as if an iron rod went through her body. The room she brought me to had dresses hanging on three walls, a full-length mirror on the fourth wall, and a stand in the center of the room. Humming a melody, the woman selected a white dress and stared at my waist.

"This gown would do. Get undressed."

I studied the design, my jaw hung open. "I can't wear something showing my shoulders. It's... immodest."

"Nonsense, child. The mistress's daughter wore it last season. Get up on the stand."

She helped me remove my dress. Embarrassed to be seen in nothing but my chemise and corset, I hugged myself.

Clicking her tongue, Madam Turner helped me slide into the evening gown. The silky dress left my arms and shoulders bare and even the top of my chest was showing. I felt naked.

Lady Linden swept into the room. "How are we doing?"

Madam Turner fastened the hooks in the back. "Not a perfect fit, but acceptable."

"Please, madam," I begged. "Can I wear something more modest? I'm only an accompanist, not a singer or dancer."

The hostess chuckled and put her hand on my unclothed arm. "Oh, such naivete. While some of my guests appreciate music, most feast on entertainment with their eyes. Delicate shoulders and lush golden hair in combination with girlish shyness. Charmante! Don't squint your eyes so much, they are lovely as well."

I fidgeted as Madam Turner inserted pins to adjust the waist. "I can't help it. I have poor eyesight after surviving smallpox a couple of years ago."

"And yet, you can play? Oh, you will make the ladies weep. Speaking of smallpox, we need to apply some paste and powder to cover the scars."

Do rich ladies have a trick to fill in the pits on their faces? My arms tingled with surprise.

Madam Turner led me to a chair. As she applied a thick paste over my face, her mistress patted my back. "I caught smallpox in my twenties. The blisters did not come right away, but fever had me shaking. Determined to perform, I drank a pitcher of cold water. I knew that young Lord Linden was in the audience to see me. After the pirouettes, I fainted right on stage."

My head swiveled to her. "You are a dancer?"

"Stay still!" Madam Turner commanded.

The hostess laughed. "I *was* a dancer. When Lord Linden and I married, it was a terrible scandal. We left London and hid away here. I put my dancing shoes away and learned my new role of Lord's wife. But I still use the paste to cover the scars."

The powder Madam Turner was spreading got into my nose, and I sneezed. "That's a beautiful story."

"You have a story as well. How did you meet a Jewish boy and started playing music with him? My guests will want to know."

I told her how I lost Ma and came to live with the Fridmans. When I finished speaking, she squeezed my hand.

"Oh, my guests will love you! An orphan playing with her adopted brother. How sweet! Practice your curtsies. You will be doing many tonight."

When she left the room, I needed Madam Turner to direct me to the privy. My bladder threatened to loosen from anxiety.

Wrestling with my skirts made my forehead sweat. When I finished smoothing them, I checked my reflection in the mirror, leaning in close. The girl who looked back at me was so stunning that I had to wave my hands to confirm that it was me in the glass. I was transformed into a beauty.

When I returned to the room, Madam Turner grabbed my arm. "They are ready for you. Come quickly," she urged.

I did not get a chance to practice the curtsy as Lady Linden suggested.

Chapter 19

adam Turner ushered me upstairs to a circular room of white and gold, spacious enough for a theater production. A white pianoforte stood in the middle of the room. Moishe stood next to it, tuning his violin. His borrowed black jacket and cream cravat sat elegantly on him. The guests were seated in the rows of chairs, chatting among themselves, and sipping from their crystal glasses. Most of the ladies had dresses styled like mine, revealing their shoulders and arms. Many had diamonds and other gems decorating their necks and hair.

While I gawked at the audience, Moishe studied my dress. I could just see him flinch at the immodesty of it.

Blood rushed to my head. I wanted to dart to the doors, but Lady Linden announced, "And now, we'll have our entertainment from promising young musicians, Moishe Fridman and Abigail Jones."

The guests clapped and Moishe led me to the piano bench. It occurred to me that this white iceberg I was expected to play might be quite different from the pianoforte we had at home.

Maybe an Italian or a German instrument, not a British one. The keys may feel and sound different than what I was used to. I gave Moishe a wide-eyed glance as my breaths shuddered.

He read my alarm and placed my right hand on the middle C. "It's the same sixty-one keys."

Easy for him to say: he brought his own instrument. With a curt bow to the audience, he started playing his solo. The piece he selected for tonight was one of his compositions, with a difficult part for the violin and a straightforward accompaniment in the second part. The piece showed off his skill, including the left-hand pizzicatos that used to make his fingers bleed. I never liked this piece much. The melody didn't move me, and I pitied his tortured fingers. I wondered if the audience would appreciate his effort.

While he showed off his technique, I found the keys for my opening and counted in my head to the beginning of my part. I came in at the right moment. To my horror, I could barely hear my sound. The keys were stiff under my trembling fingers, not willing to sing for me. With my heart in my throat, I pushed harder at them, and they yielded, giving the volume I needed.

After a few weak notes, my fingers found their rhythm. The hours of practice paid off. My sound was tenser than at home, my hands had to press harder than I was used to, but the instrument was essentially the same. *I could play in any room that had a piano, anywhere in the world.* Freedom rang through that thought.

I glanced at the audience, glad I couldn't see their faces. To comfort myself, I imagined they were grinning at me. The piece was more melodious and ear pleasing with the accompaniment. I exhaled and smiled but then... *Oh my Lord, no*. My finger slipped and hit the wrong key. My heart skipped a beat together with the music. My hands froze.

Forcing myself to breathe, I waited for a good moment to pick up again. Moishe's shoulders tensed along with his sound. I suspected that he itched to turn to me, but his challenging spiccato required all his concentration. Telling myself to keep calm, I came in at the crescendo, right near the end.

The audience gave us lukewarm applause. Heaven help me, they noticed my amateur mistake. It couldn't be for anything Moishe did; his playing was perfect. When he lowered his head, I wanted to go home and cry in Papa's lap.

He bent down to me with his face distraught, and my chest ached.

"I'm sorry," I said quietly enough only for him to hear. "I ruined everything."

Moishe shook his head. "It's not you. They didn't care for the music. They looked bored the whole time."

"But..." *Didn't they see what it took to play such a piece?* Well, if they were not musically trained, they probably didn't.

"Ladies, gentleman, let's show more appreciation," a tall man with a red mustache boomed. "Such an ambitious piece would challenge any virtuoso. Bravo!" The uninterested audience livened at his command. The applause rang with enthusiasm.

"Maybe we should play something they would know? From Vivaldi's Four Seasons?" I offered.

Moishe frowned. He practiced nothing but his own compositions the last few weeks, and he hated changing his plans. I considered how to convince him when Lady Linden approached us.

"My friends have a request. Could you play a waltz?"

I blinked. Even if we heard the piece, they couldn't expect us to play it impromptu.

"A what? I've never heard of it." Moishe answered.

Lady Linden lowered her voice. "That dance is the latest craze. It would be a treat to hear after such ... an intense performance you gave us."

He shifted his feet. "If someone would sing the melody I might..."

"It goes la-la-la, one-two-three." A former dancer, she had an ear for the rhythm.

Never one to bypass a challenge, Moishe nodded. "I can improvise. Abigail, you do this." He whispered the series of chords he wanted me to play.

"You are not serious," I stammered, but he stepped away and picked up his bow.

In a minute, he was playing, while I was doing my best to keep up. The dance was simple and measured, much easier to play than the pieces we rehearsed. It had an instant charm.

The red-mustached gentleman brought the hostess out to the center of the room. To the applause of other guests, they faced each other and danced a few graceful steps. My eyes widened at the close position of the couple, the man holding the lady by the waist while her hand rested on her partner's shoulder. Two other couples joined them on the dance floor and spun to the music. When we ended playing, and the dance partner bent Lady Linden into a dip, the claps and cheers boomed.

Moishe and I exchanged looks, unsure what to do next. He whispered that we should play another one of his pieces. I sensed that we should continue with better-known melodies. After a brief discussion, we compromised. We played Mozart, Bach, and Clementi, and finished with another of Moishe's compositions. This time the audience listened attentively.

Excited by his success, Moishe suggested to play another piece. I sensed that the audience got tired, and we should take our leave. The hostess chose for us.

"Well, that was marvelous," she said, extending a hand to me. "Please take a well-deserved bow." I bobbed a couple of awkward curtsies, and Moishe bent his head to vigorous applause.

A young man handed me a magnificent rose bouquet. "My mother, I, and especially my sister enjoyed your performance," he said and nodded to the women next to him.

I suspected they brought the flowers for the Russian dancer, but I was happy to accept them.

"Do you sing, Miss?" The older woman asked. "My daughter needs a voice teacher."

"I'm sorry, but I don't sing," I said. I sang prayers and Yiddish songs, but I did not think that counted.

"You played with such passion," the young woman said. "I wish I could show that much emotion in my singing."

I gave her a timid smile and curtsied again.

Back in the changing room, I was overjoyed to don my own dress. Madam Turner fixed my hair and bid me to wait for the hostess, who was saying goodbye to her guests.

Left alone, I replayed the evening in my head. It was exciting, even exhilarating. Moishe was right; it was a night to remember. Now I was tired and craved to be home.

Lady Linden glided into the room. "Success! They loved you, like I knew they would."

I thanked her for the opportunity and for the dress, but she waved me off and rang the bell. A servant woman brought a tray of sandwiches.

"You must be famished. Help yourself," Lady Linden said.

At the aroma of food, my stomach rumbled. But seeing meat slices next to the cheese, I stopped my hand from grasping at them.

"I'm sorry, but I follow kashrut. Please don't be offended."

Lady Linden shrugged. "No one is offended, dear, but you need to eat after a performance. Is there anything we can serve you?"

"Fruit and water."

"That will be easy." She nodded to the serving woman. In mere moments, she brought a new tray with grapes, apples, and oranges.

"Now listen, Abigail," the hostess said after I muttered the *bracha* and stuffed an orange slice into my mouth. "The high society think themselves good judges of musical talent, but most just clap for anyone famous. The gentleman who danced with me, Mr. Campanella, can distinguish between a diamond and a fake. He was awed by Moishe's technique. Mr. Campanella is an impresario. He wants to arrange a tour for him to perform around Europe. Venice, Vienna, St. Petersburg."

I beamed. "That's wonderful. Moishe will be so happy."

"Oh, how sweet." She pinched my cheek. "You are so glad for your music partner that you don't ask about yourself. Don't you have ambitions of your own?"

My toes curled up. "I know there are better performers than me. I prefer to play at home for my family and give lessons to children."

Lady Linden snorted. "Nonsense. Every girl dreams to travel the world. While Mr. Campanella said you were a mediocre pianist, I believe you can make Moishe shine. Today, you charmed the ladies. And the gentlemen." She pointed to the bouquet.

My cheeks and neck grew hot. I gulped down a glass of water.

The hostess chuckled. "Yes, the gentlemen. They were ogling you, and that's usually a good thing for a performer. But I sense that you are uncomfortable with this kind of attention. And Moishe was riled by it as well, I noticed. Is he always so protective of you?"

"I don't know. I suppose he is."

"Hmm..." She cocked her head. "As a former entertainer, I want to give you some advice. Marry that boy before the tour. A female performer on the road receives unwelcome visitors in all hours of day and night. A married woman carries more respect and protection. Think about it."

"It's impossible. He and I are not in love," I explained. Agreeing to a tour with Moishe would be madness. David would return soon and we'd announce our engagement.

"No? Could've fooled me." She stroked my arm. "I just wanted to help. I look forward to seeing more of you and your music partner. And here is a little gift from one artist to another." She offered a basket with a couple of round containers. "Paste and powder for your face. There's also a note with the address of the shop where you can purchase more."

Rising, I thanked Lady Linden for an unforgettable evening and followed her to the antechamber. Moishe was there with Lord Linden and Mr. Campanella, all three in a heated discussion.

"We will not perform Friday evenings or Saturdays before sundown. And our meals must be kosher," Moishe said with his arms crossed.

Lord Linden scratched his chin. "Friday is a prime evening for concerts. And the food..."

"I'm sure the great impresario can accommodate," the lady of the house said. "He once organized a tour for an actor who insisted on bringing his goat along. Right, Mr. Campanella?" She whispered into my ear. "You will learn to use your charm as well. Men love praise."

I had no such confidence, but I admired how she disarmed the arguing men.

"Artists have such peculiar tastes." Mr. Campanella raised his hands dramatically. "We'll sort out the details later. It will require me a couple of months to schedule the tour. I will write when I have news."

The hosts insisted that we travel home in their carriage. Clutching my bouquet, I sat across from Moishe and gauged his mood. A triumphant evening, yet I perceived no excitement from him.

"Are you angry about the dress? I had no choice," I said.

He chewed on his nail. "When we go on tour, I will detail all requirements into the contract, including that we wear our own clothes. They will not make you look like a harlot again."

Tears welled up in my eyes. "I was dressed the same as the other ladies. Are they harlots too?"

"This wasn't your fault. I'm sorry I spoke so harshly." He touched my arm. "You saw for yourself how vulgar those people are. And they are frauds. They understood nothing of my composition."

I suppressed a sigh. *His pride and stubbornness will bring him trouble.*

"They are not Jews. Their customs are different. And they are not musicians. Lively and familiar tunes give them more pleasure."

He sneered. "More pleasure. What about the technique? The art?"

God help me convince this bigheaded boy.

"Do you remember Papa's story, how he played on the ship to England? Do you think he chose the most challenging and artful compositions?"

"No... He played folk songs and dances."

I smiled. "Those simple melodies gave people hope and cheer."

"That's different." Moishe threw his shoulders back. "Papa played for weary travelers like himself. We performed for a wealthy crowd who know nothing of hunger and grief."

"Then we should play music that would soften their hearts to those who are less fortunate."

Moishe stared at me and grabbed my palms. A long breath deflated his chest. "This is why I need you. Even if I play each note perfectly, I will fail without you. I love you. Without you, the tour is meaningless. Marry me and go as my wife. Please."

I almost blurted about Lady Linden's advice. Instead, I paused and lowered my voice. "Moishe, if only I could love you like I love David." My heart ached as I said the words.

He brought my palms to his face. "You and he are two people I love the most, and you vex me to madness. While you await like Penelope, your Odysseus is pleasuring himself with Circe. David will return with a Gentile wife... If he returns at all."

"You are cruel!" Hot tears ran down my cheeks, and my throat convulsed with sobs.

"You are cruel too!" He pushed my hands away. "I spoke to you of my love with words, with flowers, with music. When David cringed from your scars, I played my violin by your window. When you gave up on music, I showed you how you can play without seeing the keys. A simple 'no' isn't enough for you. You must torture me by bringing up David."

Lord in Heaven, he loves me. I thought he wanted to win me from David like a prize in a game. *But he loves me.*

"I'm sorry," I whispered.

He studied my face. "Sorry for bringing up David? Or sorry that you don't love me?"

"Both."

"You wait for David," he said after a pause, "and I wait for you."

When I said nothing, he exhaled and passed me a handkerchief. "Wipe your face. We are almost home and it's past midnight. Brace yourself for Mama's fury."

My weak stomach, subject to several trials that evening, tightened again.

Chapter 20

Mama massaged my belly, helping the tense muscles relax.

"Abigail, if your stomach still hurts that much, we should fetch Dr. Kaplan again." Mama made a tsk sound. "He said it's only nerves, but five days is too long. Are you sure you didn't eat treif at that Gentile's house? Their food can make us sick."

Sprawled in bed, I twisted from the ache in my gut and the memory of walking in after the audition. "Only an orange. Mama, you said that you could've died of apoplexy, I... I'm so sorry." I blinked away tears.

When Moishe and I returned from our performance, we found Mama slumped on the sofa, holding her chest. Moishe scoffed and said that Mama was being dramatic, but Papa shook his head at us and said we gave them a terrible fright. My heart grew heavy as if a great stone was crushing it. After much crying and apologizing, I staggered to bed, where I pictured Mama cold and stiff, like Ma when she died. In my dream, I saw both of my mothers being lowered into the dark grave. Each morning this week, I woke up before dawn with my pulse racing and my gut roiling.

Mama put her warm hand on my cheek. "You are lucky you don't have parents like mine. I sneaked out of the house to glance at the man they chose for me to marry. Afterwards, I was moaning and groaning in bed as well. From the bruises on my *tuchus*." She made a swishing sound and swung her arm with an imaginary whip.

I swallowed. "I deserve a punishment. When I lost my Ma's pearls, I thought she would never forgive me, yet she did. But you... our thoughtlessness could've killed you. You can't forgive that."

"Excuse me, I'm tougher than you think." Mama raised her chin. "You had me worried out of my wits, but I wasn't ready to leave this world."

Exhaling, I sat up. The pain in my belly was melting away. "You forgive me?"

She kissed me and held my cheeks. "I told you I forgive you. I forgive you a million times."

My eyes widened. "I heard someone say this before. Amelia's mother, Mrs. Hearts, at the hospital."

Mama stood. "You'll tell me about that some other time. I need to go to the dairy. Should I fetch the doctor on my way?" She tilted her head. "Or did I just cure you?"

I ran my hands over my abdomen, no longer wincing from cramps. "I think I'm better. I'll get up soon and help in the kitchen."

When she left, I counted in my head how many days David had been gone. Sixty-five. *David, where are you? What's taking so long?*

Moishe poked his head in the door. "Are you finally better?"

"You need to knock!" I pulled the blanket over me even though my night dress covered up to my throat. "Yes, I'm just about to get up. I'll make breakfast and feed Murka. Or did you fill her bowl already?"

His shoulders jumped. "I haven't seen Murka this morning. Come to think of it, I didn't see her yesterday either."

Ten minutes later, hastily washed and dressed, I was outside. My heart was in my throat. The Lord was teaching me a lesson about how parents feel when their children leave with no notice.

"Murka!" I shouted, willing my eyes to spot the agile shape of our black cat in the bushes. "Murka, where are you?"

Papa laid his hand on my shoulder. "I don't see her anywhere. Sometimes, when old animals feel their death coming, they go away."

"No! Not Murka!" I sobbed. Dear Murka, who warmed my feet at night, who lay on my forehead when I had a fever. She couldn't leave us already.

He touched my wet cheek. "Don't cry, *libling*. Moishe or I will find her. You stay here near the house."

"Aren't you going to the docks?"

"Not when my daughter is so upset. You have endured a difficult week already."

My shoulders fell. "It's about to get worse. I can feel it."

"I'll search the street and then the shops that may attract her." He patted my head. "I will likely run into Mama at the dairy. And if I see Moishe, I'll tell him to keep looking."

With my throat constricted, I walked a circle around the building, calling for Murka. When I returned to the front, I found two women shifting their feet as they stared at the house.

"If they live here, they must be the rich Jews, such who charge interest on loans and profit from the troubles of others. Vicious people," the older of the two said. Her face was red, and her breath labored. Heavy cases burdened her sturdy hands.

The other woman, who held a small basket, shook her head. "That's an unkind remark, Mrs. Armstrong." Her voice and manner were of a young woman, easily half the age of the other one, yet she spoke to her like a patient teacher to a child. Her white hat and gloves reminded me of the mothers from the church school I once attended. "Doesn't the Gospel say, 'Do not judge, or you too will be judged?' Let's take that wisdom to heart."

The young woman's quiet boldness impressed me.

Her companion sobbed. "You bring up the Gospel, Miss Caroline, when you..." Her wails did not let her continue. The young one stroked her on the shoulder and whispered to her.

Gawking, I tried to sort out who they could be. The younger woman eyed me as well as I approached. She opened her mouth to say something when Moishe came toward us, shaking his head.

"I walked the whole length of the street but could not find her," he said. Noticing the women, he faced them. "Ladies, did you happen to see a black cat?"

"Did you hear that, Miss Caroline?" the older woman said through tears. "The first words from these people to us are about a black cat. It's an ill omen. Please, come away at once!"

"Father taught me not to believe in omens." The young woman rummaged in her basket and asked Moishe, "Does your cat like ham?"

Moishe and I shrugged. Since ham was forbidden to us, we never fed it to Murka.

"Come kitty!" Caroline held out a slice of sweet-smelling meat. "I brought ham slices for the road. It's all I wanted to eat the last few days," she said with the casual tone of an old friend. "Would you like some?"

Moishe gagged as if he was nauseous.

Trying to show politeness to this well-dressed, helpful girl, I responded, "No, thank you. I'm sure it's delicious."

"My mother's famous Christmas ham. It's my favorite, and she baked it for me despite the wrong time of the year." She giggled with a nervous note. "Oh look, is that Murka?"

Murka and a large gray tomcat flew to us, meowing loudly at the treat. My mouth opened wide. Not because our cat was found. Because the young woman knew our cat's name.

"We didn't say her name is 'Murka'. How did you know it?" Moishe crossed his arms.

Caroline gasped and lowered her head. "What a blunder. I'm sorry. I should've said something. I'm just unsure how to start. I am—"

A premonition resonated through me. I held my breath waiting for her to speak.

"Thank you, Lord, Murka is found!" Papa's voice boomed. He walked towards us, holding hands with Mama and carrying one of her shopping baskets. Mama carried another basket in her other hand.

"Murka and her friend seem to like my ham." Caroline offered the cats another piece. Murka and the tomcat devoured the meat from the girl's palm.

Mama clicked her tongue. "My children's unruly behavior has spread to the cat. She found herself a paramour and tasted pork. She won't get any fish from me today!"

Papa petted Murka and passed her to me. I hugged her tightly and buried my nose in her fur.

"Thank you for your assistance, Miss." Papa addressed Caroline. "I don't believe I've seen you here before. May I be of service to you?"

"Yes." Caroline touched her face. "I mean, it's not exactly a service. We were looking for someone. I don't mean the cat..." She reddened and broke off her speech.

"She knew our cat's name," Moishe spat.

I fidgeted and hugged Murka for comfort.

"Well, that's strange," Mama said. "Do you know our names as well?"

The young woman glanced at all of us in turn, as if trying to choose, finally resting her gaze on Papa. "I'm terrible at making a good first impression, no matter how much I try. I'm sorry. Yes, I know your names and more. This is so awkward." She hung her head.

"You certainly intrigue us," Papa said. "What is your name?"

She curtsied. "Caroline Flowers. This is Mrs. Armstrong." She turned to the older woman, who kept her gaze on the ground and gave no reply.

"How do you know us?" Mama asked with chill in her tone.

"Oli... I mean David... Did he never mention my name?"

Ice slid down my neck.

"No," Mama and Moishe said together.

Papa leaned in. "We know David is visiting a family in Seatown. Is it your family?"

Caroline bobbed her head. "Yes. My brother invited him. He's been staying with my parents, sisters, and me."

"Is he well?" My heart was palpitating.

"Yes, he's much better. Walks and sunbathing restored his health."

Everyone exhaled a collective sigh of relief.

"Then we should show you the same hospitality your family has given our son," Papa said. "Let's have tea and you can tell us what brought you here."

"That would be wonderful." Caroline glanced at the older woman. "Mrs. Armstrong, would you like to come up for tea before you go?"

"I beg you one last time to reconsider." The older woman's voice quivered.

Caroline lowered her basket onto the ground and wrapped her arms around the woman. "Dear Mrs. Armstrong, let's say goodbye. Have a safe journey home, and please give all my love to my parents and sisters. My regards to your husband and son too. Thank you for all you've done for me."

The woman's voice broke into weeping. After extracting herself from Caroline's embrace, she placed the luggage by the door and trudged away with her head down.

"She was my nursemaid when I was a baby and has served our family ever since. This is hard for her," Caroline said to no one in particular. "Hard on my parents as well, but they are supportive."

"We don't know why you've come," Moishe reminded her.

Caroline's shoulders dropped. "Right. I'll explain everything over tea. I stopped by Shira's bakery and bought a cake."

"Very considerate of you," Papa said. "Moishe, please take the lady's things."

Moishe lifted the luggage and Caroline's basket. He looked inside it and dropped it.

"The cake is touching the ham. It's not kosher now."

Caroline flinched. "Oh, I'm sorry. Did I do something wrong?"

"You better leave the basket outside our door. I don't want my house defiled," Mama said.

Caroline nodded and left the basket on the porch. I felt a little sorry for her. But a knot in my belly reminded me that this woman came without invitation and was acting in a strange manner.

We walked into the house and ascended the stairs. The gray tomcat attempted to follow. Mama shooed him away. "Enough unexpected guests already," she muttered.

In the dining room, Caroline gazed around. "What a lovely home. You keep it so tidy. I'll be happy to lend a hand. Shall I brew the tea?"

My head pivoted toward Mama, as I thought she'd send me to the kitchen. Her legs were wide apart while her arms were crossed on her chest.

"The tea can wait a few minutes. Are you planning to stay with us?" she asked sharply.

Caroline shifted from one leg to another.

"I can stay at the inn if you prefer. But then, we'll be family soon, so..."

The air in the room became a few degrees colder.

"Family?" Mama echoed.

"I'm your future daughter-in-law." Caroline exhaled and stretched her arms toward Mama.

A piercing scream and then a curse came from Mama's throat. The room spun, and I grabbed the wall for support.

"Oh dear, I frightened you," Caroline shrieked, turning from Mama to me. "I should've written and explained. David and I will marry after I become Jewish."

This woman stole my David away from me. A Gentile, like Mama feared. I wanted to lunge at her and wrench her long neck.

Leaning on the wall, I exhaled a long breath and wrapped my head around the situation. British law required marriage by a religious authority. In a marriage between a Jew and a Gentile, the bride or the groom had to convert before the wedding. David kept to his conviction not to hurt his family by baptism, and thus Caroline chose to become Jewish. Fortunately, the conversion for her could take a year. *I have time to get rid of this woman, especially without David here. Where is David?*

"You are the woman he wrote to?" Mama demanded.

"Yes. He wrote me such witty and charming letters. I read each a hundred times, and they never stopped amusing me. Then a letter, that came two years ago, said he won't write anymore. I was saddened and confused, and wrote back several times. My mother became afraid that while pining for him I would waste my chances of finding a suitor. My oddities scared the gentlemen away."

Well, she is odd. Or maybe uncommon? David was not an ordinary man. I tried to see Caroline through his eyes. She was two or three years his junior and about his height. Her voice was melodious. Her manner approachable. She was refreshing in her peculiarity and self-criticism.

"Oh, yes, I'm awkward and clumsy, as I'm sure you've noticed. My mother's quest to find me a suiter was doomed. There was one fellow who asked me if I liked rainy days. I thought he would be interested in the flask I used to collect the rainwater and measure its level. After I showed him the notebook with my observations, he remembered an urgent meeting and left."

Caroline babbled on, waving her hands. "My next suitor was composing a poem about stars. Trying to help, I explained to him which stars were visible in the summer, and which in the winter. I then showed the chart of the night sky my brother and I drew as children. When I fetched the telescope, he bid a hasty goodbye and never called on me again. Goodness, I don't know why I'm going on about myself. I came to find out more about you."

I summed up what I learned of her: intelligent, curious, educated. David would love to converse with her about star charts and rainfall measurements, and probably did.

"We'll get to that," Mama said. "How did you and David meet?"

"He treated my brother in Plymouth. It was a grim time for my family, but David was such a caring and kind doctor."

I envisioned her next to a sickbed, holding a young man's hand. David would be moved by a compassionate sister. My legs weakened, and I collapsed on the sofa next to Moishe. His body tense like a drawn arrow.

"After my family returned to Seatown, I received the first letter from David," Caroline continued. "He asked after my brother, but he clearly expressed interest in me. Which was surprising because he met my sisters Julia and Audrey, who are much prettier. We corresponded for two years."

"But didn't he say goodbye to you twice? First in his letter, and then in person?" I shook my finger at her as I spoke.

Caroline hugged herself. "Yes, he came to see me intending to explain why he stopped writing. David revealed that he is Jewish. But a few days after he explained why we could not marry, I weighed all he said and saw a solution. He can't bear to hurt his family by converting. But my family isn't religious and would allow me to convert. My mother is overjoyed that I won't be a spinster."

"Where is David now?" Papa asked, stroking his beard.

Her hands tugged on her collar. "In Scotland. My father is a prominent dentist and occasionally receives visits from other medical men. He introduced David to a professor from Edinburgh. Turns out, the professor read the publication about the appendectomy on a pregnant woman. He was so impressed that he extended an invitation for David on his return to the university to give a few lectures at the upcoming seminar. As the new term was due to begin, they set off rather quickly."

"But why did David send you here?" Mama queried, fanning herself.

Caroline dropped her head. "He didn't send me. He left abruptly, and I didn't get a chance to tell him that I chose to convert." She paused, then raised her head and squared her shoulders. "But as I was thinking things over, I decided to come here to learn about Jewish customs. I should've written to you to explain. I just couldn't find the words... It's a big change, as my family goes to church twice a year. I have much to learn."

Everyone stayed quiet. Moishe chewed his nails, while Papa scratched his beard in thought.

Leave. You are not wanted, my mind screamed. *David didn't invite you here. Maybe he doesn't want to marry you.*

"Come to the window," Mama said to Caroline and pulled her by the hand. "I need more light to see your face."

I couldn't imagine what Mama needed to see, but to my surprise she ran her hand over Caroline's forehead and cheeks.

Fidgeting, Caroline chortled an anxious note. "You must think that a woman who wooed your brilliant son must be a great beauty. Alas, I'm plain. And I'm having this unpleasant breakout of pimples..."

Mama's hand pressed on Caroline's belly.

The girl staggered back. "What are you doing?"

"You are with child," Mama announced with the gravity of a judge delivering a verdict.

Black spots danced before my eyes. Moishe grabbed my arm. "Don't swoon," he whispered.

Caroline touched her face and then her belly. "No, no. It can't be... It was only one time... Oh dear. Is that why I'm craving ham?"

Mama had her hands on the hips. "Didn't your mother teach you not to open your legs before the wedding?"

Caroline hid her pink face in her palms. "She did, I assure you. Oh, what have we done!"

With David's baby inside her, there would be no way to get rid of Caroline. My heart was as heavy as a stone.

David vowed to marry me! I should be the mother of his children.

Papa cleared his throat. "Leah, that's enough. If this young woman is pregnant with our grandchild, I'm sure our son had much to do with this." He walked over and stretched his hands to Caroline. "Welcome to our home. We were going to have tea, but I'm in the mood for something stronger. It's a day for a celebration."

"What are we celebrating, Isaac?" Mama snapped. "That our son fell for a *shiksa* and left a baby in her belly?"

"We'll celebrate that David found this steadfast and brave young woman. We feared that our son would abandon our ways and leave us forever. Instead, Caroline came to us to join our tribe." He raised his fist. "*Mazel Tov!* We'll dance at the wedding, and if there's a child on the way, that's a double blessing."

A wedding. A child. My world shattered into pieces. Only Moishe noticed my anguish and squeezed my hand. "David is lucky he's not here. Or I would've murdered him," he whispered.

Caroline threw her arms around Papa. "David said you would be happy for us."

"Well, *I'm* not happy!" Mama stomped her foot. "The reputation of this family is in danger. She must convert and marry David before she starts showing. I will explain the circumstances to Rabbi Cohen in confidence. And you," her pointed finger almost touched Caroline's nose, "will write to David and tell him to forget whatever he's doing and get here at once."

Caroline bobbed her head with fervent agreement. "I will... I'll write to him right now."

Mama snorted. "It's dinnertime and you are famished from the road. I'm not letting you starve my grandchild." She snatched Caroline's arm and charged her to the kitchen.

Chapter 21

Caroline's gaze darted around the synagogue as she took in the view from the balcony. We sat slightly apart from other women, ensuring our conversation didn't interfere with their praying. Wearing a dress she made, Caroline blended in, but still attracted curious glances. Despite staying with us for a month, this was her first visit to the temple. Most days she suffered bouts of morning sickness.

"This is quite different from being in church," she said, looking down at the men below us. A group of them were opening the arc to bring out the Torah for today's reading.

"I know. I've been to church with my Ma," I stammered through my teeth. As if Caroline's mere presence in the house wasn't awful enough, Rabbi Cohen thought that I should bring her into the fold. One convert could teach another. She followed me all day, asked questions like a child, and jotted careful notes. Her persistence was suffocating. Moishe shared my feelings and hardly appeared at home. It had been a *very* long month since Caroline appeared in our lives.

"Why are we separated from the men?" She craned her neck watching them.

"To avoid distracting them. They shouldn't see or hear us when they pray."

She giggled. "But we can watch and listen. Isn't that distracting to *our* worship? David has a beautiful singing voice."

He sings to her. I hadn't heard him sing since that time in the hospital when he sang me his lullaby. I clenched my jaw so hard that it hurt.

"It's fascinating how the Jews kept the Hebrew language and traditions since Biblical times," she said as we listened to the Rabbi reading the Torah. "Can you understand everything he's saying?"

"No. I catch only some words that I know. The boys study for years to read the Torah."

"And the girls?"

I rolled my eyes. "We don't read from the Torah. Our mission is to become wives and mothers."

"Well, I've made a good start on that." She touched her belly. The baby didn't show yet, but she talked about it constantly.

The little *mamzer*. One should not loathe an innocent baby, but I couldn't help it. That child sealed her and David's future and my unhappiness.

Meanwhile the prayer service ended, and the congregation began to disperse. Caroline rose to her feet. "I'll say hello to the Rabbi and ask him about conversion."

I nodded absently. As soon as she left the balcony, the women circled me, all talking at once.

"Was that David's betrothed?"

"Where's she from?"

"Did they set a wedding date?"

Each question was a peck of a sharp beak. My mouth went dry. Mrs. Cohen, the Rabbi's wife, petted my arm and asked the ladies to stop pestering me. They backed away, but not far, and watched Caroline ascend to us with her head bowed. By convention, the rabbi would reject her plea to convert three times before accepting.

When Caroline returned, Mrs. Cohen extended a hand to her and introduced herself. "I hope you're not upset. My husband is following an ancient tradition. We are all glad to have you."

Caroline grabbed her hands. "Thank you. I'm looking forward to meeting everyone."

Mrs. Simons, the Hebrew teacher's wife, approached. "Do you sew or embroider? The Women's Guild meets every Sunday. We are going to make a new cover for the torah."

"I'm not as talented as my sisters, but I can lend a hand," Caroline said. "I made my dress."

Mrs. Simons leaned forward to inspect it. "Beautiful work. I say you'll be our best seamstress. Please come to my house on Sunday at five. Abigail will show you the way."

I inhaled a sharp breath. I couldn't sew well because of my vision, but I also didn't like how some people excluded me from their gatherings.

Caroline touched my shoulder. "I think I'll need Abigail with me. She has great taste. I would've never designed this dress without her help."

All I did was show her a few of Mama's and my dresses to copy the pattern. I didn't know if I should thank Caroline for getting me invited, or to sulk about spending Sunday evenings with her.

"That would be wonderful." Mrs. Simons nodded. "I'm going to be purchasing materials later today. Silk and velvet, if we can afford them."

"Oh we must have the best for the torah cover." Caroline unhooked the money purse from her belt and offered Mrs. Simons a handful of coins. "In case you are short, here's my share. Would this be enough?"

Mrs. Simons gasped. "How generous! I can purchase excellent fabrics with this money."

The ladies bid us warm goodbyes. "She's a dear," Mrs. Simons murmured to someone, and others whispered in agreement.

She bought your friendship, I thought with disgust.

As we walked home, I craved silence to contemplate my misery. The pleasant August sunshine failed to lift my spirits. Caroline, however, was in a chatty mood, asking me about the various shops and houses we passed. I grunted my answers, hoping she would stop prattling.

"Did this shop close?" She pointed at an abandoned storefront, two doors away from Shira's bakery.

I shrugged. "It's been empty for years."

She approached and peered into the dusty windows. "It looks spacious enough for a medical practice. What do you think?"

I shrugged, unsure what to say. "It's on a busy street."

"Right. Being next to Shira's bakery is perfect." Her hand rested on mine as she laughed. "Oh, I don't mean that people would need a physician after enjoying her treats." I flinched at her touch, but she didn't seem to notice. "A location on High Street is visible and convenient. As for the space... The practice will need a sitting room, an exam room, a surgery, a dispensary with a medicine cabinet and a table to make remedies, and several beds for the patients. In the back, we could build a study where David would write notes or read. And look, there's a flat upstairs for us and the baby."

She gestured with animation as she spoke. No doubt she saw herself helping David with building the practice and preparing a home for her new family.

"How do you know what the practice needs?"

"Didn't I tell you that my father is a dentist? I've been helping him since I was a child. I kept the schedule, ordered supplies, and prepared remedies. Father didn't keep an assistant, insisting he didn't need one while he had me."

She had the experience and the confidence to assist David. While she stared inside and pointed where the various rooms would be, my teeth bit down on my bottom lip. *Could this woman be any more perfect for him?*

"David said he has little in the way of savings, but we could spend my dowry to purchase the building. The baby and I don't need much." She patted her stomach again.

That bean inside her had to be mentioned every minute, as if it was some miracle. Surely other women made less fuss about their pregnancy, especially when it happened before wedlock. Still, we heard nothing from David. Maybe he wanted nothing to do with Caroline and the baby.

Shira popped out from the bakery's door. "Caroline, we need you! Come help!" When we rushed over and stepped inside, she added, "We are trying to make the meringue glaze from your recipe, but it won't set."

Naomi handed Caroline an apron and ushered her into the kitchen.

Turning to me, Shira wiped sweat off her forehead. "What luck that I saw you. We've been slaving over that meringue all morning. It may be just what we need for the new menu."

"Since when are you and Caroline bosom friends?" I crossed my arms.

My sister cocked her head. "Oh... Come, have a cup of tea with me. The kettle just boiled."

I sat down at the table in the corner. Shira brought a tray with the tea set, milk, and honey. She offered pastries, but I declined.

"Sister." She swiveled her head toward the kitchen for a moment and then back to me. "I'm sorry. We thought you were over David. When you disappeared with Moishe for the evening, we guessed that he finally got your attention."

My trembling hands lifted the cup to my lips. "Who's we?"

"Naomi, Miriam, Hannah, and I. The more we get to know Caroline, the more we see her as a great match for David. Even if she wasn't carrying his child."

My sisters sided with Caroline. They talked behind my back about how perfect Caroline was for David. And how pathetic I was for clinging to him.

Shira clasped my hand. "Abigail, you are mistaking love for other feelings. You are overwhelmed with gratitude for him saving you from poverty. David harbors guilt for letting you get sick. This is not the kind of love that a marriage can be based on. If he made you some promise, it was for wrong reasons."

The memory of David agreeing to marry me pierced my chest. He was exhausted and broken after his voyage, the one that failed to make him forget Caroline. Hopeless to have her, he gave in. Maybe he decided, *'Since Caroline is forbidden to me, it doesn't matter who I marry. Could as well be Abigail'.*

I took a careful sip to relieve the dryness in my throat. The cinnamon and clove tasted bitter on my tongue. "At least Mama and Moishe are still on my side. They don't treat her like she's a gift to the world."

"We are all on your side and want you to be happy." Shira leaned toward me. "But my brothers deserve happiness as well. Moishe is more suitable for you than David. You are closer in age and play music together. You should give him a chance."

If only I could love him like I loved David. I lowered my head. "He asked me to marry him and join him on his tour."

She nibbled on a pastry. "Getting away may be good for you. Not to marry Moishe or perform concerts but to forget David."

"I'd go to the moon to get away from Caroline."

Shira shook her head. "If she gets on your nerves this much, you should stop being her teacher. Send her to bake challah with me tomorrow. You look sad and exhausted."

I was sad and exhausted. And furious with my sisters who sided with my enemy.

Caroline came out of the kitchen, shaking the flour off her hands. "Problem solved. You should use caster sugar for this recipe. The regular kind doesn't work as well."

"Oh, that makes sense. Thank you." Shira rose.

"We'll get going," I said, getting up as well. "Thank you ...for the tea."

Shira opened the door. As I passed by her, she whispered into my ear, "Stop torturing yourself."

Chapter 22

Caroline and I sauntered home, greeting neighbors as we passed. Several stopped us to chat and invited us to visit. "What a nice town. Everyone's so welcoming," Caroline said.

She was fortunate her shameful pregnancy didn't show. *Or would even that be forgiven for her agreeable manner and easy smile?*

When we got home, Mama kissed my cheek, and scowled at Caroline.

"I'm taking some dinner to Miriam's. Please set the table for four in case Papa joins us. I will serve brisket and new potatoes." Mama fixed my collar and pinched my cheeks.

Caroline bounced on her tiptoes. "That sounds delici—" But Mama swept past her without a reply.

We went to the kitchen. Murka sat there, warming herself by the stove. She raised her head, studying us.

Caroline opened the drawer for meat utensils. "*Fleishig* is for meat," she murmured as if rehearsing a lesson.

I was tired of being her mentor. *Why should I help her?* Better everyone see that she's not fit to run a Jewish household.

"No. *Milchig* is for meat," I said.

Her hands hovered over the knives. "But… You said *milchig* is for dairy. I even thought that would be easy to remember because the word sounds like 'milk'."

I crossed my arms. "You got it wrong."

Rubbing her forehead, she went up to her room and returned with her notepaper. "It says *fleishig* is for meat."

"Then you weren't listening when you wrote down your notes."

She sighed and closed the meat drawer. "I heard that a woman's mind plays tricks during pregnancy. That must be it."

After she spread the *milchig* tablecloth and set the table with the plates and utensils meant for dairy, I asked her, "What brachot are you going to say before we eat?"

"I so appreciate you pushing me to learn." She glanced at her notes. "*Hamotzie lechem myn ha'aretz* for the bread. *Boreiy pree ha'adamah* for the potatoes. And *Shehakol Nihyah bidvaro* for the meat."

"No. You have this wrong as well. *Boreiy pree hagafen* is for the bread and *Boreiy pree ha'etz* is for the vegetables." I ignored the churning in my breast.

Glancing from the paper to me, she read her notes again. "I'm so confused," she muttered.

Good. No more bowing to the usurper.

Mama entered humming to herself. "The grandchildren asked me to visit again after dinner. They are preparing a surprise for me." She gaped, staring at the table setting. "This is for *milchig*. We are having meat."

"Caroline mixed them up," I cried before Caroline could protest.

Mama put her hands on her hips. "Then she better fix it."

"Of course. I'm sorry." Caroline bowed her head.

In my mind, I dared her to point a finger at me, but she gathered the utensils and plates without a word. Only her slumped shoulders revealed her disappointment.

Papa walked in and greeted us. "How is everyone today?"

"The dinner is being slightly delayed," Mama answered. "Caroline confused the silverware and the dishes for a *fleishig* meal."

"So sorry about that. I'll bring the other set," Caroline said.

"Abigail, why didn't you correct her?" Papa inquired.

Because I hate her! Because I want her gone, my mind screamed.

"I... asked Abigail not to help," Caroline interjected. "This was a test, and I failed miserably." Her self-deprecating laugh rang with unease. "As usual."

"*Milchig* is for milk." Mama clicked her tongue. "Any fool could remember that. How will you run a kosher kitchen when you are my son's wife?"

With her head low, Caroline sighed. "I'll keep trying."

"I'm sure you will learn," Papa patted her on the shoulder.

After Caroline reset the table, Mama and I brought out the food.

"Now Caroline will say the brachot," I said as we sat down to eat.

"You are a zealous teacher, Abigail," Papa observed.

With a shaky voice, Caroline recited the two wrong brachot I told her to say.

Leaning back, Mama shook her head. "We are not having wine and fruit."

"Goodness. I've befuddled everything." Caroline threw up her hands.

I wanted to laugh at her falling for my prank. But somehow it wasn't funny.

"It's the intention that matters the most." Papa waved his hand dismissively. "When you learn Hebrew, the blessings will be easier to remember. The last one you said means, 'Blessed are you our Lord, King of the world, who creates the fruit of the trees.' Isn't it poetic?"

Caroline exhaled. "Beautiful."

With vigor in his voice, Papa led us in reciting the proper brachos. Everyone dug into the juicy meat, while I picked at my food. The shifts of my emotions were bad for my appetite.

"It's been a month, yet David still hasn't come or written back," Mama remarked as her knife clinked on the plate.

With one hand holding her belly, Caroline sipped her water. "I hope he's all right."

"Your letter to Scotland could've been delayed on its way," Papa said.

"And if it's so delayed that the baby starts showing?" Mama scoffed. "I won't allow our family to be humiliated. Caroline will go back home."

"No," Caroline moaned. "My sisters... Their chances at marriage will be ruined."

"Leah," Papa put down his utensils with a clink. "Caroline is David's betrothed. This makes her our family."

My eyes dashed from one parent to another. The food on my plate was getting cold.

With a humph, Mama shoved a forkful of meat into her mouth. "What evidence have we seen of their agreement? David may have no intention of marrying her. Maybe the baby isn't his."

Shifting on her seat, Caroline clenched her belly. "It's David's baby. There was no one else."

"His absence is suspicious." Mama shook her finger.

After pushing his plate away, Papa rose to his feet. "Our son wouldn't abandon his child."

"Our family's reputation is hanging by a thread." Mama stood abruptly, making her chair tip. "If David doesn't return by the time her belly swells, she must go back to her parents. Let them deal with a fallen daughter."

Her shoulders shaking, Caroline hid her face in her hands.

Hope swelled in my chest. With a little luck, we would be rid of Caroline. If David would deny fathering the baby, life would go back to how it was before. We may announce our engagement.

Massaging his temples, Papa tapped his foot. "If David doesn't return soon, it may be best to shelter Caroline from gossip. We'll find a place for her away from the town."

"When he learns about the baby, David will return. I will write to him again," Caroline said with a quiver in her voice.

Mama pointed a finger at her. "Do it today."

No one was eating anymore. Caroline and I gathered the dirty plates. Papa kissed us both on our foreheads, pecked Mama on the lips, and left to finish his workday.

Sighing that we didn't eat enough, Mama covered the leftovers. "I'm going back to Miriam's," she announced and rounded on Caroline. "Write that letter."

After Mama left, slamming the door on her way out, Caroline rubbed her abdomen. "Something feels odd."

"With the baby?" I stared at her stomach. "You should've told Mama."

"She's upset with me. She has every right to be, of course. I haven't given her any reason to trust me. Anyway, it was only a pinch. I'm sure it's nothing."

"I don't know about these things." I shrugged. "I'm going to practice my piano."

Caroline nodded. "I need to write that letter to David, but I'd like to do some studying first. Do you have any books that explain the kashrut and the brachos?"

"Check in the bookcase next to the pianoforte."

In the music room, I sat down at the piano and played the scales to prepare my mind and fingers for practice. Caroline caressed the spines of the thick books.

"Oh, what a wonderful collection. David mentioned some of these classics. Can I borrow a few?"

"Suit yourself. But please don't talk."

I warmed up my hands with a simple exercise, then played an accompaniment to one of Moishe's pieces. As with most of his music, it required my full attention to get the notes and the rhythm right. Since I turned down the tour and his marriage proposal, Moishe rarely rehearsed with me. With our routine interrupted, my playing had suffered. I missed my music partner's cutting criticism that vexed me, but ultimately made me better.

Caroline muttered about something she was reading. I drowned out her voice by playing louder. With happy abandonment, I lost myself in the music, when a sob interrupted my bliss. I hit a wrong note.

"Caroline, do you mind?" I said, still playing.

"I... I'm sorry." Her shaky reply came through weeping.

I stopped playing and twisted my body to look at her. Her hands shook as she stared at some letters. Several papers were scattered on the floor.

"It's rude to read other people's letters," I said. "And could you please be quiet so I could concentrate?"

She nodded with a sigh, gathered the letters, and shoved them behind the stack of books. Whispering apologies, she stepped towards the door. There was a dark red puddle in the spot where she just stood.

My hands froze over the keys. I jumped to my feet. "What is that? Blood?"

Caroline turned on her heels, looked where I was pointing, then shyly raised her skirts. Her white petticoat was stained with red spots. I approached to see better. The metallic smell made me gag.

She dropped her skirts. "I didn't feel the bleeding. Just something pinching in the belly."

Breathing heavily, I tried my hardest to stay calm. *Do I fetch Mama or Dr. Kaplan?* I decided on Mama, since she was nearby, visiting Miriam. My knees shook. "You go lie down. I'll bring Mama."

Her hands rubbed over her abdomen. "But your parents said you should never walk anywhere..." She doubled-over with a gasp. "By yourself. It's too dangerous. Let's wait."

"I'll be fine."

My feet hurried down the stairs and brought me to the street. As a coach rolled past, my pulse pounded in my ears. My brain showed me visions of people trampled by horses.

Before leaving for Seatown, David visited Haim, the boy who was run over and ultimately lost his leg. "The child lay there, badly hurt, and the driver didn't even stop," David retold us the story of the accident with his voice trembling. "I've seen even more devastating injuries at the hospital. Shattered bones, broken spines. Drivers and riders can be terribly irresponsible."

My hair lifted at the nape of my neck as I remembered his warning. Mama's anxious voice sounded in my head as I watched the carriages speed by. "Abigail, never go by yourself. Wait for someone to take you." When I disobeyed Mama, unfortunate things happened.

I didn't have to do this. Mama would return soon enough. *Maybe that cramp and bleeding is nothing serious.*

I turned back. Mama would be proud of me for obeying her. I should not risk myself for Caroline. Or her baby. Her and David's baby. My heart clenched. For David, I'd do anything, even if it killed me. Pivoting, I returned to the road.

The rush continued as riders and carriages hurried past me. I timed my move after a cart on squeaky wheels rolled by me. Holding my breath, I reached the middle of the road. A rider on an enormous black horse was coming from another direction. I hurried to get out of the way. My shoe stepped into something foul and slippery, and I fell forward. My knees and elbow hit the cobblestones. A horse whined above my head. *This is how I die.*

"Watch it! Are you blind?" The rider snapped as he maneuvered the horse around me. Panting, I struggled to rise. Pain shot from my limbs, but I managed to hobble to safety.

At Miriam's door, I knocked and yelled for Mama. My oldest sister flung the door open and led me in. I found Mama on the rug with her grandchildren in the middle of a game.

"Abigail? What's wrong?" she cried, catching a toy tossed by one of the children.

She threw on her shawl as I explained about Caroline. Miriam sent her husband to fetch Dr. Kaplan while Mama and I hurried out on to the street.

I clutched her hand as we waited for the coaches to pass. "You warned me not to cross by myself, but ..."

"You did the right thing. I trust you were careful." She must've missed the mud on my dress.

My hand in Mama's, we crossed the road together. Walking with her gave me a warm feeling of safety in a perilous world. If only I could hold on to that arm forever.

"Is such bleeding always bad?" I asked as I ascended the stairs behind her, clutching the railing.

Mama grunted as she touched the door handle. "It could be bad, but not always. Sometimes the woman is not pregnant, and the bleeding is her normal menses. It happened to me once."

I gasped. *Please let it be so.* If there's no baby, I could still have a chance with David.

"Bad!" Mama shouted as she crossed the threshold. She ran inside, and I rushed after her. There was a crimson trail under my feet. Next to the dining room table, Caroline lay in a pool of her blood.

Chapter 23

"What's happening, Mama?" I hugged her waist when she came out of the bedroom. Caroline's moans echoed in my chest. Dr. Kaplan was with her, speaking in a soothing voice.

Mama circled her hand around my shoulder. Tears flowed down her face. "The baby is gone. She miscarried."

No baby. David had lost a child and didn't even know it. Shallow breaths shook my body.

"I feel like I lost someone too," I said.

Mama hugged me tighter. "I already saw myself rocking that little one in the cradle."

"How's Caroline?"

Mama sighed. "We are doing all we can to save her. She lost a lot of blood. Poor girl. I regret I was so hard on her."

She may die. Didn't I wish her to be gone? Yet my chest was heavy, as if weighed down with rocks.

Since my sleeping space was transformed into Caroline's sickroom, I stumbled into the boys' room and collapsed on

David's old bed. His pillow carried a faint scent of his hair. I closed my eyes and pictured him returning to learn that his betrothed had perished in our home. At some point, after the initial shock and grief, he'd want to talk about her time with our family.

What could I tell him? I could say that until the moment she explained who she was, I liked her. She stood up to her hateful nursemaid and helped us find our cat. It was brave of her to come to us, as she suspected that we may not react well to her appearance. Her efforts to learn our ways were earnest.

I could tell him that she had a vision of their future medical practice. She would've been a partner in his work, as well as a loving wife and mother. Despite the unexpected pregnancy and the shame it could've brought her and his families, she adored that baby.

I could tell him that Caroline tried hard to befriend me. She ensured that people included me. When I tricked her into saying the wrong brachos and using the wrong utensils, she never pointed a finger at me. We could've been friends, even sisters—if only we didn't love the same man.

With my lips trembling, I whispered a prayer for the sick. As I prayed, I wondered if I should ask Our Lady for help as well, as I used to when I was a child. Caroline had not converted to Judaism yet, and her baby... Was it Jewish or Christian? Where would that tiny soul go?

I started making up my own prayer. I asked Our Lady to guide the child to Rachel and the other children that my family had lost. Soon, I was in a blooming garden full of children who awaited their parents.

The morning sun peeked through the curtains when I pried my eyes open. I was still in my clothes, my head feeling heavy and sluggish. Mama poked her head inside as soon as I raised my head. I wondered if she checked on me before.

"Ah, you are awake, Abigail. Papa just left for the morning service. He'll pray for Caroline's recovery."

I stretched my arms, stiff after sleeping on David's hard bed. "How is she?"

Mama rubbed her cheek. "It's a miracle that she lived. But she's been agitated, crying all night. That's dangerous in her state. I'm going to the apothecary to get medicine to calm her nerves. Would you stay with her?"

I scrambled out of bed. "What do I need to do?"

"She finally fell asleep. If she wakes, give her water or broth. Comfort her. She keeps asking to be taken to her parents. That's out of the question for now. More bleeding or an inflammation would kill her."

After the door closed behind Mama, a rustling sound came from the bedroom. I hurried to check on Caroline. She was up on her shaky legs, her hands on the wall to steady herself. My heart clenched.

"What are you doing?" I called out. "Go back to bed."

She grabbed a dress from the closet and tossed it on the bed. Then she reached for a hat. "I'm going to get dressed and go home. Someone will come for the rest of my things later." Her hand touched her stomach, and she sobbed. "Without the baby, there's no reason to stay."

"You can't go in such a state. You'll die before you reach Seatown."

She stomped her foot. "Does it matter to you? You think I'm thick and don't know that you told me the wrong brachos and showed me the wrong utensils on purpose. You planned to embarrass me in front of your parents. How petty."

I stared down at my skirt. "That was a mean trick. I'm sorry."

Her hands dropped to her sides. "No need to apologize. I don't know what came over me. It was a harmless prank, something a little sister would do." She sank onto the bed. "You saved my life yesterday. My parents and I will be forever grateful. Please visit us in Seatown with all your family. Except for David."

"Except for David?" I echoed in surprise.

A sob escaped her throat. "He's not the man I thought he was. I have to leave before he finds me here."

She had gone mad. That was the only explanation I could find for what she said. "David would never do you harm. Even if you don't love him, he'd want you to stay and get better."

Caroline stood up, grabbed her shawl, and added it to the pile of clothes. Moaning, she bent over and collapsed onto the bed.

I rushed over. "What's wrong?"

"My head is spinning. It will pass."

I fetched her a cup of water. "Caroline, you are not fit to travel. You need to stay here till you recover."

She shook her head. "I must go. Abigail, why don't you come with me to Seatown? It may be best for you to be away from him as well."

My eyes widened. "Away from David? Why?"

Caroline sat up and clutched my shoulder. "Listen to me. You love David like a kind older brother, but you can't trust him. He's not a good man. Yesterday, I accidentally found his letters and learned his secret. I'm not the first woman he has gotten pregnant. There's a Christian woman named Verna Bax who had two children with him. Julian and Josie."

My heart squeezed at hearing those names. "They are—"

"Do you see a pattern here?" She threw up her hands. "He told me about his cat, for Heaven's sake, but he never mentioned those children and their mother. He must've been eighteen or so when he fathered them, but youth is not an excuse. Now I know why he has no savings to open his medical practice. He may think it's enough to send money to feed and clothe these children, but they don't even know their father."

My throat went dry. Much time had passed since I thought of my brother and sister. I long forgot that David promised to support them. It never occurred to me that the arrangement with Verna hurt his financial situation.

"No, you are wrong."

Her hands shook as she brought them to her face. "I saw the letters with my own eyes. He means to abandon me, like he abandoned that woman and the children he fathered."

Let her believe this nonsense. Let her grow to resent David. She'll leave, never learning the truth, a voice whispered in my head. I squashed the voice.

"They are not his children. Julian and Josie are my brother and sister. David supports them out of kindness."

Caroline studied me. "This is not a trick?"

"I would never lie about something like this."

She put her hands to her chest. "Oh, my Lord. Of course. How could I imagine him doing anything so despicable? He has the most generous heart." After wiping her tears, she threw her arms around me. My muscles tensed, but I forced myself to exhale and return the hug.

After we laughed and cried with relief, I urged her to rest. She laid down on the dining room sofa because the light was better there for reading. Propped on her pillows and covered by a quilt, she leafed through a heavy book on Judaic philosophy.

A click of the lock sounded from the front door. I sped down to greet Mama. "Caroline is reading in the dining room. She's feeling better," I said as the door opened.

My breath stilled. David was on the threshold. Tanned and no longer gaunt. "Caroline's here?"

I nodded.

He gave me a momentary glance before he flew past me without a hello. I followed, heavy with premonition of the scene I was about to witness.

"My love." David breathed, staring at Caroline. "You are so pale. Is that because of the baby?"

She extended her hand and sobbed. "I'm so sorry. I've lost our baby. Abigail and Mama saved my life, but our child is gone."

"I'm sorry I couldn't come sooner." He kneeled by her and covered her hands with kisses.

She was his *bashert*. I could not hate her anymore. And I could never hate David. The easiest person to hate was myself.

Chapter 24

All day I started one task or another, just to find myself dreaming on my feet, the chore forgotten. Twice, I tripped over Murka as I staggered from room to room. When Moishe's violin cried a sweet tune, I followed the music, like a charmed creature drawn to the piper. Since Caroline's arrival, he slept at one older sister's house or another and rarely appeared at home.

Moishe halted his practice when I came into the music room. "I received a letter from Lord Linden. I wanted to open it with you."

"All right." I gave him an encouraging smile.

He lifted the letter from the piano and broke the seal. Pacing, he read through it, then raised his head.

"Mr. Campanella arranged a tour of Italy. Rome, Florence, Venice. Depending how that goes, he will arrange more. Any requirements I have will be in the contract."

I forced a smile. "That's wonderful news. I'm happy for you."

He stepped close to me. "Happy only for me? What about us? Do you want to play our music, and travel the world? Or do you prefer to stay here and torment yourself by watching David and Caroline? Even when they move out, you will be running into them everywhere."

He was right. I'd see Caroline at the synagogue, at the market, at the shops. The town was small, and the close-knit Jewish community made it feel even smaller. As David's wife, she would be at every family celebration. My hands went to my temples.

"That would be torture."

He wrapped his arms around my shoulders. "Then go with me on tour, away from here."

Isn't every girl supposed to dream of traveling the world? Lady Linden said so. And Shira said distance would help me get over the heartbreak.

"Yes," I said.

Moishe lifted my chin with his finger. "You must marry me first."

I stepped back and studied him. Could I accept Moishe as my husband? When David despaired about Caroline, he opened his mind, if not his heart, to me. Allowed himself to see me as someone he could learn to love. So I could learn to love Moishe. He resembled David physically, only he was younger and taller. Most women would find him the more handsome of the two. His musical talents and prospects of fame didn't hurt either. Rigid and arrogant at times, but kind and understanding when it mattered most. And Lady Linden advised that we marry before the tour.

I sighed. "Yes. I will marry you. Let's get away from here."

The words came out heavy, like rocks tumbling into the water.

He wrapped his arms around me. "You could try to sound happier about it."

Two weeks later, I sat in my room sketching, my fingers free to do as they wish. The picture took shape from my scattered strokes. A girl, possibly me, deep under water. For some reason, the bottom wasn't sandy, but hard and smooth, like a tiled floor. Her body relaxed as she smiled. At least, that's what my mind saw in the picture. To anyone else, it might look like indiscernible shapes.

Mama's head appeared in the doorway. "Abigail, do you mind drawing in the dining room while I cook dinner? The lovebirds need to be reminded they are not alone in this home." She said the last part in her full voice for everyone's benefit.

They were likely kissing again. Bile filled my mouth. Because of their embraces, I avoided them at mealtimes and forced food down my throat in the kitchen.

"Leave them alone, Leah." Papa came up behind her. "They are in love."

Her hand on her hip, Mama faced him. "In our days, young people never permitted themselves such liberties. To allow my betrothed a kiss at my future in-laws' house... never."

Papa chuckled and hugged her shoulders. "But that's exactly what happened when my mother went to tend the cows. Did you forget?"

"Oh goodness, Isaac." Mama gasped, "That was your fault. At least you stole that kiss in private, without your parents there. Abigail and Moishe are betrothed as well, and they are behaving all proper."

"Too proper, unless they are being sneaky." Papa shook his finger.

Mama and Papa received the news of Moishe's and my engagement with enthusiasm. They agreed that if we were to go on tour, we should get married first to protect each other from troubles that could happen to young people abroad. There were sighs of relief in their congratulations. David and Shira brought up concerns about our youth and quick betrothal, but Mama said her favorite word, *Bashert*. There's no escaping fate.

"Enough! This is not a joke." Mama stomped her foot. "At this speed, another child may be conceived before the wedding.

Abigail, go sit in the dining room and anytime David has his hands on Caroline, cough loudly."

"Yes, Mama." I smiled at her, as a lump in my throat threatened to choke me.

Caroline and David were seated on the sofa, their hands intertwined and her head on his shoulder. They did not look up when I sat at the table with my sketchbook and charcoal. I braced myself to witness their kiss, happy for once that my vision was blurry. Instead, Caroline wiped her eyes.

"We'll have many children," David said in a soft voice. "At least five."

"Why five?" she whispered back.

"I don't know. Seems like a good number."

She remained silent for a while. "What if there's something wrong with me? What if I can't carry a child?"

My cheeks grew hot. Hearing her share her innermost fears twisted my heart. While I couldn't even bring myself to tell Moishe I get bellyaches before performing.

David slid his arm around her neck, resting his hand just above her bosom. I coughed, but they didn't react.

"There's no reason to think you can't. Many women lose their first pregnancy but then have healthy children. Next time, I will watch over you."

"What about your job at the university? You will not be here all the time."

My ears pricked. David and Caroline had already discussed the purchase of the building for the medical practice. The university job was something new.

"That's not for a while. Our medical practice will come first. That building you found is perfect for it. And we'll make our little nest in the flat above."

I had a coughing fit, a genuine one.

This time they noticed me. Caroline leaned away from David and sat up with her back straight, as if I were her teacher or a governess.

"Abigail, we didn't hear you come in. Sorry, we are in our own little world." She touched her cheek, which was no longer pale. Quite pink instead.

David groaned. "Did Mama send you to watch us? Tell her not to worry."

Since David returned, he attempted to speak to me several times, but I refused to hear him out. What good were his apologies and explanations to me? I already knew far more than I wanted.

Caroline extended her hand to me. "Please, come sit here. Let's talk bride to bride."

When I sat down next to her, angling my body away, she asked, "Are you sure you want to have the same wedding day as us? I know you must marry before the tour, but with some effort, we could plan separate weddings."

"If you feel rushed, I could talk to my brother," David added. "You should not be pressured into marrying."

"No, everything is fine," I said with my palms open. "Sharing the wedding day is an excellent idea. Shira and Naomi will make food for everyone. Your family will arrive. No sense to do it all over again on another day." Busy with my own duties as a bride, I will avoid watching David and Caroline take their vows under the chuppah.

"I'm glad. Our day will be even more special. Do you want anyone at the wedding besides the people we invited?" Caroline nodded encouragingly.

"I don't have anyone... Except for my brother and sister, Julian and Josie." If Caroline hadn't found Verna's letters, I might've forgotten to invite them.

How old are they now? With a shock, I realized that they were nine and eight, slightly younger than I was when Ma died.

What sort of children were they growing up? I envisioned a boy and a girl with sandy hair like mine, dressed in fine clothes, greeting me on my wedding day. Despite the years passed, we'd known each other.

"Of course, they should be there. You must miss them terribly." Caroline clutched my arm.

David ran his hand through his hair. "I'll see if I can persuade Verna to bring them."

Caroline glanced toward the wall clock. "The Women's Guild meeting is in twenty minutes. Abigail, you must come. They plan to discuss the wedding decorations."

"Decorations?" My breath quickened. "I thought this would be a quiet affair."

"Well... The group has some ideas."

She dragged me to the meeting where the guild ladies gushed about ribbons, flowers, and other nonsense. They insisted on preparing the large room of the synagogue for food and dancing. The women would gather early to congratulate Caroline and me, and the men would come later, in time for the *chuppah* ceremony.

Over the next two weeks, Caroline and I prepared the menu for the feast, consulted the rabbi, penned invitations —that last job was all Caroline with her fancy handwriting—and sorted through replies. Most days, I was vexed and anxious, apparently a normal state of mind for a bride, according to the women from our prayer group. Whenever Caroline asked me to sample a dish for the wedding table, the food tasted like ash. Flowers she offered me to choose from smelled like rot. My lips would stretch into a smile and my voice rang high, but each bridal task we performed together was a spoonful of poison I downed in secret.

Caroline seemed excited and a little overwhelmed. "How lucky for our grooms!" she said with pretend scorn. "All they have to do is go to mikvah and wear their best clothes."

Using her dowry, David completed the purchase of the building and worked on furnishing the upstairs flat. He wanted to have the lodging finished before the wedding. "Our honeymoon nest," they called it.

My honeymoon would be our tour, starting with Venice. Somehow, a city comprised of canals did not appeal to me. I kept thinking about falling into one and disappearing in the darkness.

Moishe practiced in all his free time and swung between hopeful and irritated that I wasn't putting in the same effort at the piano. To satisfy him, I rose at dawn to play. I slept little anyway, often waking up sweaty and shaking from a nightmare I couldn't remember.

Overwhelmed with wedding planning and a rigorous music routine, I canceled all lessons with my student, Miriam's daughter. My throat ached as I lied to the tear-streaked child that we'll resume soon. If the tour proceeded by the plan, I wouldn't see her in many months.

One morning, Caroline brought me to a coach station but refused to tell me why. When we passed the city boundary, I threatened to jump out if she didn't tell me where we were going.

She laughed with glee. "I'm stealing you to London. Don't worry, Mama knows where we are. With all the excitement, we neglected the most important thing. Our wedding dresses."

"We have our dresses." I huffed. "I'm getting married in my dress with mother-of-pearl buttons. And you brought that yellow one with you."

My head snapped to the window when I remembered Caroline trying on her dress. My sisters oohed and ahhed over it, and even Mama admitted that the color suited Caroline. "She's a ray of sunshine," Naomi said. Biting my lip, I told Caroline that she was beautiful. Because it was true. Immediately I regretted my words because she swept me into an embrace and held me. "We are two lucky brides," she whispered into my ear as I blinked, willing myself not to burst into tears.

Caroline sighed, and I turned back to her. "My sisters keep up with the fashion. They informed me in their letter that my dress is out of style for the season. They insist that I visit their favorite London shop and order something new. And your dress... lovely, but so modest. Perhaps there will be something else you prefer."

I rolled my eyes. "Jewish brides are supposed to be modest. No open shoulders or bare arms in the temple."

"We'll go to Madam Pointer's. They'll alter any dress to our requirements. Whatever you choose is my gift."

Her chatter kept me from brooding. As we rode in our shaking coach all morning, Caroline told me stories of her family. Her brother Jamie, two years younger, and sisters Julia and Audrey were younger by six and eight years, respectively. They were all born in London, where their father held a successful dental practice. The family moved to Seatown because of Jamie's health. The new practice her father built was even more prominent, and the children benefited from the sea air and exercise.

When we entered the crowded streets of London and breathed in the stench of the river, I understood the family's motivation to move.

Caroline wrinkled her nose. "I forgot how bad the city smells. And the soot! No wonder we were sick all the time. It's not all bad though. There are lavish parks, museums, and famous theaters. Each year, my mother brought us back to the city to attend parties and to refill our wardrobes. I would beg her to let me off at a bookshop. But now that I'm away from her and my sisters, I cherish the fun we had together."

Mama and I never go anywhere for fun. She would think it idle and extravagant to visit a theater or stroll in a park. But listening to Caroline, I wished we had these adventures to share.

We descended from the coach in front of a small shop with rose bushes planted in front. Low cut gowns and feathered hats decorated the windows. Two ladies, holding hat boxes and parasols, gawked at us as they sauntered out of the shop.

"Never seen Jews in this part of the city before." One of them continued to stare.

"Perhaps they came to ask for work," the other answered.

"At Madam Pointers? Christian women need jobs."

Caroline and I exchanged wide-eye glances. Perhaps we should've been offended, but we were breathing hard not to laugh. Caroline grasped my hand and led me inside.

For a moment, I was lost in the world of lace and velvet. Caroline brought me to a stand with pastel fabrics and encouraged me to run my fingers through the silk. "Doesn't that feel divine?"

"May I help you?" A woman's voice sounded harsh and irritated.

Caroline pivoted. "Hello Madam. My future sister-in-law and I require wedding dresses to be finished in less than a week. They must cover the chest, shoulders, and arms, but still be elegant and fashionable."

The modiste, tall and slender in her sleeveless gown, uttered a grunt. "Is this a joke?"

"Not at all." Caroline fidgeted. "We have the means to pay."

"Then why are you clothed like you just left your Polish village?" The woman crossed her arms. "Let me show you some designs English brides wear. This season, bare shoulders are a must."

"Caroline, I don't think this shop is for us," I said. "Let's go somewhere else."

She squeezed my hand and turned back to the modiste. "You misunderstood. I'm converting to Judaism and want to look every inch a Jewish bride. My sister is a convert as well. We require you to make dresses that will be the talk of the town."

Madam Pointer leaned back, sniggering. "Madam Pointer's to be the talk of a Jewish neighborhood? We'd be a laughing-stock and lose our best customers. There are shops at the East End that will help you better. That's where your people live, near the docks."

I tugged Caroline's hand. "Let's go. We don't deserve this."

"That's right. We are leaving." Caroline squared her shoulders. "Nothing in this shop is good enough for us anyway. These silks are rubbish."

Before the modiste could protest, Caroline brought a piece of bone-white fabric to her lips and spat on it. Then she grabbed my hand and we flew out. For a few minutes we were running, lifting our skirts, and gulping air. Reaching a dead end, we stopped to catch a breath.

Caroline slumped against a wall and covered her face with her hands. Her shoulders trembled.

I knelt next to her. "Caroline, please, don't be upset. That woman isn't worth it."

"I'm not ... upset," she said, gasping for air between words. She burst out laughing. It spread to me, and I giggled, clutching my belly. Her laughing fit continued for a good five minutes. The tightness in my chest I'd carried for weeks eased a bit.

"How she said... about our people... living at East End," Caroline labored to speak. "Our people. I belong with the chosen people now."

I snorted. "You become Jewish when you immerse yourself in the *mikvah*."

"That's only a week away. Let's go together the morning we are to be married."

Only a week away. While Caroline squeezed my hand with her excitement radiating through fingers, my heartstrings cried, breaking one by one.

Chapter 25

"**D**ear Murka, we'll never forget you." My voice quivered as Moishe shoveled dirt over our cat's little curled up body. Poor Murka refused food and water the last few days. This morning, Moishe found her in the bushes. He offered to bury her alone, but I threw on a shawl and rushed down to the yard. What an ominous sign the day before our wedding.

My hands already missed her soft fur. I hugged myself, trembling from the wind and the chill inside me. "You were a member of our family. We all loved you." My eyes blinked away tears.

"She was quite old, you know." Moishe set the shovel down. "And had a great life for a cat. When David found her, she was scrawny and couldn't step on one paw. He patched her up, and then Mama spoiled her."

She was a foundling like me, rescued by David and Mama. My lungs squeezed from a terrible premonition.

Leveling the grave, Moishe shook his head. "If you wanted a ceremony for the cat, why didn't you tell me to wait for everyone?"

With the wedding only a day away, my family was caught in a swirl of preparations. Caroline and David went to greet her family arriving for the festivities. Papa was consulting the Rabbi about the Torah reading, while Mama ran some last-minute errands. Everyone was busy so hadn't noticed that the cat was gone.

I placed a stone on Murka's grave. "We'll tell them later, after the wedding."

"Because everyone should be happy tomorrow. What about you?" He circled his arm around my neck. "What can I do to lift your spirits? Please tell me."

My body leaned into his, feeling his warm breath on my ear. For a moment, I let him hold me and make me feel safe. Until I pulled away. "I'm just sad about Murka. But tomorrow will be grand. The ladies from the prayer circle say it will be the finest wedding our synagogue ever hosted."

He let his hand drop. "Once we settle somewhere, we can get a cat of our own. A Persian with long fur, if you wish."

I don't want another cat! I want Murka, my mind screamed. "Yes, someday." My voice was toneless. Dead.

Ma was calling me from the darkness. Her shape was vague, as if underwater, but her voice pierced my ears. "You forgot Our Lady. You forgot me. You even forgot little Julian and Josie."

My body was buried under a weight that crushed me. *I didn't. They are coming to the wedding.* Hot ash filled my mouth.

"You don't even know them."

My eyes snapped open. My blanket twisted around my legs and the pillow was drenched with sweat. Panting, I sat up. The dawn of my wedding day illuminated the window, but my thoughts were darker than a thundercloud. Every moment of this day would be torture. I can't be happy for David. I don't love Moishe. And I hate myself for it.

"Abigail, are you awake?" Caroline's voice chirped from beyond the door. "I could not sleep a wink."

"Me neither. Except for one dream." I cringed, remembering that I agreed to go with Caroline to the *mikvah* the morning of our wedding day. *What's one more spoon of poison when I've drank a hundred?* "Let's get ourselves clean."

As before, I washed myself thoroughly and instructed Caroline to do the same. When we entered the inconspicuous building behind the synagogue, the attendant Ditza greeted us at the door.

"*Shalom*, my brides," she said with a singsong voice. "Let me give you another rubbing for a good measure."

After scrubbing our skin pink, she gave Caroline a robe. "I will start with Abigail," she said and held my hand as she walked me to the room with the *mikvah* pool.

As last time, I carefully descended the steps. When my feet found the bottom, I dove under the surface. Submerged, my body and soul became heavy. The stones on my chest were pulling me down. I was drowning under their weight. Bubbles escaped my lips. Terrified, I forced myself to rise and breathe. When I repeated the blessing after Ditza, my voice trembled.

I took a minute to compose myself before I submerged again. Telling myself that I was frightened over nothing, I opened my eyes underwater. The pool was the loveliest shade of green. This color enveloped me with warmth. I almost didn't want to rise, but my lungs forced me to emerge and breathe. When I broke the surface, my body was seized by a chill. I said the second bracha through chattering teeth.

The last plunge was effortless and serene. Enlarged by a visual illusion, the mosaic of the tiled floor appeared to me in its ordered detail. As it sparkled, the water reflected the rows of silver light. I recognized my sketch. There was no doubt that I drew myself in this *mikvah*.

The dark canals of Venice Moishe spoke about emerged in my mind. Even hundreds of miles away from David, I could not run away from myself. I would be homesick and unhappy, ruining Moishe's tour and life. He deserved better than a wife who only pretended to love him. But at the bottom of this sacred pool, my love and my torments left me alone. *I am at peace.*

I slowly rose to breathe. On the third bracha, my voice sounded like it belonged to a stranger.

"Are you alright?" Ditza asked when I grabbed her hand and ascended the stairs.

I forced a smile. "Fine. Just nerves on my big day."

"You are shaking like a leaf. Dry yourself off before you freeze."

She gave me a towel and a thick robe and ushered Caroline in. "Do you know what to do?"

"I think so," Caroline said. She touched my shoulder before she disrobed and descended into the *mikvah*. I crept behind her to the pool's edge. While Caroline bobbed her head in and out of the water and bellowed the prayers, I stared into the water, entranced by its glimmer.

The water darkened, and then a shape made of light came together. My eyes saw details, as they did before smallpox. Ma, staring at me with longing. I tiptoed towards the water.

"Abigail, be careful, you are right by the edge." Ditza's arm pulled me back, and the vision disappeared. "Why are you staring at the water like that?"

"I... lost a ring," I stammered the first thing that came into my mind.

"What ring?" Caroline threw on her robe. "Did you drop it in the water?"

"You can't wear any jewelry when you immerse in the *mik-vah*," Ditza said with disapproval.

I fidgeted. "It was an accident. I left it somewhere here, near the edge."

"I've never seen you wearing a ring. What did it look like?" Caroline asked.

"Um…"

Ditza waved dismissively. "I will find it later. You won't believe the things women leave behind here, especially the brides. Get dressed, ladies, and best wishes. I'm planning to eat plenty of Shira's sweets and dance till morning."

"Personally, I'm horrified at the notion of being lifted with my chair," Caroline said. "For sure I will fall off."

Ditza laughed. "It's important to do that dance early, before the men are drunk. *Mazel tov*, my lovely brides."

Dried and dressed, we came out to be surrounded by the majority of the Jewish female population of the city, including Mama, Miriam, and Hannah. We received hugs, kisses, congratulations, and marital advice. Mrs. Cohen, the rabbi's wife, whispered in my ear. "Do you remember our conversations on what's expected of you tonight?"

"Yes." My cheeks heated. Like many religious couples, Moishe and I decided to wait until the wedding to have our first kiss. Nothing inside of me craved it, let alone what Mrs. Cohen implied. I swallowed hard.

Caroline hugged Mama. After the *mikvah*, she changed into the yellow dress that made her face glow. The lace covered her neck, wrists, and feet, and yet she was no less striking than the fashionable ladies at Lady Linden's. When Mama cupped Caroline's face and kissed her cheeks, bile crept up my throat. Even Mama accepted her as David's bride. His *bashert*.

After we received congratulations and instructions from Mama, Caroline wrapped her arms around me. "We are truly sisters. I've shared dolls and secrets with Julia and Audrey. But with you... we are sharing the most important day of our lives."

A good person would've loved her with no reservations. Yet, pricks pinched my skin as I embraced her. "David and you deserve happiness," I whispered.

She pulled back and stared at me. "Is something wrong?"

"No, no." I forced a grin. "It's just... David is a wonderful person... And so are you."

Her hand patted my shoulder. "You are so sweet. I wish you and Moishe all the happiness you deserve as well." She turned to the women gathering around us. "Ladies, please help Abigail to get ready. I will join you soon."

"Where are you going?" Mama asked.

"I... have a question for the Rabbi. He's waiting for me in his study," she replied and rushed away.

The women whisked me away to a room in the synagogue designated for us. No men were allowed. Mama sat me down by the mirror, spread the paste to hide my pox scars and brushed my hair. Members of the Women's Guild applied finishing touches to table decorations. Guests greeted Mama and me then found places to sit or fix themselves up before the ceremony.

"To me, you are the most beautiful bride," Mama said. She wrapped her arms around me and kissed me on top of my head. "I love all my children, but you've long been my favorite. You stopped David from going to war. Helped Moishe find his purpose. Recently, Shira told me how you talked her out of running away. What others fail to see with their eyes, you see with your heart."

"Oh, Mama." I began to cry.

"Why so sad, dear? Tell me."

I wished to tell her the truth, as terrible as it was. That I loved David even though I shouldn't. That I agreed to marry Moishe when I didn't love him. That all these people came to celebrate our wedding, and I didn't want to be married.

My stomach spasmed from my nerves. I doubled-over from pain.

She patted my head. "You need chamomile tea to settle your belly. I'll see if I can make it here."

"Mama, wait," I said, but her mind was on her mission. She gave me a peck on the cheek and sprinted out of the room at an impressive speed given her age.

As always, she thought she knew what I needed better than I did. What tea I needed to drink, what coat I needed for chilly weather. But she didn't know my heart. Even if I told her how I felt, she'd convince me to go through with the wedding. Moishe and I were a good match. *Bashert*. But Moishe deserved better.

"*And you deserve worse!*" Ma's voice exploded in my ears. Her face appeared in the mirror, her eyes fixed and her skin bloodless, like the morning I found her dead. I shrieked and hid my face in my hands.

My scream was drowned out by the chatter of the guests. When I lowered my arms, the vision was gone. Paralyzed, I sat with my heart pounding, waiting for it to slow.

"Abigail!" Shira waved to get my attention and signaled me to come with her. My legs shaking, I followed her to the table full of scrumptious dishes.

"Are you all right? You are pale as a ghost." She peered into my face.

"Mama must've overdid it with the powder. I'll add some rouge."

She led me toward two white cakes, with tiers upon tiers of icing. "This one on the right is yours," she said. "We made roses and carnations from spun sugar."

I inhaled the sweet aroma of vanilla and cinnamon. "It's beautiful. Thank you. You went through so much effort."

"Want a taste? I have a piece to sample."

My head shook. I've had no appetite for days. To trick Mama, I've thrown food from my almost full plates out of the window. Stray dogs ate it up. "I'm saving room for the feast," I said, patting my stomach.

"I'm glad they turned out this well. Mama said a cake this tall would collapse. I can't wait to see her face." She giggled with delight.

Her back slumped from kitchen work, and the skin on her hands dried, but still that rebel spirit in her held, ready to prove others wrong. If I had her courage, I would've told these people to go home. But they were here not only for me. They were here for Caroline, who managed to charm much of the town in the brief time she stayed with us. I did not hate her anymore, but I couldn't be happy for her. Watching her take her vows with David was going to break me.

Shira touched my shoulder. "What's wrong, sister? Your expression just now... it scared me. Are you all right?"

A lump hurt my throat. I wanted to show her how much she meant to me. "I was thinking of the scones you baked the day I came to live with you. Of all the things you baked over the years, I loved those the most."

Shira sniffed in tears. "I was never sentimental, but you are making me cry. Why didn't you remind me you love scones? I can make a batch for the wedding. There's plenty of time."

I waved my hand. "Don't. You've already worked so hard. I was just reminiscing."

"No, it's only fair. I've baked meringues for Caroline but didn't make your favorite dessert. Naomi is still at the bakery. We'll bring back a batch in a jiffy, and I'll save some for you for tomorrow morning. You and Moishe will be hungry." She laughed and pinched my cheek.

"Please give my love to Naomi." I lowered my voice. "I'm glad she's in our lives and making you happy."

Shira threw her arms around me. "Give it yourself when she comes. She's so excited about the wedding." She hurried out.

I glanced at the rest of the women gathered in the room. My sisters Miriam and Hannah, and their oldest daughters joined hands with other women to practice a dance. Talia, Rivka, Ester, and other young women of the town were in that circle. Mrs. Cohen, Mrs. Simons, and a few other ladies gathered in a pack to share some of the latest gossip. This day would feed them for weeks. Some of them stared at a group of Gentile women, dressed in ball gowns with low cut necks and open shoulders. The three blond women were Caroline's mother and sisters.

I had trouble placing the fourth woman with short raven hair. In my mind, I reviewed the guest list Caroline made. When the realization hit me, I smiled. The slender woman in a gown of eye-catching red, with her arms loose at her sides was Ella Parker. We met when she disguised herself as Alan, a medical student. David mentioned that she became a ship surgeon and had wild adventures, inspiring him to join the navy. Despite the stares from other women, she held her chin high and her back straight, but not too stiff. Her head spun in my direction, and she stepped toward me, but Caroline's mother asked her something, and she turned back.

Children chased each other through the room. Scanning the faces, I looked for Julian and Josie. I was sure I would recognize them despite the years apart. My heart would tell me. But they were not here. My chest squeezed from one more of David's unkept promises.

I gave all the women a final sweeping gaze and a casual wave and turned to go. Some women answered my wave. They likely assumed I was going to the privy or some quick bridal errand.

In the doorway, Caroline bumped into me, breathing heavily. "Abigail, where are you going?"

I answered with the first lie that came to mind. "I... I'm still searching for my ring."

"Let me look with you. We can ask others to help."

Her sisters flanked her. "Caroline, there you are. Let's get you ready," the older of the two blond girls said.

"Oh no!" the other one gasped. "You are missing a button, and the bow is about to fall off."

With her cheeks flushing, Caroline threw up her hands. "I always manage to ruin my clothes. Luckily, I found the button." She removed it from her satchel and showed it to her sisters.

"Good. We brought our sewing set," the older one said. "Let's fix your dress."

Her sisters pulled her away.

"Can we do this later? I need to help Abigail..." she protested feebly as they fussed over her.

With my head down, I stepped out of the building. Cool air hit my face. Leaves rustled under my feet as I trudged the short distance to the *mikvah*. I gathered rocks into my pockets as I walked.

Rocks in my pockets and rocks in my chest. This load was too heavy for me. There was a road to cross, but I was no longer afraid.

The door was unlocked. I did not see Ditza in the rooms that I passed. I had an excuse ready in case she was still here. I'd tell her that I returned to search for the ring I supposedly lost. Hopefully, she'd leave me alone to look. All I needed were a few minutes with everyone distracted elsewhere. And the rocks in my pockets.

The pool, bathed in the noon sun, was tranquil and inviting. One could imagine a siren living in a place like this and beckoning people for a deadly plunge. I gave one last thought to Mama and Papa, David, Moishe, and Shira. They will be sad, but they've lost Rachel and two babies, and found a way to go on. This was to be a merry day, but Jewish weddings are not only feasting and dancing. A groom would break a glass to signify the destruction of the Temple. Our rituals remind us of our sorrows even on the happiest occasions.

At my conversion, Ditza said that *mikvah* is a ritual that links us to all Jewish women from Biblical times. I wondered if any woman ever drowned in a *mikvah* before. Probably not. Suicide was forbidden. The Christian Bible said the souls of those who commit it will be damned to Hell for eternity. Judaism was vague about what happened in the afterlife. I hoped to see Ma and beg her forgiveness for forgetting her. Maybe Murka would be there as well.

Fully dressed, with the weight of rocks in my pockets, I descended into the *mikvah* to perform my final transformation. My clothes expanded around me like angel wings. The heavy skirts and the ballast pulled me under the surface, and I sank to the bottom. The water filled my nose and ears. Pain and fear shot through me. *Don't do this!* my mind shouted. My hands flapped helplessly. I coughed, exhaling any air still left in me, but more water rushed in.

I don't want to die! My mind resisted my will. Dying was scarier and more agonizing than I imagined.

The oblivion I craved wouldn't come. My limbs no longer moved. Only my mind refused to shut down, to stop telling me to save myself.

Death, take me already. I want this pain to be over.

From the darkness, a figure of light appeared, advancing on me. With trepidation, I recognized my mother. My eyes no longer impeded me, and I could make out every detail of her white clothes, even the pearls I lost as a child.

"Abigail, come to me. We'll be together at last." I craved to stretch my arms to her, but they wouldn't move.

Another figure blocked my mother's way, then faced me. She was young and had a heart-shaped face, a classical beauty.

When she pursed her mouth like she tasted something sour, I recognized Amelia, the beggar who turned out to be an actress and a daughter of rich parents.

She shook her head at me. "No, you need more time. Rise! Live!"

Time for what? I've lost him. I lost David. What do I need to live for?

Ma and Amelia disappeared, and the pitch-black darkness crept toward me. Suffocating, boundless. Every fiber of my body screamed for air; every shred of my mind told me to fight.

"When you find yourself at the bottom, the only way left is up." Papa's voice boomed in my ears. Energized by his wisdom, I emptied my pockets of the rocks, one by one. My sluggish limbs made an attempt to push my body up. A crushing weight sunk me back down.

It's too late. I can't save myself.

Darkness was upon me. My heart gave a faint beat, likely my last one. And then, when I surrendered, something tight squeezed my hand. Arms were pulling me up. Shadows receded and a shimmering light filled my eyes. *Angels are taking me to heaven.* My body relaxed, letting them lift me.

The gentle glimmer of light became blinding. My eyes squeezed. Screams assaulted my ears.

"Turn her over! On her side!"

Someone smacked my back. Water poured out from my mouth and nose. My chest convulsed and I coughed. With a breath in, sweet air rushed into my lungs. I coughed again, and more water spilled out.

"Goodness! She tried to drown herself in the *mikvah*. On her wedding day." I recognized Ditza's voice.

"No! That's not what happened." That voice was Caroline's, higher pitched than usual. "She was searching for her ring and slipped into the pool. Oh Abigail, why didn't you wait for me to look with you?"

The women helped me onto my hands and knees. I shivered and my teeth chattered.

Caroline's hands rubbed my back. "Ditza, fetch some towels. Then find David or Dr. Kaplan. Tell them Abigail suffered an accident. But don't start any stories about what happened."

Thick towels wrapped my quivering body. Caroline embraced me, giving me her own warmth.

"Why? Why did you do this?" she whispered into my ear.

My voice was weak and shaky, no louder than a whisper. "I love David... Always have... I can't live without him."

More water rushed from my throat and nose. The contents of my stomach gushed out, most of it landing on Caroline's wedding dress. Caroline's hands left me. When I finished hacking and spitting, I looked up at her.

She sat on her knees, unmoving. "This is my fault. I drove you to this."

Part 3

Chapter 26

Present Day

Where am I? My head pounds. My throat and my chest burn. *What happened to me?*

When I remember, my cheeks heat, and I break into sweat. *I almost committed the most terrible sin. Suicide.* Tried to drown myself in the sacred pool.

My sluggish mind attempts to remember. Did I imagine Ma being angry at me? *I'm sorry, Ma.* In my heart, I know she was not the reason why I wanted to die, even if the vision of her made me step over the edge. *But how did I come to be here, on my bed?*

I will my heavy head to make sense of what happened after I let the rocks sink me. My lungs compress as I remember the weight of the water. Struggling for air, I had the first of my visions. When I lost hope of saving myself, Caroline pulled me out. Coughing and retching at the edge of the pool, I lost consciousness. My arm throbs. While I slept, someone must've brought me home and fetched Dr. Kaplan, who bled me. The treatment probably made me faint again...

Between those events, I relived much of my life.

The voices from another room make my head hurt more. I squeeze my eyes closed, shutting out the world. If Mama or Papa see me awake, they'll start asking me questions. Worse, they'll tell me how disappointed they are in me.

Mama is yelling. "Who knew about this? Who knew that she's obsessed with David?"

"I was sure she'd get over him eventually," Shira says.

"I hoped if she married me and joined me on my tour, she'd forget David," Moishe adds.

My ears strain for David's reply. His voice is quiet and full of pain. "Before going to see Caroline, I promised to marry her. I was hopeless about marrying my true love, and I wanted Abigail to be happy."

"You told me nothing about her love or your promise," Caroline cries. "If I knew, I would not have come here. I thought she was lonely and needed a friend. I took her everywhere with me. She must've hated me... and yet, she saved my life."

"You paid her back today. She'd be dead if not for you," he answers.

Mama grunts. "No one told me or Papa. Do you see where your secrets lead?"

No one speaks for a while, and I pray I can fall back asleep.

"David and Caroline, you need to get back to the synagogue," Mama says. "The guests are waiting for you."

Caroline's voice breaks. "No. Could someone tell everyone that they can help themselves to the food and go home? We cannot celebrate today."

"You are not getting married?" Shira asks. "Are you sure?"

I hold my breath. *Is this what my vision of Amelia meant? Is there still a chance for me?*

Caroline's voice chimes with a worried note. "Where is my dress? The yellow one I wore earlier?"

"I tossed it into the laundry pile. There's vomit all over it," Mama answers.

Hurried steps sound, and then a heavy silence.

"There," Caroline says. "For a moment, I thought it was lost. It was in the folds of my wedding dress."

"A ring?" Mama says.

My brow wrinkles. *What ring?*

"My wedding ring. David and I were married this morning, in the Rabbi's study. We decided to have a part of the ceremony just for the two of us. After the mikvah, David and I signed the *ketubah* with Rabbi Cohen and two witnesses. I was going to put the ring on later, during the celebration."

My stomach roils as I ponder what Caroline's announcement means. This is why she excused herself to consult the Rabbi after the *mikvah*. David and Caroline were married, by Jewish and British laws. After signing the legal document, it's customary for a newly married couple to have *yichud*, a few minutes without witnesses. The torn button... Caroline's flushed cheeks when she returned to the gathering... Realizing what occurred between them, I twist and swallow bitter bile.

A coarse hand takes mine and another pats my forehead. I muster the courage to open my eyes and gaze into Papa's. Everything in me wants to reach for his face and kiss it until his eyes won't look so sad and lost.

"Abigail, how are you feeling? Are you cold?"

In my body, I don't feel any pain or chill, only numbness. My mind is sluggish, and my tongue won't obey me.

Papa props me up with another pillow and brings over a bowl and a spoon. "We kept some broth warm for you."

Like a helpless baby, I open my mouth, and he spoon-feeds me the lightly salted liquid. My throat, irritated by coughs and vomit, welcomes the soothing goodness of Mama's cooking. It warms me from the inside, and I breathe easier.

"I'm sorry," I mouth.

My chest constricts at the lost stare he gives me. Despite studying the Torah and reading books on religion and philosophy, he has no wisdom to share with me at this moment.

"Let's have David examine you." He squeezes my shoulder and leaves the room.

David comes in a minute later, holding his doctor's bag. He collapses on the chair next to me.

"Do you know where you are?" he asks, studying me. I remember that Dr. Kaplan asked me the same question a few hours ago. I think it was a few hours. It could have been another day.

My voice croaks. "My room."

His fingers shake slightly as he prompts me to open my mouth and stick out my tongue. Then he listens to my chest. This reminds me of being his patient in the hospital, when he was a student. Back then, he often checked my throat twice, unsure if he saw everything the first time. Now, his movements are efficient and practiced, but his breaths are fast, and his chest is caved in.

"Dr. Kaplan was eager with his lancet. Not a treatment I favor, but your heart and lungs sound better. Your mind is what worries me... Frankly, I'm terrified. I hid all sharp objects out of sight. Mama locked up any medicines that may be dangerous." He leans away. "What were you trying to do? Break Mama's and Papa's heart? If you wanted to stop the wedding, you should've told them."

"I couldn't find a reason to keep living if you don't love me. If you'd asked me to release you from your promise, I would've found a way to go on." A wave of anger gives me energy. I sit up and face him. "While I waited for your return from Seatown, Caroline appeared here, pregnant with your child. Didn't I deserve at least an explanation, a letter of warning, if not an apology?"

His arms go limp. "Abigail, I tried to talk to you, but you avoided me. And you've convinced everyone, including me, that you want to marry Moishe and leave with him. What happened between Caroline and me is private. But just know that in my wildest dreams, I didn't imagine her coming to this home. When I gazed at Scottish mountains and lochs, my heart was breaking from the thought that I would likely never see her again. Part of me dreaded that Caroline may be pregnant. I would've betrayed my family and religion for her and our baby. That thought weighed heavily on me. Of course I would've written if this occurred."

My eyes are bone dry because I have no tears left. "If she weren't pregnant, would you've returned to marry me?"

He clasps my hands and shakes his head. "After seeing Caroline again, everything became clear. She's the one for me …in every way. If I'd married you, we'd both be miserable."

I fall back on the pillow. "So it was easier to stay away in Scotland, give lectures and teach other doctors than face me and tell me the truth?"

"No!" His shoulders jump. "Is that what you thought? I left within the hour Caroline's letter reached me. It made me cry tears of joy but also hit me like a hammer. I was throwing my belongings into my bags as I finished reading."

His head drops. "I'm sorry for the promise I should've asked you to release me from. I was weakened by a disastrous voyage and disease and brokenhearted about the love of my life. My judgment was muddled. I'm sorry for how you learned about Caroline. I'm sorry that I could not get here any faster. For Caroline's and our baby's sake. And for yours."

He lowers his voice. "Since the time I cared for you at the hospital, I felt a tender emotion for you. We have a special bond. But it's not the same as love between a husband and a wife."

I exhale with a hiss, letting my anger dissolve. "I forgive you. Please forgive me as well. It wasn't only my despair at losing you. I've been seeing strange things. I'll tell you later."

His hands clasp mine. "We almost lost you. Please promise me you won't try again."

The burning in my throat and chest makes me wince. "I promise. It was terrifying, but then, I saw my mother... and Amelia as well. Remember her, the girl with consumption who came to the hospital with me? I watched that night and many other days and years of my life."

He leans back. "Blimey, that's incredible. Some people have powerful visions when they are close to dying. I saw Amelia recently. I'm supposed to give you her letter. I was trying to tell you, but you wouldn't hear me out."

"You saw Amelia?" My eyes widen. "Please read me her letter."

He shakes his head. "Not tonight. You need rest."

"At least tell me how she is."

He turns away without an answer.

"She died, didn't she? It's all right. I won't cry. I thought that she died years ago."

"Amelia lived much longer than her doctors predicted. I was at her deathbed right before I came back. She died peacefully and painlessly, with her parents holding her."

I sighed. "A good ending for her at least. How come you were with her? Where was this?"

"At Churcham. After I gave my last lecture in Edinburgh, the president of my alma mater, Professor Harris, approached me. He invited me to apply for a job in the medical school where I studied. They are changing their policies and opening their doors to men of all religions. Dr. Miller, their most celebrated professor, resigned over this change, and they were looking for new instructors. I traveled with Professor Harris back to my old university. This is why Caroline's letter, addressed to my lodging in Edinburgh, didn't find me for a while."

"Did you get a teaching job at the university? Caroline mentioned it."

"Yes, but I will not teach regularly. I'll oversee the changes they are implementing. The admission process, the learning opportunities, and the final exams need to be the same for everyone, regardless of their background. There's a lot to do, and not everyone is receptive to new policies."

My chest warms with pride for him. Caroline is likely full of ideas on how to help him. I can only admire his success.

"You are helping people who were barred from your university. You had to change your name to study, and now you'll make sure that others won't have to do the same."

He nods. "Professor Harris introduced me to Amelia's mother, Mrs. Hearts. She's the biggest donor of the hospital. When I told her that I met her daughter, she invited me to visit them in their home. Amelia was close to death, but she recognized me. I came by every day to ensure her comfort until her passing. Her mother was grateful despite her grief."

Even though I haven't thought of Amelia for years, the image of her dying while holding her mother's hand brings tears to my eyes.

David inhales sharply. "You can't upset yourself. I should've said nothing."

"It's all right. She lived a good life with her parents, didn't she? Maybe she got back her horses and fancy carriages."

He gives me a handkerchief to wipe my eyes. "It wasn't like that at all. After her mother found and forgave her, they traveled to countries where the climate is beneficial to consumption patients. Amelia improved, and not only physically. She noticed that most people were not getting as much medical care as her. I knew her as a foolish and selfish young woman but she changed. She convinced her family to use their wealth to benefit others. Traveled with her mother extensively and they helped renovate hospitals in impoverished places."

I gasp. "I was the one who told her mother how to find Amelia. I'm glad that my tiny part in their reunion meant they could go on helping many other people."

"Very true. Eventually Amelia's health began to fail, and they returned home. One of Amelia's last efforts was to build a ward for consumption patients in the university hospital. Her mother carries on this project with the hospital board."

"I can't believe we are talking about the same Amelia. And she wrote to me?"

"Yes. She was too weak to write, but I took her dictation." He glanced at the window. "I'm not going to give you the letter now. You need rest. I'll give you medicine to help you sleep."

He takes out a bottle from his bag, measures a spoonful of the red potent liquid, and brings it to my lips. I wrinkle my nose and wince at the bitter taste.

"Sorry, I don't have raisins." He chuckles.

Moishe's head pops in the doorway. "Can I see her?"

David gives him a long stare. "Only if you leave your anger at the door."

"Don't I have a right to be angry? It's my wedding day."

"Yes, it's my wedding day as well. But her wellbeing comes first."

Drowsiness creeps through my body but I will my tongue to work. "I'm sorry, Moishe. And please tell Caroline that I'm sorry."

David shushes me. Their voices sound further away from me. My eyelids close.

"Come sit with her, brother," David says. "Take her hand."

Moishe's warm hand covers my palm. His long fingers intertwine with mine. His voice sounds farther and farther away.

"I'll cancel the tour," he vows.

"No," I mouth.

"Nonsense," David says. "You'll go. Music is your calling, like medicine is mine. Abigail will recover while you are gone."

He breathes through his teeth. "I don't want to play without her."

"But you still should," David says. "You'll play with a different accompanist for a while. I'm sure there are many talented pianists who'd be willing." His chair creaks as he stands. "I need to go now. Stay with Abigail, don't leave her alone. If you get sleepy, have Mama sit with her. And I repeat: no talk of your hurt pride, no anger, no tears. Just hold her hand. She must feel how much we all love her."

Moishe gives a sob. "I thought my love would be enough for us both."

That's what I thought about David and I. But it was not enough.

My eyes are shut but in my dreamlike state I see David hugging his brother's shoulders. "I said, no tears. You have something special together. She may realize it someday. Perhaps in a few years, we'll celebrate your wedding after all. Mama's intuition is rarely wrong."

The warmth of his hand spreads to me. "I love her. I'm so angry that I want to shake her. But I still love her."

Before I drift off, I feel David's touch on my cheek. "Goodnight, I'll check on you in the morning. Now I'm going home with my wife."

All night, through my sleep, I feel Moishe holding my hand. But when the sun's rays warm my face and the smell of fried eggs and freshly baked bread wafts into my sickroom, he is not there. The first meal I gobble up with appetite in weeks gives me energy to leave my bed, and I walk to Moishe's room as quickly as my legs carry me. I must tell him all the visions and dreams I saw yesterday. There's so much to understand, and I need his logical mind to make sense of them. My hands fall when I see his bed stripped and his travel clothes and his violin gone.

Chapter 27

David offers me his arm as we stroll through the Bishopscourt garden in Rochester, in the shadow of the old castle. I admire the autumn scenery. A large sycamore rains down its golden leaves. The crab apple trees boast their fruit. David brought us here for light exercise, which he deems good for me and Caroline. After spending the High Holidays in the sickbed, I'm happy to be in the sunshine of this radiant October day.

Flapping in the wind, Caroline's skirts swish behind us. Like a proper Jewish wife, she has her hair covered under a headscarf. David keeps looking back at her and his anxiety seeps through his smile. I feel awkward that David is walking next to me instead of Caroline, but she insisted, saying she prefers to examine various plants. Each time she bends down to collect some leaves and roots into her satchel, David turns to watch her.

The shrubs in the garden are planted in perfect geometric designs, and the yellow and gold leaves cover the grass like a lavish rug. *Why didn't I come here before? I should invite Mama to walk here with me.*

"Are you cold? Do you want my gloves?" Caroline asks me, catching up to us.

"I'd like to sit down." I walk towards a bench, shaded by a large oak. When my chaperones sit down next to me, I turn to David. "I've been taking all the remedies you prescribed. I sleep for ten hours each night and nap in the afternoons. I play piano in short stretches and only the pieces I enjoy. I drink goat milk, eat cow heart and liver, and sample every fruit and vegetable Mama buys. Can I finally see Amelia's letter?"

"You've been a good patient." He chuckles. "I thought you'd ask me on this walk, so brought it with me." He glances at his wife. "My love, do you mind making a circle on your own? Just don't tire yourself. Or would you rather sit, and we can go talk somewhere else?"

"I'll collect some chestnuts." She gives David a kiss on the cheek before she leaves. As she passes me, I notice her paleness and thinness.

"How is she?" I watch her figure disappear, almost as fragile as the day after she lost her baby.

He shakes his head. "Not well. She hasn't slept a full night this week. Insomnia, nightmares, tears into her pillow. Valerian root and the pills from the apothecary are not working well enough. After losing the baby, her nerves were strained already, and well ... you gave them another shock. I'm hoping your recovery will make her better as well." He rubs his forehead with a fist. "She blames herself for what happened."

A tightness in my throat makes me wince. "I didn't mean for anyone to blame themselves. Or for Caroline to become sick."

"I don't want to imagine the sorrow we'd all carry if Caroline didn't find you in time. But I don't blame you for anything other than not telling us how you felt. You drove yourself to a sickness of the mind."

His gaze shifts, and I follow it to see Caroline walking back to us with a determined gait.

"Is something wrong?" David asks.

She stops in front of him, wrinkling a wilted flower in her hands.

"You said you have no secrets from me anymore. Then why do you ask me to take a walk when you are going to read a letter?"

He stares at his shoes. "This is not my letter. I'm only the messenger."

I understand her worry. She already paid a hefty price for my and David's secrets. "It's all right. You can listen. This letter is from an old friend who recently passed away."

"Thank you." Caroline smooths her skirts to sit on the edge of the bench. She bends her head. "My condolences about your friend."

David takes out the creased letter from his pocket and starts reading.

Dear Abigail,

You were my steadfast companion the night we could've frozen. When I look back at that fateful Christmas Eve, I'm horrified at my selfishness, making you beg in the cold instead of asking someone to take you in and feed you. I could've been the death of you, but instead you saved me.

When you told me the story about the stolen pearls to encourage me to apologize to my mother, and then directed her where to find me, you gave me an invaluable gift—a gift of time. Before that night, my life of a spoiled wealthy girl—then a failed actress—then a pauper, had significance only to my parents. Because they had the means to improve my health and more wealth than they could ever spend, I was able to do virtuous deeds and alleviate the suffering of others. I thought I knew hunger and illness, but meeting people who lost everything and had no one to turn to for help gave me perspective.

My time in this world has almost run out, but I have no regrets leaving it, knowing I used my last years well. My mother will continue our charitable efforts. I'm glad to hear that Dr. Oliver Higgins (or I should say Dr. David Fridman) is opening a medical practice, and my family is giving him enough to get it started.

I hope your brother and sister are well. You should pay them a visit. Even if their godmother provides for their needs, they may still need their sister.

My regards to you and to the wonderful family who raised you.

Be well,
Amelia

A tremor goes through me as I listen. The vision in the *mik-vah* was prophetic. Amelia said I needed time. Not for winning back David but for doing something valuable with my life. Her letter hinted where to start.

"You should've given the letter to Abigail as soon as you arrived," Caroline chides David.

"I wanted to, but first she was unwilling to talk to me, and then she was too fragile. Are you all right, Abigail?"

I shake my head. "David, you were going to bring Julian and Josie to the wedding. What happened? Are they unwell?"

He avoids my eyes. "They are healthy. But I'm afraid Verna didn't believe the trip to be appropriate for them."

"What was inappropriate about their sister's wedding?" I say, but David stays silent.

"David," Caroline says, "the letters I've read from Verna were mean-spirited. She sounds angry and greedy. Are you sure that she cares for the children?"

He grunts. "You haven't seen her most hurtful letters. Those I've burned. But her accounts about her purchases are detailed, and she includes receipts. The children have food, clothes, shoes. When they were sick, she sent me the physician's bills. I wish she used a different tone in her letters, but she sees to the children's needs."

Heat rises to my head. "They are *her* godchildren. Why is she anything but thankful for the money she receives from you? If my siblings are a burden to her, I will be happy to relieve her of that burden. I'm sure Mama and Papa will support me in this."

He taps his foot. "This worry is not good for you. Let's go home and have you rest. Same goes for you, Caroline."

David stands up and offers us his arms to rise. I give Caroline a pleading look. I need her as an ally.

She grabs my palm and squeezes it. Her voice is sharp. "How convenient for you to assume the doctor's tone and avoid the conversation. It won't work this time. We'll stay here until you give us answers. You may give us extra doses of your smelly potions later."

"I can't fight a united front." He chuckles and raises his open palms. "What do you want to know?"

I ball my fists. "What was in the letters you burned?"

As he sits back down between us, his shoulders tighten. "Abigail, my aim was to protect you."

"Yes, that's often your intention, but things don't turn out the way you hope. Please, tell me what she wrote."

He rubs his face. "All right. In the beginning, her tone was civil, although never warm. It became icier when you stopped attending church school. She wanted you to go to the boarding school, as the mothers' committee offered. More than once she said you would be better off in the orphanage than living among Jews. The worst came when you were ill with smallpox."

"You wrote to her that I was sick?"

He nods. "I thought we should prepare for the worst outcome. I asked her to have the children and herself inoculated and come to see you. I had to tell her about your wish to convert because you spoke of it any time you were lucid. In her reply, she said that she told Julian and Josie that you died. She wrote that your death would be better than conversion."

My throat convulses and tears flood my eyes. Immediately, Caroline is at my side, her shoulder supporting my head as she rocks me like a baby.

"How could you let this woman lie like that? Letting the children mourn their sister when she's alive?" Caroline says to David.

He sighs. "That's what my own parents would do if I converted to Christianity. In her eyes, Abigail condemned herself to damnation. She preferred the children to think their sister was dead and gone to Heaven. But I burned that letter for a different reason. I hate to tell you this."

"Please. I want to know everything." I plead through my sobs.

"She added a letter from Julian and Josie. With crooked letters they've only learned to make, they'd written all kinds of anti-Jewish sentiments. Called us dirty, greedy, and soulless. Profiting from the tears of Christians and damned to Hell. This broke my heart."

A shudder goes through me. David passes me a flask of water. As I gulp, water mixes with tears in my throat.

Caroline's arms pull me tighter into her embrace. "They are only children. She forced them to write things they don't understand. David, you don't have to put up with her. She continues to accept your money while teaching the children to hate us."

David shrugs. "Lots of people hate Jews. I tried to reconcile with Verna and persuade her to send Julian and Josie to the wedding. She didn't bother responding."

I give my voice forcefulness. "I don't want my brother and sister to grow up with hate. Let's take them away from their vile godparents and teach them to be kind to all people."

As he pulls out his pocket watch, David takes my wrist. "I should've kept my mouth shut. This talk upsets your nerves. A fit could negate all the progress we've made."

Drawing deep breaths, I will my pulse to slow. "Now I know why I need to keep living. I will be strong enough to face Verna. My brother and sister will come home."

Caroline squeezes my hand again, and her cheeks flush. "Abigail is right. For all of Verna's accounts for food and clothes, I doubt the children hear a kind word from her. They need their sister and a loving family. We'll all care for them."

David puts away his watch. He glances at the passersby, then gives Caroline a kiss on the lips and me a brotherly peck on the cheek. "We will all go."

Chapter 28

My heart pumps as I glance around the familiar room. Most of the furniture is different, but the bed where Ma and I slept is still there. A bunk bed stands where the babies used to rock in their cradle. The plants on the windows have withered, and one could draw on the layer of dust.

"You said you have another flat downstairs?" David asks Mrs. Levy, the landlady who threw me out when my Ma died. "Obviously we need more room."

We are a large party. Mama, Papa, Caroline, David, Shira, Naomi, and I. We expect my two siblings to join us tomorrow. We slept last night at a roadside inn and planned to arrive during the day, but the coach broke down, delaying us by a few hours. Mrs. Levy spotted us as we walked through the town, looking for a place to spend the night. If we go to Verna at this late hour, we'll likely frighten Julian and Josie, and Verna's children as well. Better we spend this night in my old lodging and see my brother and sister in the morning.

Mrs. Levy's tone is agreeable. "Yes, let me show you. And if you give me an hour, I'll clean up here."

"I hope so," Mama says with her arms crossed. "This place needs a proper scrubbing."

"It sure does. Like I said, I usually rent to Gentiles who barely scrape up for the rent. They don't care about the dirt."

I ball my fist. My Ma swept the floors and dusted in the evenings, after working a twelve-hour shift at the mill. I'd helped her since I was three.

Caroline, Shira, and Naomi follow the landlady to see the other flat. I sit on my old bed. The mattress sags just how I remember it.

David bends down to me. "We don't have to stay here. If this is too much for you, we'll find lodging somewhere else. I can ask Amelia's mother."

"We shouldn't barge in on her at night. This place is fine."

Mama shakes her head. "I will tell this Mrs. Levy what I think of her for putting a child out in the cold. Her meanness gives our people a bad name."

"Wait till we are leaving. We need this place for the night," Papa says.

The landlady comes back with a load in her arms. "I brought candles, fresh towels, and clean linens. I also put a brisket in the oven. While you eat downstairs, I'll tidy up here. So good to have our people stay. What luck that I spotted you at this hour."

She lights a couple of candles and puts them on the table, the light reflects on her face. Moved by a glimmer, I draw near to see better.

She flinches from my stare, but I recognize the beads dangling from her ears. "The earrings. They are my mother's."

Her hand touches her earlobes. "These? Someone left them behind years ago."

"No, they belonged to Nellie Jones." My lips tremble. "She lived here with three children. She... she died."

Mrs. Levy scratches her face. "Ah, I remember. That woman coughed all over the place and then perished... She hadn't paid in two months, and then I couldn't find a lodger for two more. Who are you to her?"

I stomp my foot. "You threw me out into the cold the day she died. You said someone needed a room."

She fidgets, staring at me.

David approaches and puts his hand on my shoulder. "You will give her those earrings and anything else you took from her mother."

With her hands shaking, she removes the earrings, and puts them into my open palm.

"You should be ashamed," Mama says. "Haven't you suffered? A Jewish woman must have compassion."

A sob escapes from Mrs. Levy. "And who had compassion for my boy in Russia when the army passed through our village? They forced him to join their ranks. My son wrote that they beat him until he converted. A year later he was killed for the tsar who cares nothing about our people." She cries into her apron.

Papa passes her a handkerchief. "May earth be soft as feathers for your son, but that's no reason to close your soul. A sick mother with three children had nothing to do with your sorrow."

She nods and leaves the room. Minutes later she returns with two dresses over her arm and a wooden box. "I'm sorry. I did not mean to throw you out in the cold. I thought your mother's friends would care for you," she says to me. "This is all I still have. I also took her shoes, but I gave those away."

Holding my breath, I open the box. Inside, there's a beaded bracelet that matches the earrings. Mama made these beaded trinkets herself. They are worthless but invaluable to me. Now I have something of hers to hold and remember. Or to show Julian and Josie when I tell them about our Ma.

"There's something else." Her hands are cupped, holding something white. "These pearls are your mother's, aren't they?"

My heart skips a beat. This cannot be. The same necklace I foolishly showed to the girls who would not play with me.

"This necklace was stolen. How did you get it?" I stammer.

She gazes down. "I saw it in the window of a pawn shop. These pearls called to me whenever I passed. It was like I heard a little whisper in my head that I must buy it. Yet whenever I wore it, I felt this heavy sadness, and I couldn't wait to get it off me.

Just now, I remembered your mother wearing it. You resemble her."

I resemble my mother. The thought makes me open my shoulders and smile. She's been gone for almost eight years but she lives in me. I wonder if my brother and sister look like her.

While the landlady makes our supper, we rest from our trip and freshen up. The smell of roasted meat wafts into the room. In an hour, Mrs. Levy calls us downstairs to a set table with a white tablecloth I've never seen her use. The brisket and vegetables are in the center, looking as appetizing as they smell. With her eyes down, Mrs. Levy trudges upstairs to clean our room. By the time we finish eating and come up to retire, the lodging is spotless.

Later that night, after Mama and Papa fall asleep, I sit down on the chair by the table. I pretend to be calm, but sweat is rolling down my forehead. Naomi holds me by the shoulders. Shira heats our longest needle over a candle. Her hands tremble a bit.

"I can do it if you like," Caroline says. "I've done it for my sisters."

Shira grunts in answer.

David watches the scene from the corner of the room. "Perhaps, you better let me do it?"

Naomi laughs. "A surgeon isn't required here. Women have done this for ages without men helping."

I sense Shira's nervousness as she stands next to me. "Ready?"

"If you are." I inhale a lungful of air.

"Don't move your head!"

The hot steel pierces my right earlobe. I flinch and scream, but Naomi's strong hands force me to keep still. Another moment and the needle goes through my left earlobe. We all exhale with relief. I touch my ears, and a drop of blood rolls onto my hands.

Shira washes off the blood with a wet rag and puts the earrings through the holes. Then she lifts my hair and slides the pearls around my neck. Caroline passes me a handheld mirror. I hold it close to my face to see my reflection. The memory of Ma smiling as she put on the necklace and earrings stirs in my mind. I mostly remember her weary or ill, but that day she was rosy-cheeked and with a sparkle in her eyes. She was going to a church picnic that she had talked about for months.

"I look like my mother," I tell Shira.

"She must have been beautiful." My sister hugs me.

That night I go to sleep with earrings in my ears and the pearl necklace under my pillow. When my eyes close, Ma stands by her grave. It's overgrown with weeds and buried under leaves.

"It wasn't your time, Abigail." Her voice is a gentle wind blowing the colorful leaves. "I miss you. But I'll wait." She makes a sign of the cross over me.

"I'm not Christian anymore," I say. "I became Jewish."

"Our Lady still loves you. And I love you. Why don't you pray for me anymore?"

"I can't. I'm sorry." I shake my head.

When I wake up, my pillow is wet with tears. The scarlet of the dawn bleeds through the curtains.

Shira, who is sharing the bed with me, stirs. "Is it morning already?" she murmurs.

"I'm going to visit my mother's grave," I tell her.

"Wait until we get up and go with you."

I throw off the covers. "Thank you but I'm going alone. This town is where I grew up. Churcham is small and there's no traffic at this hour. The cemetery is just down the street. I can't get lost."

Dressed in my warm clothes, I walk through the cemetery. I haven't been here since the day Ma died. When I can't find her resting place among the other unkempt graves, I get a feeling that no one's visited her since she was buried. My blood boils.

Verna, wasn't she your friend? Aren't you supposed to bring your godchildren to visit their mother's grave? I demand in my thoughts. But then, I didn't visit either. I never asked my family to bring me here. In my desire to leave my hungry and cold childhood behind, I neglected the responsibilities of that life.

Mama and Papa were shocked to hear about my brother and sister. "Why didn't you tell us about them? We'll make some sacrifices, but they should live with us," they said. It was hard to be honest with them, and even harder to be honest with myself. I didn't want to mind babies. I didn't want to share Mama's and

Papa's love. Over time, I convinced myself that they were doing well with Verna and growing up good Christians.

To protect my heart from longing for them, I built a wall around it. Those walls were made of heavy rocks that weighed on my chest. With my secret love for David and jealousy of Caroline, the walls grew taller. Threatened to crush me. They almost drowned me. But when I told my family that I must take Julian and Josie away from their godmother, the walls broke, and my heart was free.

I recall my dream, trying to remember where Ma was standing. Behind her, there was a gravestone with the figure of an angel. Elaborate monument that stood out as a surprising luxury among the humble graves. A shape in the distance could be of that angel. As I approach, my skin tingles. The angel is exactly how I saw it in my dream, a long-haired woman with wings. She even reminds me of someone.

I walk past the angel and stop by a row of graves covered in weeds. Most have no markers. I run my hands through the grass and leaves. When my palms touch wood, I rip out the weeds around my find. Soon, a cross just a few inches tall, made of two boards tied together, becomes visible.

The name 'Nellie Jones' is carved into it with a knife. I don't have to see it to know it's there. As a child, when I asked Ma's friends how anyone would find the grave, they helped me make that cross and carve her name.

My mother's grave shouldn't be neglected. I grab the tallest weed and pull on it. Thorns prick my hands, but I'm glad for the pain.

That's what you get, Abigail Jones, for abandoning your Ma. For letting your brother and sister grow up with their mean god-mother. For letting her teach them to hate people who are not like them. I channel my anger into my work. One by one, the weeds fall to the ground.

There are many more weeds to pull, but I'm tired. Catching my breath, I consider what prayer I should say. *If I say a Christian prayer, will the Lord accept it? If I chant a Jewish prayer, will it offend my Ma?* I close my eyes, hoping for a sign that would tell me how I must pray.

"Are you all right, child?"

Startled, I open my eyes to see a woman in a black dress and a veil.

"I didn't mean to scare you. Please pardon my awkward question. Obviously, you are grieving. As am I."

"My mother is buried here." My fingers tremble.

She pats my shoulder. "I'm sorry. My daughter Amelia is buried nearby. It was her wish to be interred in a common cemetery because death does not care whether you are rich or poor. I visit her grave every morning, and then I take a walk around."

"I'm sorry for your loss as well. Amelia was my friend. I saw you at the hospital years ago and told you where to find her."

She gasps. "I remember. Amelia talked about you and so did your brother David, when he tended to her. You are Abigail!"

"Yes. And you are Mrs. Hearts." I rise. "I saw Amelia in a vision."

She steps back. "A vision? What do you mean?"

I draw a long breath. "I felt lost and tried to take my own life. She spoke to me as I was dying. She told me I needed more time."

Mrs. Hearts puts her arm around me. "Of course, you need more time. You have so much life yet to live. Amelia once gulped down sleeping pills over something trivial. That scare didn't teach her much. But when an incurable disease slowly drained life out of her, she used her last years to help others. I truly believe that her work kept her alive longer than any treatments the doctors prescribed."

"I was given another chance at life, but I don't know what to do." My head drops. "I only know that I need to find my brother and sister. While I grew up with a loving family, I left them behind with an unkind woman as their guardian. I recently learned that she teaches them to hate Jews. They think I'm dead."

Mrs. Hearts strokes my hair. "Poor child. It sounds like you shut the door on your past. You didn't visit your siblings. You left your mother's grave uncared for." She stares into the distance toward the grave with the angel. "But now you've returned to make things right."

"I saw in my dream last night that Ma wants me to pray to Our Lady again. But I'm Jewish now. We say different prayers."

She shakes her head. "Again, you are shutting doors. Honoring your mother doesn't take anything away from your new life. Why can't you pray to the Virgin Mary and the God of Abraham?"

I shrug. "I don't know anyone who does that."

"There's so much we don't know about life and death, dear. All we can do is pray for forgiveness. Let's say a Hail Mary together."

She drops to her knees, and I kneel next to her. Our hands lock as we chant, "Hail Mary, full of grace, the Lord is with thee; blessed are thou among women, and blessed is the fruit of thy womb, Jesus. Holy Mary, Mother of God, pray for us sinners, now and at the hour of our death."

I breathe, "Amen."

Something warm caresses my soul. Maybe it's a hug from Ma.

"I'm sorry, Ma." I whisper. "I will never forget you. I'll tell Julian and Josie all I can remember about you. Each night, we'll say a prayer for you together."

I forgive you a million times, I hear on the wind. I gasp and glance around. Then I smile through tears.

"I always loved Mary," Mrs. Hearts says as she stands and shakes off the dirt from her dress. "She's relatable. A woman. A wife. A mother."

"That's what Ma used to say."

"What was your Ma's name?"

I rise and smooth my skirt. "Nellie Jones."

Her hand goes to her cheek as she steps toward me. "Did your mother have a pearl necklace?" she asks after a pause and touches my arm.

"I'm wearing it." I remove my shawl to show her. "But how do you know?"

She leans in to see. "Did your mother tell you how she came to have these pearls?"

My eyes widen. "No. Is it from you? You knew her?"

"Abigail!" Several voices shout at once. My family has gathered at the edge of the cemetery. They are gesturing for me to come to them.

Mrs. Hearts watches them. "It looks like you need to go," she says with notes of regret. "But please visit me later today. There are things I must tell you." She gives me her address. I know her street as one of the best in town.

Mama approaches us. "Is this where your mother is buried, Abigail?"

"Yes, Mama." I hang my head. "I didn't know that her grave was uncared for."

"I will order a headstone and have the gardener weed it and plant flowers in the spring," Mrs. Hearts says. She nods to Mama. "I take it you are Mrs. Fridman. Your son David attended to my daughter on her deathbed. I visit her grave every day."

Mama opens her arms to embrace her. "I've lost children too. That wound never heals." They are strangers, but they hold each other, and cry as dear friends would.

After releasing Mrs. Hearts, Mama pats my back. "I will pay respects to your mother."

Like at Rachel's grave, she speaks as if Ma were here. "Mrs. Jones, thank you for letting me raise Abigail. She's a joy to my heart... most of the time." She gives me a light shove. "I know you must miss her, but please don't call her to you yet. Not till she's a hundred and twenty, as we say. Our girl is very loved. And we'll love and care for your younger children as well. Let the ground be feathers to you. Please be at peace."

Mama picks up a round stone and places it on Ma's grave, next to the cross.

"That's what we do when we visit loved one's graves," I tell Mrs. Hearts. "The stones keep evil spirits away and show that we paid homage to the deceased."

"That's a beautiful custom. Please put a stone for Amelia. It's the one with the angel. She asked for a simple grave, saying the money should be donated to the poor, but... I wanted to give her one last gift."

I find a smooth pebble and walk over to place it next to the angel. Mama follows me and puts down another stone. "Thank you for showing me what I need to live for," I whisper. "I will take Julian and Josie away from Verna."

Mrs. Hearts gives me a hug. "Abigail, please come later today. I must tell you a remarkable story that involves your mother and you. And your necklace."

Chapter 29

After bidding goodbye to Mrs. Hearts, Mama and I join the rest of our family to walk to the address written on Verna's last letter. David shared that the addresses changed three times over the years they corresponded.

Verna answers the door. She's yawning, and her hair is uncombed, but she's wearing a nice dress, much prettier than she wore when she worked at the mill with Ma. As she studies us, she makes a throaty groan.

Her eyes land on David. "Ah, it's you. You are late with the payment. Why didn't you send me a check?"

"There will be no more payments. We want Julian and Josie. We are taking them with us," David answers.

"This is not the agreement." She crosses her arms. "You are to pay me until the children are eighteen."

I step forward. "Verna, do you remember me? I'm Abigail, their sister. Let them go with us."

She peers closer at my face and scoffs. "Our Lord punished you for turning away from the true faith. Gave you ugly scars.

Nellie must be turning in her grave, knowing that her daughter became a Jew."

"You wouldn't know. You don't visit her grave," I retort.

"Don't talk this way to Abigail." Mama hugs my shoulders. "If you cared about her, you would have raised her yourself."

"I had enough mouths to feed." Verna shrugs. "I birthed two more children, and then my husband started drinking after work."

My throat tightens. "Are my brother and sister going hungry?"

"The money I send every month is plenty to feed and clothe them," David says. "Are you using it for their benefit? Or are they eating crumbs from your table?"

I suppress a moan. My stomach hurts like it did when I starved. Are poor Julian and Josie waking up with this pain in their empty bellies?

Verna draws herself to full height. "The children are fine."

"We will see for ourselves," Mama says. "And *Hashem* help you if they are underfed."

"I said they are fine." Verna plants her feet wide. "Didn't I send receipts every month? I buy them all kinds of things. They love me like their own mother." False notes sound in her voice.

"We don't believe you." David steps toward the door. "We are taking them with us."

She blocks his way. "This is not what we agreed to. Swindling Jews. I need that money."

David's face reddens. "I'll give you money. All that you would've received over the next two years. I'll send more later."

"Son," Mama hisses, "don't give that snake another farthing. Let me deal with her."

"No. A deal is a deal." David takes the roll of bills from his money bag and starts counting them. My heart pinches because he's using the money that was supposed to go toward his medical practice.

Verna's hand reaches towards the bills, but David takes a step back. "The children."

Her arms fall to her side, and she shakes her head. "I don't have them anymore."

My head spins. I lean on Mama, and she cradles me in her protective grip. Shira and Naomi soothe Caroline, who is sobbing.

"What have you done with the children?" Papa bellows. "If they are harmed, you will answer for it."

She raises her hand. "They live at the orphanage, St. Anne's. They are fed and schooled."

Pain twists my chest so hard that I gasp. My brother and sister are living at the same orphanage where I was sent years ago. Beaten for breaking rules or bullied.

"Why did you send the children to the orphanage when my son covered all expenses for them?" Papa's voice booms.

"You sent me receipts," David adds.

Her lungs deflate with a hiss. "Any mother would do the same in my place. My three children must eat. They grow through clothes. My oldest had measles last winter."

David touches his flushed cheeks. "You wrote that Julian had measles. I paid the physician's bills. We could take you to court for your deception. If you end up in the poor house, your own children would go to the orphanage."

She bristles for a moment, but then straightens her shoulders. "This is a Christian country. The word of a churchgoing woman has weight in court. More weight than the words of swindling Jews."

"That orphanage is more like a prison than a home for children," David cries. "How long have they been there?"

"Two years. Look, they are better off there. They are growing up good Christians. I visited them recently and brought them gifts. They were healthy enough." She cocks her head. "If you give me the money, I'll bring them nice things every month."

"What a *schlump*," Mama mutters under her breath.

Papa's face is red, yet he manages to speak in a calm voice. "Thank you for telling us where the children are. We'll take them home with us. Goodbye, Madam."

Mama takes my hand. We turn to leave.

"I've warned the orphanage that you may come." Verna calls after us. "They won't let you have Julian and Josie. Give me your money. I'll take the children back."

None of us looks back at her as we walk away. Her voice starts to quiver.

"Please, one last payment. My husband drank through his wages last night. I don't have enough money to pay for rent. Or to buy food."

"Serves you right," David yells back.

"She has children," Caroline says. "David, please. Give her something so they don't go hungry."

David takes her hand and kisses it. Then he approaches Verna and throws several bills and coins on the ground. We turn and walk away. When I gaze over my shoulder, she is frantically running around the yard, struggling to catch the money as the wind sweeps the bills away. Her legs get tangled in her skirt, and she falls flat on her face.

An hour later, we stand by the orphanage's railing. The façade is even more rundown than seven years ago. Several windows are broken. The yard is empty of greenery or people.

"Is this where you took Abigail before bringing her to us?" Mama asks David. "Obviously you couldn't leave the child in such a gloomy place."

"What I saw of the people here convinced me more than the rundown building," he answers.

"Should we all go?" Shira asks, examining our clothes. "That woman said they won't give us the children. She probably told them that Jews may come for them. What if David and Caroline pretend to be a Christian couple hoping to adopt?"

Papa rubs his beard. "They are forewarned about us. Deception will only confirm their suspicion. Hopefully, the money will persuade them. That roof must leak, and the broken windows let in the cold."

"Let's all go," I say. "It may take all of us to convince the people in charge to let us take Julian and Josie."

My heart hammers as we wait for someone to answer the door. My siblings were babies the last time I saw them. *Will I recognize them?* They were told that I'm dead and will likely be frightened of me.

The locks click from the inside, and the doors fly open. A heavyset woman in a soiled dress studies us. There's more gray in the hair that peeks from under her bonnet, but I recognize her. She's the woman who hit a boy for taking the teachers' bread.

"What do you need?" she barks.

"We are here to take two children from your care," Papa says. "And to make a donation benefiting the orphans."

"Come inside."

Her voice lacks civility, but she leads us through the corridor. I catch a glimpse of a dining room with long tables and benches where the children in gray clothes are slumping over their plates. Their spoons clink against the dishes as they eat in silence. The smell of burned porridge makes my nose wrinkle.

She brings us into the office, and points at the two chairs next to the table covered in papers. A cabinet with more papers stands behind her. Papa and Mama sit, while the rest of us remain standing. She takes a seat across from us.

"I'm Mrs. Mulligan. Are you looking to adopt a baby? A six-month-old boy came here three days ago."

Papa shakes his head. "We are here for Julian and Josie Jones."

"Some children get new names here, but..." She rubs her forehead. "Oh, I remember. I haven't had my coffee, or I would've caught on. You are the Jews their godmother warned us about. No, you won't have them. We allow only Christian families to adopt our charges."

The pulse beats in my ears, and I force myself to breathe.

David takes out his money purse. "Would a donation persuade you? The building needs repairs, the children need better food and new clothes."

Her voice is flat. "We are doing fine. Look, I'm following the rules. The Jews cannot adopt here. And I can't accept your donation."

"Shame on you," Mama exclaims. "The children eat burned porridge and stale bread, and you won't take the money to feed them."

Papa and David raise their voices in objections, while Caroline pleads for woman's mercy. A tremor goes through me. I have an urge to leave the stuffy room, to find my siblings and hug them with all my strength.

I slip out and run into the dining room, where the children are eating. The boys sit at the two back tables, and the girls at the front two. A strict-looking woman walks between the tables, hushing any child who dares to talk to their neighbor.

"Can I help you?" she asks me.

I approach one of the girls' tables. The girls stop eating and gawk at me. Their faces are a blur to my damaged eyes. Many could be eight years old. Several are blond like me or chestnut-haired like Ma. *How could I not know my sister?*

"Josie," I call.

None of the girls answer but more eyes stare back. Mrs. Mulligan said the children may have new names. Did my sister and brother forget the ones Ma gave them?

"Mistress, are you adopting?" A red-haired girl with two braids asks. "Pick me. You can call me Josie if you like."

"You don't want Francine," a tall girl next to her says. "She smells. I'm bigger than her and can help you with any work."

Their neighbor jumps to her feet. "Don't listen to them. I can sew the fastest."

Several more speak at once, telling me about their good qualities. A girl of four grabs my skirt with her tiny hands. My heart beats faster against my ribs. Another child falls to her knees in front of me. Several girls fold their hands and pray. The noise makes it hard to think. The youngest children begin to cry.

The woman who supervises the meal marches toward me. "Do you see what you've started? Get out!"

Nausea is coming up my throat. "Julian," I cry out to the boys.

The boys have been watching, and one rises. "I'm Julian," he says.

My breath catching, I grasp my skirt away from the children holding me and run to him. When I see his wide shoulders, I halt. He's at least thirteen.

"He's lying," another youth says. "I'm Julian."

Behind me, the woman is threatening the girls with punishments if they don't quiet down. Once they are silent, she rounds on me. "Leave right now."

My hands clench. "Please. I'm looking for my brother and sister."

"Obviously, you don't know them. Go away."

I plant my feet wide. "I'm Abigail," I yell to the children. "Our mother was Nellie Jones."

The woman drags me by my arm. "Stop it," she hisses.

"You were raised by your godmother Verna Bax before you came here," I keep shouting.

Many eyes stare back at me. *Which of them belong to my brother or sister?* Desperately I try to remember the last time I saw them. *The day Ma died.* They were still babies. Before we parted, I sang Ma's cradle song to them. It was the song they heard every night.

My arm breaks free from the woman's grasp. Drawing air into my lungs, I start singing Ma's song.

The children listen, gaping, to my soft and gentle singing. When I don't know the lyrics, I hum the melody. Francine, the girl with red hair, weeps quietly and her neighbor hugs her.

As I come to the end of the song, the woman shatters the spell. "Enough. Go before I call someone."

She pushes me into the corridor. I look about, trying to remember the way back to Mrs. Mulligan's office.

A child's cries come from a room further away. There must be more children here. With my heart swelling with hope, I follow the cry.

Chapter 30

I pass a couple of dormitories with at least twenty beds in a row, all empty so I keep going. The cry leads me further to another room. I walk in and scan my surroundings.

There are only a few beds in this stuffy dormitory, heated by a blazing fire of the hearth. The smell of vinegar reminds me of the hospital. This must be the sickroom. One bed is occupied with a boy, whose weeping brought me here. A gray-haired woman stands by him with a bowl and a spoon.

"Dear, you must eat. Just a bit," she says to the distressed boy, who looks around two. He bites her hand, and she cries out. The spoon drops to the floor with a clatter. She puts the bowl down on the nightstand and turns to pick up the spoon. Her body freezes as she notices me.

"I've seen you before, perhaps when you were a child," she says after a pause. "Don't tell me... That's right. Abigail."

With her voice, the memories of a kind woman who nursed me at the hospital rush to me. "Mrs. Grace?"

She opens her arm to embrace me. Her hands run over my face and hair. "It's good to see you. All grown up."

"You work here?" I give a tentative smile that lifts higher as the realization sinks in. This kind woman will help me find my siblings.

"Yes. It was time for me to leave the hospital and move on. I've been here for a week. So much to do, I don't know where to start."

"I'm looking for my brother and sister, Julian and Josie. They're nine and eight now. They were not at breakfast with the other children. Where can they be?"

"Hmm. I don't know. Are you sure they were not in the dining room?"

"Yes. I would've recognized them."

She lowers her head. "Then it may be sad news. Five children were taken to the hospital with scarlet fever. I got word this morning that they all perished."

My body convulses. *No, I can't be too late!*

Mrs. Grace hugs me. "I will check the records. We will find out what happened to them."

The boy in the bed wails and throws off his blanket. Mrs. Grace hurries back and tries to soothe him, but his howls only get louder.

My heart pounds. I remember the hospital ward, the dying children, the bags Mrs. Grace sewed for the tiny corpses.

Did my brother and sister have a kind doctor like Oli or a compassionate nurse like Mrs. Grace to comfort them in their final hours? Or did they die all alone, thinking that they have no one in this world who loves them? Tears pour from my eyes.

Mrs. Grace's touch on my arm startles me. "Abigail, were you singing earlier?"

I nod.

"I'm sorry to ask this of you, but would you please sing for Harry? This poor boy has not eaten since he came here two days ago. When you sang, he stopped crying and let me feed him a little."

My throat is closed. As I breathe to open it, I remind myself that Mrs. Grace nursed little patients even though her own children died. Maybe I can't save Julian and Josie, but I can still comfort this boy.

Wiping my tears, I approach the bed and start singing to the child. At first, my voice is drowned by his weeping, but by the end of the first verse, Harry quiets and watches me. He opens his mouth, and Mrs. Grace catches the moment to insert her spoon into it. The boy winces but swallows the porridge. I keep on singing while Mrs. Grace feeds him a few more spoonfuls.

I pause to catch my breath. Then a quiet sound startles me. "Help! Help us!" A muffled child's voice pleads. I don't know where this voice is coming from. My heart pinches.

"Did you hear that?" I ask Mrs. Grace.

She frowns. "Did I hear what?"

"Children pleading for help."

Harry whines, but I strain to hear the voice. I hold my breath as I listen.

Mrs. Grace shakes her head. "I'm afraid you've imagined it."

I bring a finger to my lips. Then I hear the voice again. "Help us!"

"Didn't you hear?"

"No." She touches my arm. "Abigail, I'm concerned for your mind. Why don't you sit and rest? I'll check the medicine cabinet for something calming."

My head is shaking. "There's nothing wrong with me. My vision is poor, but my hearing is excellent. The children are calling for help. Listen."

This time the voice is louder. "Open the door!"

"These children are locked up!" I grab Mrs. Grace's sleeve. "They are pleading for someone to open the door. Please. Where could they be?"

Mrs. Grace gasps. "Mrs. Mulligan must've punished them. Wait here while I find the keys to the closets." She hurries away.

I pace between the cots as I wait. Little Harry tosses in his bed and howls.

Shira and Naomi enter the room holding hands. Their heads are bowed, and their shoulders are slumped.

My body shudders. Mrs. Mulligan must've told them that Julian and Josie had perished. I grab the wall for support.

"I'm sorry, Abigail," Shira says. "We argued with that wicked woman, but she won't let us take the children. Caroline had a nervous fit. Mama took her out for air."

"But they are alive?"

Naomi flinches. "Of course, they are. Mrs. Mulligan said several times that they are fine. What made you think they are not?"

My knees hit the floor as I thank the Lord. Harry howls, drowning out my voice.

Shira watches him, then perches at the edge of his bed and takes him into his arms.

"What are you doing?" Naomi demands, approaching.

Shira rocks the boy. His wails change to quiet sobs.

"Now I know what I have been missing," Shira says. "I want a child."

Naomi grips the railing of the bed. "I knew it. You will leave me so you could be married and birth children?"

Shira cradles Harry closer as he shudders from sobs. "I don't want to marry. But a child, who we would raise together... Let's adopt this boy. Both of us would be his mothers. Oh, but they won't let us, will they?"

Naomi shakes her head. "Even if they don't suspect... We are Jews. We have no husbands. They won't let us adopt."

My chest caves in. This is so unfair. Shira and Naomi would make wonderful mothers. This little boy would be much better off with them than in the orphanage.

Voices echo from the hall. "Open the closet, Mrs. Mulligan. Where are the keys?" Mrs. Grace is demanding.

Bunching my skirts, I run into the corridor to find her, Mrs. Mulligan, Papa, and David next to the door in the back. Children's voices sound from beyond it. When I come close, I hear them clearly.

"I'm scared." A girl's voice is quivering. "If it's her, she must be a ghost."

"Or an angel. Her singing was so nice. And I remember that song," a boy answers.

My heart leaps as I crouch by the door. "Julian, Josie, is that you?"

The children fall silent. Then both of them whisper, "Abigail?"

My throat closes and I can't speak. Tears flood down my face. Papa's hand squeezes my shoulder, comforting me.

"Get the keys for Heaven's sake!" David yells to Mrs. Mulligan.

While Mrs. Mulligan strides to her office, I speak to Julian and Josie. "I'm Abigail, your sister. Alive and well. I'm here for you."

Their sobs sound through the door. Mrs. Mulligan returns and thrusts the key into the lock. When she opens the door, a boy and a girl stagger from the tiny, dark room.

I kneel by them and caress their pale cheeks. Their small noses and chestnut hair color resemble Ma's. My brother has a swollen lip, and my sister's neck is bruised. I hug them and kiss their faces. Their tears drip onto my hands.

"We will take you away from here. You'll have a big family who will love and care for you. You'll never be hungry or cruelly punished again," I tell them.

"How long have they been in there?" David asks Mrs. Mulligan.

"Not long. Since seven this morning."

"Four hours? Outrageous. They need water."

"And breakfast," Julian adds.

Papa ruffles Julian's hair. "Clever lad."

Mrs. Grace takes the children's hands. "Let's get you something to eat and to drink."

We follow her into the sickroom where Shira is holding Harry in her lap while Naomi feeds him porridge.

"What are you doing?" Mrs. Mulligan exclaims.

"When he stopped crying, he let us feed him," Naomi says. "He was hungry."

"Thank you for taking care of him," Mrs. Grace says as she pours cups of water for Julian and Josie. "You must be very good with children."

Shira clenches Naomi's hand and whispers to her. Naomi shakes her head.

When my brother and sister perch on a cot, drinking water and chewing bread, Mrs. Grace turns to Mrs. Mulligan. "Please prepare the paperwork for Julian and Josie Jones' adoption. They are going to live with an excellent family."

The red-faced woman puts her hands on her hips. "These people are Jews. We can't let them adopt our charges."

Julian and Josie stop eating and stare at Mrs. Mulligan. I hug and comfort them, while my insides are quivering.

Mrs. Grace huffs. "Nonsense. I've known Dr. Higgins since he was a medical student, and I can vouch for his character and his piety. I trust that he and his family will be excellent guardians for the children. And the donation they pledge is most helpful for the urgent needs of our charges. Please do as I ask."

Mrs. Mulligan, red as a radish, paces between the beds. "I will write to the board about this. They will hear that you have allowed Jews to take the children."

"I'm in charge of this orphanage." Mrs. Grace straightens to her full height. "Things are about to change here. You may write wherever you wish, but I take my orders from my Lord Jesus Christ who was once a Jewish carpenter. I will tell anyone that I saw Dr. Higgins at worship every Sunday when he was a medical student. As their guardian, he will take the children to church and enroll them in a good school. Won't you, Dr. Higgins?"

"Absolutely," David replies. "And we are most grateful."

Mrs. Grace nods. "Did you hear that, Mrs. Mulligan? Please do your job."

The large woman gives us a sweeping gaze and walks towards the door at an exaggerated slow pace.

I smile through tears as I hold Julian and Josie. "Soon we'll be home."

Shira, who's still rocking Harry, tugs on Naomi's sleeve. "Please," she mouths.

"Excuse me," Naomi says to Mrs. Grace. "I am a widow. My late husband and I weren't blessed with children. May I adopt this little boy?"

"If you have the means to care for the child, I'm more than happy to let you adopt him." Mrs. Grace extends her hand to Naomi. "It looks like you have a supportive family to help you raise him."

Mrs. Mulligan steps back into the room. I wonder if she was eavesdropping. "Do you need that headache? That child isn't normal. He cries all the time and bites his caretakers. His parents died in a mental asylum, and he belongs there as well."

"No!" Shira rises, clenching Harry in her arms. "He's just scared."

Naomi draws her fists. "You plan to send a little boy to an asylum? You are the one who belongs there. Give him to me." She takes Harry from Shira and nestles him on her shoulder.

"These ladies are nice," Josie whispers. "Will they come with us?"

"Yes, they will," I answer. "Shira and Naomi are very nice. They will bake you all the sweets you want. David will heal you if you ever fall sick. Caroline will sew you new clothes. Mama will feed you delicious food, and Papa will read to you. When Moishe visits, he'll play you the violin."

Their mouths hang open and their eyes are full of wonder.

"And who'll take us to church? We go every Sunday," Julian says.

"I will take you." I instinctively know that it will be my job to help my expanding family navigate the customs of our two religions. "I will play piano and sing for you too."

Mrs. Grace pats my shoulder. "It's a blessed day. Three children have found a home. Mrs. Mulligan, are you still here?" She mocks surprise in her voice. "I thought you left to pack the children's belongings. Please add Harry's name to the paperwork and pack his things as well."

Mrs. Mulligan storms out, her steps thunder down the corridor.

"I'm afraid we'll have a vacancy soon," Mrs. Grace murmurs to herself.

"You should sack her," Julian says. "She hit me on the lip and gave Josie her bruise."

Mrs. Grace clicks her tongue. "I'd sack her immediately, but she has friends on the board. I was speaking of myself. If Mrs. Mulligan tells on me, the board will likely dismiss me. But it's nothing for you to worry about. I've done my duty today and will be going to bed with my heart singing."

Papa and David approach us, and I introduce them to my siblings. The next thing I know, Josie is sitting on David's shoulder, while Papa is crouching next to Julian and telling him a story.

"What do we have here?" Mama says, entering. Caroline holds on to her arm as if she's too weak to walk on her own.

"I found them," I say. "My brother and sister, Julian and Josie."

Mama studies them with her gaze. "Well, of course they are. They look like you, only smaller and skinnier. They need to be fed better."

"They are beautiful," Caroline says. She gives her hand to Josie, who is hugging David's neck, and then to Julian, who is engrossed in conversation with Papa. Then her hands go to her belly, and she turns away with a sob.

David lowers Josie down and puts his arm around his wife. "I know, darling. No one can replace our baby. But we'll have fun spoiling these two."

"Mama," Shira calls. Harry is now restless in her arms, twisting his little body. "We are adopting this little boy."

"I'm afraid we have no idea what we're doing." Naomi spreads her arms.

"No new mother does, but everyone learns." Mama tugs on Shira's ear and then on Naomi's. "Will you finally start listening to me and take my advice?"

"We will, Mama," Shira says.

Mama extends her arms to Harry. The boy whimpers but lets her pick him up and hides his face in her generous bosom.

"Shalom," she purrs. "I'm Leah Fridman, but everyone calls me Mama."

"I can see why," Mrs. Grace says. "As the old saying goes, 'God could not watch after every child at once, so He invented mamas.'"

Less than an hour later, we barely fit in the stagecoach that we've hired. I'm flanked by Mama and Caroline. Julian sits by the window on Papa's lap and Josie is across from them on David's. Shira and Naomi are sitting together and taking turns holding Harry, who's whimpering feebly. Shira tries to sing to him. Writhing, the boy turns away from her scratchy voice. I sing a little of the cradle song, and his body slacks against Naomi's.

"Sing some more. He's falling asleep," she whispers.

I keep singing until my mouth dries. Mama passes me a flask with water and an apple. "Your song lulled all the children to sleep," she says, gesturing at Julian, Josie, and Harry, all slumbering.

David shifts my sister on his lap to make her more comfortable and covers her with his coat. "I remember you nodding off like this on our way to Chatham."

Tears brim my eyes. "I'm so fortunate you didn't leave me at that orphanage and instead gave me a family."

Mama pats my arm. "You made us very happy. And with more children joining our family, we'll be even happier. *Mazel tov!*"

Naomi caresses Harry's head as he stirs and gazes at Shira. "We both are mad. You saw this boy you knew nothing about and decided on the spot that you loved him. And we adopted him just like that. What if he won't love us?"

"He's our son," Shira's voice quivers. "I knew it when I saw him. It's *bashert*. Our destiny."

"He loves you already," Caroline says, wiping tears from her cheeks. "I can feel it. I could feel that my baby loved me. I know that's impossible, but it's true."

David extends his hand to her. "I am sure our baby loved you. And I love you more than I could ever say or do." Caroline clenches his hand and brings it to her cheek.

Unlike before, I feel no urge to cringe or grunt. Instead of a prick, a warm sensation runs through my skin. Their love was meant to be.

"As I love you, more than I can say," Shira whispers to Naomi. "I will never leave you."

"*Hashem* works in strange ways sometimes," Mama mutters.

"Love is a great force," Papa says. "It can destroy us. Or it can make life worth living."

"Our family love helped me survive. You showed me love and compassion, cared for me, and taught me so much." My chin drops to my chest. "But I was selfish in my love. I wanted it all for myself and not share it with my brother and sister. Because of me, they suffered with Verna and at the orphanage."

"You can't blame yourself," Mama says. "You were only a child."

"There's an unlimited supply of love," Papa says. "We'll love Julian, Josie, and Harry without taking any love away from you, or from our other children or grandchildren. Today, you set things right."

"That's what Mrs. Hearts said." I jump in my seat. "Oh no! Mrs. Hearts! I promised to see her."

"We already passed the town border," Shira says looking into the window.

"No, I must speak to her." I clutch my necklace. "She knows something important about my ma and me."

"Turn the horses around! We are going back!" Papa bellows to the coachman.

Chapter 31

We ride on a street of houses that are massive and showy, decorated with columns and balconies. They remind me of Lady Linden's guests displaying their most expensive clothing and jewelry. *Why did my ma come to this part of town?*

Our stagecoach stops by the largest house. Its windows are draped in black. I marvel that Amelia used to live in such a fine home. And that she ran away from it. Apparently, an excess of material things could become as oppressive as the extreme lack of them.

Mama suggests someone comes with me, but I decline. Perhaps Mrs. Hearts wants to share her story only with me. The past is not always flattering or easy to recount.

I climb out and approach the door decorated with a wreath. A black ribbon winds through the leaves. I ring the bell.

A white-gloved elderly butler opens the door. I stiffen, remembering the attitude of Lady Linden's servant.

"I'm sorry," I stammer. "I should've gone to the backdoor."

He studies my face. "Are you Miss Abigail Jones?"

I nod.

"You are anxiously expected. Please come in."

He gives me a bow and steps aside for me to enter. After taking my coat, he leads me into the spacious parlor. "Eighteen years already. How time flies," he murmurs under his breath and leaves the room before I can ask what he meant.

The first thing that catches my eye is the mahogany grand piano. My fingers crave to touch it. Without Moishe to encourage me, they've missed the practice sessions. I wonder if Amelia played or if Mrs. Hearts pours over the keys. Music may comfort her when she misses her daughter.

I shift my gaze to the large portrait on the wall. From this distance, I see a slender figure of a golden-haired woman. Amelia. I approach to study the details of her dress. It's a splendid ice-blue gown matched by gems on Amelia's slender neck. The face is hard for me to make out, but I get a sense that the artist captured her likeness when she was young and not yet ill. The aroma of flowers arranged in vases below the portrait perfumes the room.

"She never liked that portrait," Mrs. Hearts says, entering. She's wearing a black dress, silky and elegant in its simplicity. "The artist painted it for her sixteenth birthday. That day she asked us for the new horse, and my husband said no. She posed with pouted lips and knitted brow. A spoiled princess she was most of the time. Closer to her death, I wanted a new portrait that would show her smile and beauty despite her illness. She said that the money for it would be better spent on the poor."

"As her mother, you knew her better than anyone. You can draw another portrait and hang it across the room. To show who she was and who she became," I suggest.

Her shoulders rise. "Me? I was never any good at painting even though I liked it. My teacher said I had no talent."

"Does it matter? If painting gives you joy?"

She shrugs. "I don't think anything can give me joy anymore."

"What about your beautiful piano? Do you love music?"

"It's been silent for years. I don't play. Amelia had lessons, but she was too restless to master the instrument. I have a tuner maintaining it. He always laments that such a wonderful instrument just stands there without use."

A twinge flows down my palms. "Please, may I? I haven't played in two days. That's too long for me."

"You are a pianist?" Her voice rises. "Well, of course you can play. It would make me so happy."

I do the scales to warm up my fingers. My ears instinctively strain to hear Moishe's violin. Music, without him, is a bit lonely.

When my fingers feel limber and energized, I play Lacrimosa from Mozart's Requiem, singing the words in Latin. The heartbreaking hymn celebrates Mary, Our Lady of Sorrows.

Tears well in my eyes. I missed praying to Our Lady. The church I attended as a child. The modest Christmas gifts and Easter hot cross buns. Ma's unshaken faith that the Mother of

God would understand and forgive her. Her last prayer to her protector gave her peace in her dying hour. Those experiences were as much a part of me as the Jewish feasts and fasts, the Sabbath, or the Hebrew prayers.

To be true to myself, I had to honor my past and my present. And I would love my birth brother and sister, as well as my adopted family.

"That was beautiful," Mrs. Hearts says, wiping her eyes. "Would you please play something else? You are an amazing musician. More than that, you are a healer. The pain in my chest that I felt since Amelia's funeral is all but gone. Your music helped me more than the drops my physician prescribed."

"I'm sure you are exaggerating."

"Oh, you don't know your full value," she says. "You have a gift that goes beyond the technical perfection others strive for. You play with your soul."

Heat warms my face. I don't really know what to make of her praise. "Well, thank you. I'd love to play more for you, but I can't stay long. We just rescued my brother and sister as well as another child from a miserable orphanage. My family is waiting for me."

"My servants have already invited them in. They are in the East wing, having dinner. I took the liberty to order Kosher food. The Jewish cook brought all new dishes and utensils. And I've ordered to prepare beds in case the children need a nap."

She touched my arm. "Please, while they eat, join me for dinner. Just you and me."

When I nod, she leads me to the dining room with a set table. The sparkling wine glasses and silverware reflect the candlelight of the massive chandelier. The aroma of roasted meats and herbs make my stomach rumble. I fill my plate with fried fish in crispy batter and golden carrots and say the bracha. Then Mrs. Hearts and I say grace.

"Our meal is twice blessed," the hostess remarks and digs into a luscious slice of beef. "I had no appetite for days, but suddenly I'm ravenous. What do you call this, do you know?" She points at one of the dishes.

"I believe that's pickled herring."

"Well, that's a peculiar taste." She eats more but then puts down her fork. "Who am I fooling? I'm enjoying this meal because I'm not eating by myself."

I think of my family's dinners filled with talk and laughter. "Are you all alone?"

She sips her wine. "Yes. My husband left me after Amelia's death. He loved another woman most of his life. I wanted him and persuaded my father to lure him with our wealth. But we weren't happy in our marriage. He's luckier than me because he got his love in the end, while I live in the house he left me, but alone."

My shoulders slump. "I made David promise to marry me. I thought I had enough love for both of us. But his heart was with Caroline. He's wed to her now."

"I'm sorry." She pats my hand. "You are hurting, but that's better than being married to someone who doesn't love you."

I take my last bite of the fish and chew slowly. "Thank you for the dinner. I'm eager to learn how you knew my Ma."

She takes a long breath. "I met her almost eighteen years ago, when I was preparing this house for the winter ball. A small army of cleaning women from the town came to make the place spotless. A pregnant woman was among them, breathing hard as she swept the floor. I remembered that when I was that far along with Amelia, I stayed in bed all day. And here was a woman doing arduous work, sweating through her clothes. This was one of the rooms she cleaned."

Mrs. Hearts rises and walks about the room. "I had different furniture, but this wing of the house was the same as today. She was here, scrubbing on her hands and knees, her swollen belly touching the floor."

I have no trouble seeing my mother working her hardest, pushing herself through pain and discomfort. "Was it Nellie Jones, with me in her belly?"

"Yes." Mrs. Hearts nods. "I said to the woman in charge, 'why don't you send this pregnant one home and fetch someone else? I don't want her baby to be born right on my newly cleaned floors.' I thought I was doing your mother a favor."

"So was I born, right in this room, on your floor?" I stare at the polished wood. *How come I never asked Ma how I was born? Was Ma going to tell me when I got older?*

"We'll get to that in a moment. The woman in charge answered that the workers don't get paid if they don't work their full day, and Nellie Jones desperately needed money."

"For the baby," I add, biting my lip. "For me."

Mrs. Hearts paces as she speaks. "Minding my business, I went to sort through replies from my guests. My mood was agreeable because all the important people accepted my invitation to the ball.

I called my maid and had her bring me my new gowns to try on. After selecting the gown and the jewelry I would wear, I visited the nursery and told my ten-year-old Amelia that she could attend the ball if she behaved herself. Amelia stomped her foot and said that she wanted a new dress. I reassured her she would have one, even though she already had a wardrobe full of clothes.

Then I returned to check on the cleaning. Pleased with the pristine floor, I sent the women to wash the staircase. But... your mother stopped and grabbed her belly at the foot of the stairs."

My mouth dries. "Her labor started?"

"Very likely. Let me show you where it happened."

She leads me to a white marble staircase. It's magnificent. And a herculean task to clean.

"Nellie stood here, clenching the railing with one hand, and rubbing her belly with another." Mrs. Hearts points to the spot. "I asked her, 'Is your rascal trying to come out early?' She straightened with the pain written all over her face. 'No, Madam. My baby will wait for me to finish my work.' She gave her middle a caress and smiled. In answer, I praised her for her efforts. It didn't occur to me to offer her even a glass of water."

I swallow, seeing Ma bending over these stairs while cringing from labor pains. "Did her work speed up her labor? Did she have to stop because the baby was coming?"

"Oh, I wish it happened that way," Mrs. Hearts says and takes my hand. "Only now, I clearly see how foolish we all were. Letting her work to exhaustion for her meager wages. I should've paid her and sent her home. Instead, I watched her climb the stairs to join the other women washing them with soapy water. She was half-way up when she lost her footing and slipped."

"No!" I gasp.

Mrs. Hearts touches her face. "She rolled down the stairs and landed on her stomach. The women screamed like mad. I ran to her, turned her over, and held her. She was motionless, and I feared her dead. But then she moaned, and her hands went to her belly. I touched there too and felt weak stirring. The cleaning women and my servants surrounded us. I ordered the men to lift her and carry her to one of the guest rooms upstairs. Then I sent my butler to fetch Dr. Miller, who was already known as the best surgeon around."

I remember the imposing, bearded doctor. "Dr. Miller was the most important man in the hospital when I was there in the children's ward. I didn't know he delivered me."

Mrs. Hearts leads me up the stairs. "They carried Nellie to the guest wing. Away from the nursery and my chambers. My husband heard the noise from his study and came out to see what the fuss was about. 'I suppose I'll be paying the doctor,' he grumbled. 'And likely the undertaker as well.' I shuddered from his callousness, but he had a point. I sent a servant for the priest."

Beads of sweat form on my forehead. Ma could've died in labor. I would've died with her.

We enter a bedroom with large windows and handsome cherrywood furniture. A four-poster bed stands in the middle. This room is fit for an important guest.

Mrs. Hearts makes a sweeping gesture. "This is the room where my servants brought your mother. I came in as well to make sure there were enough pillows and blankets to make her comfortable. Dr. Miller arrived moments later. Thinking he was being called to attend to the lady of the house, he told the coachman to drive the horses at full speed. When he saw me standing here, and your mother stretched on the bed in her work clothes, he almost dropped his bag."

The image of the puffed-up man gaping at Ma in her soiled dress and dusty apron makes me chuckle. "Then what happened?"

"He quickly recovered from his surprise and examined his patient. Then he ordered my servants to bring him towels and clean rags, and to boil a full pot of water. I approached him and lowered my voice to ask him if the mother and the baby would survive. He answered too loudly, that he would do all he could, but likely both would die. Poor Nellie heard him and screamed."

"Oh no. My poor Ma." I covered my face with my palms.

"Angry that the doctor frightened her, I grabbed her hand and said, 'Look, you have the body and the heart of a warrior. You toiled harder than all the other women and would've kept on going if you didn't fall. Surely you have the strength to live on, and your child as well.'"

I run my fingers over the soft blankets, seeing Ma on this bed. Writhing in pain, as she watched the doctor roll up his sleeves. Clutching the hand of the unlikely friend who gave her encouragement to keep fighting. "What did she say?"

Mrs. Hearts shifts on her feet. "Her pain became sharper, and she could barely speak. The doctor hushed her a few times, telling her to push. He suggested I leave the room, but Nellie clutched my arm. I strained to hear what she struggled to tell me. Finally, between her contractions, she whispered one word, 'Pray.' I kneeled by the bed and began saying 'Our Father'. She tugged on my sleeve. 'No. To Mary.' I nodded and recited 'Hail Mary' with her. Nellie managed to say the last words of the prayer before her voice broke into a blood-chilling scream."

A lump in my throat makes me wince. In terrible pain and fear for her and my life, Ma called on Mary, Our Lady with all the strength left in her. Perhaps I'm standing here by the grace of Ma's beloved protector.

"Terrible hours crept by," Mrs. Hearts continues. "Nellie tossed in agony as the doctor commanded her to keep pushing. Despite her suffering, her cheeks were flushed and her eyes glowing. She didn't appear defeated and dying to me. The priest arrived, but I sent him away before she could see him. I didn't want her thinking of death. The doctor's alert gaze and focused gestures told me that the baby was coming. And despite his poor prognosis, I had full faith that the mother and the infant would live." She touches my face. "You see, child, you were born a survivor. Is it any wonder that you overcame death repeatedly?"

She wraps her arms around me. My heart races. Was I good enough of a daughter to Ma for the suffering my birth caused her? But then, I couldn't help it.

"Nellie and you stayed in this room for a week, recovering from the difficult birth. Servants brought her food from my table. My husband thought I was mad, letting a working woman and her baby occupy a guest room when we had a place in the servant wing. But those rooms were poorly lit and cold. Since I had no guests staying overnight, I didn't see the need to move her. And you cried little, an angel of a baby. When we had the ball, you slept through the performance of the finest musicians. Perhaps this is how you received your proclivity to music."

I smile, thinking of Ma and me slumbering peacefully to the sweet sounds of flutes and violins. Eating fine foods and sleeping on the feathered bed, Ma lived a fairy tale life. Maybe this is why Ma loved beautiful things, like jewelry. But fairy tales come to an end. "She must've been sorry to leave this place," I said.

Mrs. Hearts lowers her head. "I would've been glad if she had stayed longer. But I made a terrible mistake and drove her away."

"How? You were so kind to her."

"Not kind enough. You see, after Amelia was born, I kept trying to have another baby and couldn't. And you were an angelic child, lovely and peaceful. After the danger passed, and the doctor confirmed that Nellie and you would recover, I started spending hours by your cradle. My motherly instincts poured like a flood. Without speaking to my husband or Amelia, I decided that I wanted you as my own daughter. I offered Nellie money, work as my maid or your nurse, the best servant room in the house in exchange for you. She said she would think about it. But by morning, she and you were gone."

Her chin drops. I turn away from her slumped figure and see Ma clutching me to her chest as she slipped out of the house into the chilly night. She chose to live in poverty with her baby rather than giving me to the rich woman. A gentle wave washes over me, warm like my Ma's embrace.

"And you never saw her again?"

Her fingers run through the pearls on my neck. "I saw you and her once more. Three months later, a servant brought me a crumpled note. With thanks for my previous kindness, Nellie asked me to honor her by becoming the baby's godmother. By that time, my desire to have you as my child passed. Your birth in my house seemed a strange dream. I was getting ready for a holiday in London. Still, I wanted to be charitable. I came to the church with my head high. After the priest dipped you in holy water, I pinched your cheeks and gave your mother the necklace you are wearing. It meant little to me, but your mother kissed my hands like I was giving her the greatest treasure."

I gasp. "You are my godmother."

"Yes." She caresses my hair. "Yes, I am."

My heart squeezes. "I could've come to you after Ma died. I could've lived in this grand house and had plenty to eat."

"It's unfortunate that Nellie never told you about me," Mrs. Hearts answers, staring at the floor. "But after giving that necklace to your mother, I took no interest in you or her. Once, my housekeeper reported that a woman with a child came to apply for a job. Since she could present no recommendation letters or references, the housekeeper turned her down. Later, I learned that it was Nellie Jones. I dismissed that information and did nothing."

My head swims. "When Ma died, I had no one to turn to. Our landlady, and then my father, turned me out onto the street."

"Your father?" Her voice rises. "You knew him?"

I bite the inside of my cheek. "Mr. Howard, my mother's supervisor at the mill. He was married and had children with his wife."

"That wasn't the name Nellie gave the priest at your christening."

My mind refuses to follow. I sink onto the bed. "Mr. Howard acknowledged that he fathered my siblings but denied that I was his daughter. Who's my father?"

Mrs. Hearts strokes my shoulder. "I don't remember. But it was an unusual name. Not Howard. The priest wrote it down in the church book. I can make inquiries."

I exhale a breath I held too long. "I'm not ready to learn about him. On the night I was freezing by the church though, I had nowhere to turn. If I knew that I had a godmother..."

"I'd have given you shelter, yes. But my husband would have objected to your presence. Most likely we would've sent you away to a boarding school."

Everything happens for a reason. Boarding school would likely be better than an orphanage, but I still would've been lonely, with no family to love me.

"Thank you, Mrs. Hearts." I rise and give her a curt nod. "Please let my family know that I'm ready to go."

Her voice takes a petulant note. "Would you give your godmother a kiss?"

I kiss her cheeks. "Be well, Mrs. Hearts."

Her arm circles around my waist and her quick breaths warm my neck. "Child, stay here," she breathes into my ear. "Play the piano and sing for me every day. Any room in this house could be yours. My servants would wait on you hand and foot. Your brother and sister could live here with you. They'll have the best education possible and everything they desire."

She lets go of me. I walk through the room, touching the expensive furniture. My ma must have heard a similar offer. *Stay in this house. Your daughter will have all she ever wants.* Did Ma caress the luxurious rugs and the velvety curtains as she pondered over the decision?

"This house has a garden with fountains and gazebos," Mrs. Hearts says. "There's a library with thousands of books. We can have dances and parties. Let's throw a winter ball, the biggest one yet. You'll play and sing for everyone."

My choice is easier than Ma's. I have a family who fill me with love. My brother and sister need the same. No wealthy house could replace it.

"I can't live in a golden cage and be your nightingale," I answer. "Caged birds often stop singing. I belong with my found family. We may not have such a big house, but we have enough."

"Confound this house!" She drops to her knees and covers her face with her hands. "At night, it feels like a giant crypt. You and your siblings could bring life to it."

I kneel beside her and take her hand. "You are not alone, Mrs. Hearts. You have a goddaughter. Please visit us soon. Meanwhile, don't you have the charity projects Amelia gave you to complete?"

She hangs her head. "I write the checks, but my heart feels nothing."

"Then open your heart." I give her a hand to get up. "Those projects were important to Amelia. She wanted to ensure that people with consumption would receive treatment. Imagine her among the people you are helping."

Her breath shutters as she wipes her tears. "That's right. She left me much to do."

"I'll give you another task. The orphanage. The building is in dilapidated condition, and the children go hungry. A terrible woman, Mrs. Mulligan, beats her charges. The new director, Mrs. Grace, is wonderful, but she needs support. Otherwise, the board will sack her."

"I will go there today. You are right, I must keep busy and not let loneliness consume me. But what do I do during those long winter evenings?"

"As you said, this house has plenty of amusements. Read in the library. Hire a teacher and learn to play your pianoforte. Throw a party in the ballroom and make some new friends. You don't need me to make your home come alive. You can do it yourself."

She nods. "And painting. I will paint Amelia, as you suggested. And write her story as well."

Her arms envelop me. "This morning, I was the wise god-mother, giving guidance to my disheartened goddaughter. In the evening, you've taught me how to go on living."

I pat her shoulder. "You helped me make peace with my old life. I will start praying to Our Lady again, like my ma did. I will go with my brother and sister to church. But will also remain Jewish and live the way my found family lives. My past and my present will be combined." I want to add, 'in harmony' but stop myself. Harmony exists in music. Life is complicated and conflicting.

Mrs. Hearts cups my face. "And what of your future?"

"I don't know. No one does."

Her fingers caress my cheek. "Whatever it is, I'd like to see it. Your life will be extraordinary."

Chapter 32

A Year Later

Papa, Julian, Josie, Harry, and I are decorating a Christmas tree in the dining room. The smell of pine makes me think of winter fairy tales. Moishe described such trees in his letter from Vienna, and my siblings decided we must have one of our own. Besides the decorations such as apples and nuts he wrote about, we use wrappers, pieces of bright fabric, and shiny trinkets. Papa pins an ornament Josie made to the top, while Harry pulls down the decorations he can reach and laughs when Julian tells him to stop.

David and Caroline come in with their arms full of wrapped boxes and baskets. The children stop with the decorating and gape.

Julian runs to them. "Are all these gifts for us?"

"There's something for everyone," Caroline says. "Some of these are from my parents and sisters." She puts the gifts under the tree. The children examine the beautiful ribbons and bows. Then they lift and shake each box, trying to guess what's inside.

"Can we go to church tonight?" Josie asks. "There's going to be caroling and a pageant."

"That sounds like fun," Papa says bending down to her.

"Of course, we are going," I say. "I'm playing the piano, remember?"

My fingers get little rest these days. I play the piano at the church services and the synagogue concerts. Then I have my private students. My niece, Miriam's daughter, resumed her practices. When she comes over, Julian and Josie join the lesson. Harry doesn't talk much, but he sings with me when I play. Ester's daughter Dina can't hear well, but she claps to the music. She watches my lips and tries to imitate me. Haim, the boy who lost his leg in an accident, is my most diligent student. He'd spend all day at the piano if his parents didn't make him do the physical activities David prescribed.

I have a voice student as well. A friend of Lady Linden's hired me for her daughter to work on her singing. The young woman had instruction from a number of prominent teachers, but prefers me despite my lack of proper training. She says that while others had instructed her to sing with her mouth and throat, I show her how to sing with her heart.

Papa crouches down to hang an ornament, and Josie wraps her arms around his neck. "I want you to come to church, Papa. Please?"

He runs his hand through his hair. "I suppose I could come. I've never seen a Christmas pageant."

"Never?" Julian scoffs. "You must see the manger at our church. There will be a donkey, an ox, several sheep..."

While my brother describes the nativity set, I go down to the kitchen, where Mama, Shira, and Naomi are making latkes. Christmas and Hanukkah intersect this year, giving us a blended holiday that excites and bewilders the entire family.

"Mama mentioned you received another letter from Moishe," Shira says as she grates the potatoes. "Can we read it?"

Moishe's letters are addressed to me, but it has become a family tradition to read them together. One arrived this morning. Busy with holiday preparations and my students, I've been carrying it with me all day and had no chance to open it. I call the rest of the family into the kitchen and give the letter to Shira.

"It's from St. Petersburg," she exclaims. "Italy, Austria, and now Russia."

"*Vey iz mir*," Mama grumbles. "We ran away from Russia. Now my son is there."

Shira shrugs and starts reading.

Dear Abigail,

I'm writing from the city of tsars. Before this, I've performed several concerts in Moscow that went fairly well. I played in the theater called the Bolshoi. It was rebuilt after being destroyed in 1812 by a terrible fire. Not all the work on it is finished, but the architect has ambitious plans to make it very grand. I also gave private concerts in the homes of several noblemen.

Now I'm in St. Petersburg. I thought of Russia as a backward country, but the capital's architecture rivals other great European cities. But it's unique as well. Teams of three horses, called troikas, pull sleighs over the snow. People skate here on frozen canals. I've tried it, and it's great fun. I think you would like it here. I know I would like it much more if I had you to skate with.

Please say Shalom to everyone for me. I hope the children are well and enjoying the holidays. My gifts for them will arrive soon. But I have a special gift for you.

I've arranged passage for you and two chaperones on any ship to St. Petersburg. It's all settled with the agent at the port. I know you have your students and plans of your own, but I'm hoping you will break away from them and join me. I will wait for you in St. Petersburg till February. The city is growing as a cultural center, and there's plenty of opportunities to perform.

My heart flutters. St. Petersburg with its palaces and bridges! Horse rides and ice skating! The old me didn't ever want to leave Chatham. The new me longs to see other cities and countries—knowing I will find my way home.

"I shall go," I say.

Mama flaps her hands like a bird. "To Russia? Are you mad?"

"Perhaps. But it's a pleasant sort of madness. And you don't have to worry about me getting lost or being in trouble." I take Mama's hand. "You will come with me."

She turns away. "No. I won't even think of it. And what about Julian and Josie?"

"I'm fortunate to have a large family. My brother and sister will be well cared for while we are gone." I look at them as they stare at me with mouths gaping. "You would let your sister go on a holiday, won't you?"

"If you come back soon," Josie answers.

"And bring us presents," Julian adds.

"Abigail, you should go," Shira says, snatching a knife away from Harry's reach. "I wish Naomi and I could go with you, but Harry is too small and needs a close eye. We can't leave him or take him with us. And we have our bakery to run."

"Caroline and I could possibly go, if you want us as chaperones," David says. "I have much to do for my medical practice and the university, but my wife and I never had a honeymoon holiday." He puts his hand on Caroline's shoulder, and her face grows pink.

"I'd love for you and Caroline to take me." I've learned to channel my emotions into other things. It doesn't bother me to see David's arms around Caroline's slim waist. Well, just a little. But I can look elsewhere.

Mama studies Caroline and tilts her head. "No. Caroline won't be going anywhere in her condition."

"My condition?" Caroline stammers. "What do you mean?"

"Can it be? A baby?" David asks.

Caroline reddens deeper and touches her face. "Well... I suppose it's possible..."

"I'm rarely wrong," Mama says. "It's my gift."

David puts his arms around Caroline, resting them on her belly. "If there's any chance of pregnancy, travel would be too risky for you. Nothing is more important than you and the baby."

Caroline rests her head on his shoulder. I sense that she's accepting the news with conflicting emotions and isn't ready for congratulations.

Mama gives her a pat on the arm. "Chin up, dear. Every pregnancy is different. And *Hashem* is kind. You are a good wife and daughter, and the most active member of the Women's Guild. Everyone is still talking about the torah cover you've decorated. This baby will be your reward."

They embrace, and Mama kisses Caroline's cheeks.

"It looks like it's up to Mama and me to take Abigail on her trip," Papa says with a chuckle.

Mama releases Caroline and pivots. "You lost your mind, Isaac. Don't you remember that awful voyage to England? I would rather die than step on another ship."

Papa strokes his beard. "That's because we traveled like fish in a barrel. If we arrange for a fancy cabin, the cruise may be quite enjoyable. I want to see our son performing in his concerts. And Julian and Josie should come with us. There's much family history we could share with our children."

"We could go too?" Julian cries. "Oh yes, please!"

Mama shakes her head from side to side. "Ships break from storms. And the world is not friendly to Jews. Why leave our haven?"

"That's how it's been and may not change in our lifetime," Papa answers. "But dangers and prejudice haven't stopped our people from traveling the world. God will protect us and the children."

She smooths her dress. "When I was young, I dreamed to gaze at the Winter Palace. I'll think on it."

Shira touches my arm. "There's more to the letter, but Moishe asks that you read that part alone."

I take the letter from her and go to my room. There I get a magnifying glass, bring the paper close to my face and read.

Abigail, I know you read my letters as a family, and my gift has probably caused a big stir. While everyone is discussing if you should go and with whom, please read this part alone. I want to tell you why I need you to come. No matter how well I play, or how well my accompanist plays, people don't seem to care for our performances as much as I'd like. Mr. Campanella says everything is going fine, but I watch the faces as I play. They are bored. If I find a piece that one audience likes, I try it the next evening, but the new audience doesn't respond to it. You would know what moves them. I understand that you are busy and doing a lot of good things, but please come.

Do Svidaniya, (that means 'until we meet')

Moishe

I hold the letter to my chest. "All right, Moishe. *Do Svidaniya.* I'm coming."

The chime of the doorbell jars me from my thoughts. I go downstairs and open the door. Wrapped in a mink coat, Mrs. Hearts stands in front of me, holding a basket of oranges. "I hope I'm not intruding," she says. "My servant will come later to drop off the gifts. But I couldn't wait any longer."

"I'm so glad you're here!" I exclaim and lead her inside. "We are just about to have our Hanukkah feast. And later tonight, we have the Christmas pageant at the church. Would you like to come?"

"I wouldn't miss it for the world." Her voice sounds years younger. She flies up the stairs with the energy of a girl.

"How have you been?" I ask, catching up to her.

She glances around the dining room. "Busy. Terribly busy. I have a favor to ask. Do you think I could stay here for a little while? A month or so. Of course, I could stay in the inn, but it's so dirty and gloomy."

My eyebrows rise. "I must ask my parents, but I don't see why not. In fact, it may be most opportune. We are thinking of going to St. Petersburg. The rooms would be empty. But why would you want to stay here that long?"

"Right now, there's no room in my house. The third floor is being remodeled. And all other rooms are occupied."

I narrow my eyes. "But your house is enormous. Who's living there?"

"The children. The children from the orphanage are at my house."

My knees weaken, so I collapse onto a chair. "What, all of them? Mrs. Hearts, it's nice that you decided to adopt an orphan, but you can't take all of them. Even if they begged you."

She bursts out laughing and sits next to me. "Oh no, you misunderstood. You asked me to fix up the orphanage. When I had an architect examine the building, he was appalled. He declared it unsafe and beyond repair. It must be demolished and built again. Meanwhile, the children and staff needed somewhere else to live. I offered my house."

I cover my mouth with my hand. "Oh goodness. Have they torn the place apart?"

"Some old furniture and vases were broken, but nothing I would miss." She waves her hand dismissively. "Once the children received toys and learned what they shouldn't touch, they were on good behavior. Mrs. Grace did a fine job getting them situated with a little help from me. Most days with them are wonderful. There is laughter, music, games. But then a few more orphans needed a home, and I had to decide whether I should turn them away or find a temporary lodging for myself."

"You are most welcome here. Come greet everyone. They are downstairs, still deciding about this unexpected trip to St. Petersburg."

We step down to the kitchen. The aroma of latkes makes my mouth salivate.

Mama's voice rings a nervous note. "I can't possibly go. St. Petersburg is terribly cold. I don't have a winter coat."

"Allow me to take you shopping, Mrs. Fridman," Mrs. Hearts says. "I'll help you find everything you need for your trip."

While everyone exchanges greetings, Josie and Julian grab my arms.

"Can we visit Miriam and Hannah before church?" Josie asks. "We want to give presents to their families."

"Yes," I say. "I will take you."

Mama turns to us and clicks her tongue. Then she says. "Abigail, when you go, hold the children's hands as you cross the road. And you," she bends down to Julian and Josie, "Look both ways. Also, watch for the ice on the road and make sure your sister doesn't slip."

"Yes, Mama," my sister says.

"We already know," my cheeky brother answers.

No matter what our fears or limitations are, everyone learns to cross the street without their Mama eventually. We are not guaranteed safety when we do that, even if we look both ways. We may still step on the ice and slip. But when we shake ourselves off and complete the crossing, we find out what's on the other side.

While Abigail is getting ready for her new adventure, would you like to learn the story of David's friend Ella Parker, the woman who disguised herself as a man to study in medical school? Read the best-selling A Girl with a Knife by Alina Rubin, the winner of Illinois Soon to be Famous Author Competition.

Also By Alina Rubin

Hearts by the Sea: Hearts and Sails Prequel

An innocent game brings unforeseen consequences

In the idyllic setting of the English coast in 1800s, Jamie Flowers experiences his first infatuation when he meets Ella Parker, a mysterious girl with a troubled past. As the two rehearse *Romeo and Juliet* together, they decide to sneak out for a midnight swim. But their plans are abruptly halted by a shocking revelation, and Ella is soon gone. Heartbroken, Jamie searches for her... and himself. With unexpected twists and turns, Hearts by the Sea is a story of friendship, secret codes, and self-discovery.

A Girl with a Knife—Hearts and Sails Book 1
Women could not be surgeons. She did it anyway.

After the heartbreaking loss of her mother and a cruel attack by her drunken father, Ella Parker decides that dishonesty is fine when it serves her needs. At a time when wealthy young ladies do little more than embroidery, Ella escapes her luxurious but lonely life, disguises herself as male medical student, and finds her footing in the university.

But when she brilliantly saves a patient and gains the approval of a famed professor, she must choose between truth and lies, and distinguish between real and false friends, before her pretense is discovered.

No Job for a Woman—Hearts and Sails Book 2
She sailed against the current.

Ella Parker is determined to practice medicine despite obstacles for a woman in 1810 England. Her only choice is to join her mentor on the *Neptune*, a warship heading for open waters.

Following an accident, she is quickly thrust into the role of ship surgeon, and her skills are put to the test. Hoping to fit in with the all-male crew and make friends, instead, Ella creates chaos and suspicion among the superstitious sailors.

After a fierce battle, Ella saves the handsome officer, Robert Weston. Her commitment to her profession is tested, however, when he asks for her hand in marriage. But are Weston's intentions sincere, and would he allow her the freedom to pursue her calling?

Ella must decide where she belongs before her future sails away from her.

Friends Don't Let Friends Read Boring Books!

Thank you for reading Abigail's Song!
Leaving a review is like recommending a book to hundreds of friends. Please share your thoughts at:

Amazon
Goodreads
BookBub

Be the first to know of new releases by subscribing to the newsletter at alinarubinauthor.com

I love hearing from my readers! Please connect with me!
Instagram: Alina.Rubin.Author
Facebook: Alina Rubin Author
Email: alina@alinarubinauthor.com

Yiddish Glossary

Bashert — 1. Fate, Destiny. 2. Soulmate

Mamzer — a bastard, a child born of a forbidden sexual union.

Mazel Tov — a phrase used to express good congratulations for a happy event

Meshugener — crazy

Schlemiel — fool

Schlump — pathetic human being

Shiksa — A non-Jewish woman – often used in a critical way

Tuchus —buttocks

Vey iz mir—Woe is me – used to express dismay or exasperation

Historical Notes

Many years ago, when I was eight, my grandmother Rina Fridman gave me a dry cracker to try. It was bland, but I ate it anyway. "It's called matzah. Don't tell anyone you've had it," Grandma warned. This was my introduction to the religion of my ancestors. A simple cracker could get a Jewish family living in the Soviet Union into trouble. Or it could inspire a novel.

The beginning of Abigail's Song was easy to write. I simply expanded on the events described in *A Girl with a Knife*. I finally gave the town with the medical school its name: Churcham. The town, the university, and the hospital are fictional, but the medicine used is accurate for the early 19th century to the best of my research. The only exception is the appendectomy. While there was one successful operation in the 18th century, the surgery was pioneered by Dr. Reginald Fitz much later, in 1886. The readers of *A Girl with a Knife* may remember that Dr. Miller performed a successful appendectomy with assistance from his students, including Oli Higgins. That case was fictional but very important to Oli's future career.

After Oli (David) took Abigail to his family, I had to choose the main setting for the story. I had visions of a Jewish village, much like in *Fiddler on the Roof*. When I started searching for such a village in England, I realized it didn't exist. I was envisioning a Polish or a Ukrainian *shtetl*. In England, most Jews settled near the ports and made their living by selling goods and services to the sailors. They were silversmiths, jewelers, watchmakers, and most commonly slopsellers—clothing peddlers. The most successful of those sellers became navy agents; they provided cash to seamen in exchange for wage tickets. I gave Papa this profession and allowed the Fridman family to be well-off.

I picked Chatham as the story setting because it boasts one of the oldest synagogues built in England. The Chatham Synagogue that stands on the Rochester High Street was built in 1861. Before that, there was an older building at the same site, and some of the Jewish graves near it are from 1782. I found little details of the old synagogue and did my best to imagine it. While I found no record of the mikvah, it's reasonable to assume that there was one nearby because mikvah is central to Jewish married life.

According to *Foreigners, Aliens, Citizens* by Irina Fridman, Chatham of 1810 was diverse but not welcoming of Jews and immigrants. Jews and non-Jews were segregated groups that didn't mingle. Some Jews shaved their beards and abandoned Yiddish to assimilate. Mixed marriages often resulted in the baptism of a Jewish partner. Some adopted Christian names to achieve job advancement like David Fridman taking the name Oliver Higgins. An inspiration for my character came from my grandfather, Israel Fridman, who changed his name to a more Russian name Leonid, to enter law school in the Soviet Union. Yet many Jews in England kept their religion and way of life openly and some thrived. Minor characters in my story were named for the people living in Chatham at the time, such as the apothecary Mr. Hyman, or Rabbi Cohen.

Like the Fridman family, I'm a Jewish immigrant who fled antisemitism in Eastern Europe. My family left the Soviet Union in 1991 and rebuilt our lives in the United States. Papa's story was extremely compelling to me. The history of the Russian Empire included many massacres of Jews since the time the country acquired territories with a large Jewish population and forced many Jews to move to the Pale of Settlement.

Besides the secret matzah, the only Jewish food I remember having as a child was gefilte fish. Once my family settled in the United States, I spent a couple of years attending Jewish schools and camps and finally experienced Jewish holidays and foods. My research of Jewish cuisine in England came from *The Book of Jewish Food by Claudia Roden.*

Who knew that the early 19th century pianos (short for pianofortes) had five octaves and sixty-one keys? I didn't until I read *The Great Pianists from Mozart to the Present by Harold C. Schonberg.* All pianos were grand pianos until 1826 when the upright pianos with seven octaves were invented. One curious fact that struck me was the popularity of female pianists. The ladies composed music, gave concerts before royalty, and toured Europe, including the blind Austrian pianist Maria Theresia von Paradis.

For Abigail's Song, my main source was *Foreigners, Aliens, Citizens. Medway and its Jewish community, 1066-1939 by Irina Fridman.* Thanks to this source, I was able to envision Chatham and Rochester of 1810 and learn how the Jewish community integrated into the region. The last name of the author was an amazing coincidence. The fictional Fridman family is named after my ancestors who whispered to me as I wrote this book.

Book Club Questions

1. Nellie's cradle song and David's lullaby change Abigail's life. Did a piece of music or a song play an important role in your life?

2. In the Fridman family, parents and children struggle between the traditions of their culture and the new way of life in England. Did you ever find yourself conflicted between following the old ways or embracing change? How did you decide?

3. Many characters in this story keep secrets from their parents (Abigail, David, Shira). How can secrets affect a family?

4. As Abigail embraces her found family, she has trouble holding on to the memories of her mother and siblings. How do you keep memories alive?

5. By the end of the story, Abigail accepts responsibility

for not taking care of her brother and sister earlier. Do you think she was being selfish, or was she doing what was necessary to survive?

6. What is the most important lesson your family has taught you?

7. Do you cherish stories of your family that you want to transmit to the next generation, but younger people may have difficulty grasping them?

8. What part does religion play in the characters' lives? Does it play a role in your life?

9. Many intriguing side characters appear in this book. Which character deserves their own novel?

10. What (and whom) would you like to see in the sequel? Are you rooting for Abigail and Moishe as a couple?

Acknowledgments

This book was unplanned and unexpected. The experience of writing was magical. I would head to my computer without a vague idea of what this writing session would bring. As I added to the last thing I wrote, a curtain would rise to reveal the next scene. The characters acted out their parts, and I described what they'd done, even when they gave me a shock. So I start with a thank you to my muse who'd been so cooperative. Don't be a stranger. We have work to do.

Next, I want to thank my wonderful readers. I've been floored by the support my previous books received, especially A Girl with a Knife. People took the time to leave reviews and to connect with me. Receiving emails from readers is an incredible boost of confidence for a writer. All the best to you and keep reading! Thank you to my superfans Michelle Ross, Helen Kopner, Inessa Levina, Cynthia Florsheim, and Michael, Jamie, and Karina Rubinshteyn. Special thank you to my ARC reviewers.

This is my third book with my editor, Kirsten Rees. Not only does she make my books a million times better, but she also helps me grow as a writer.

My beta readers are a vital part of my writing process. Critiquing a manuscript is a daunting task, and I'm so glad that my tribe supported me. Tim Spadoni, Rosemary O'Brien, Sherri Fisher Progar, Julie Krinks, Rachel Callaghan, and Miriam Schulman Allenson, thank you so much for your ideas, eagle eyes, and fact-checking.

As I keep growing in my writing, the tribe of authors helps me stay on my path and overcome obstacles. Thank you to the communities of Paper Lantern Writers, Harvest Moon, Niles Library Creative Writing Club, Toastmasters, and 20 Books to 50K for help and support. A special thanks to Tami Palmer. A rising tide lifts all boats.

Teachers are never thanked enough. Thank you, Mr. Kevin Hickey, Mrs. Barbara Fryzel-Marquette, and Mrs. Barbara Schuman, among many other wonderful teachers from Prospect High School.

This book was more personal than any other novel I have written so far. I dearly miss my parents Yelena and Joseph Frumkin, and my grandparents Rina and Leonid Fridman. Writing opens me up to my memories of them, and their stories come alive in unexpected ways.

My biggest thank you to my family. Thank you to my husband Vitaly for his patience and love. Thank you to my dearest

Elanna. You've inspired this book in a myriad of ways. Always remember your family and the history of your ancestors.

As I write this acknowledgment in December 2023, my heart bleeds for two countries that I love. I pray for peace in Israel and Ukraine.

About the Author

Alina Rubin is an IT professional and a mom. Writing became her passion during the pandemic, and her characters took her on a journey beyond her wildest dreams.

Alina's debut novel, A Girl with a Knife, has won the Illinois Soon to be Famous Author Competition. Since publishing, Alina has been interviewed by Glenview Off The Shelf TV program, Ukrainian-American Magazine, History through Fiction, and many other programs and podcasts, as listed on her website alinarubinauthor.com.

Alina obtained a B.S. and M.S. in Business and Information Technology from DePaul University. She lives in Chicago with her husband and daughter. When not working or writing, she enjoys yoga, hiking, and traveling.

Follow her blog, A Girl on Adventure, and check for book releases on her website alinarubinauthor.com